Welcome
to Camelot

Welcome to Camelot

Tony Cleaver

Winchester, UK
Washington, USA

First published by Roundfire Books, 2014
Roundfire Books is an imprint of John Hunt Publishing Ltd., Laurel House, Station Approach,
Alresford, Hants, SO24 9JH, UK
office1@jhpbooks.net
www.johnhuntpublishing.com
www.roundfire-books.com

For distributor details and how to order please visit the 'Ordering' section on our website.

Text copyright: Tony Cleaver 2013

ISBN: 978 1 78279 645 9

A CIP catalogue record for this book is available from the British Library.

Design: Stuart Davies

Printed and bound by CPI Group (UK) Ltd, Croydon, CR0 4YY

We operate a distinctive and ethical publishing philosophy in all areas of our business, from our global network of authors to production and worldwide distribution.

Dedication: para Maria Cristina

Chapter 1

THE RECEPTIONIST

Gwen Price waited impatiently for her interview outside the manager's office at the Camelot Hotel, Monmouthshire. This grandly restored old country house and its surrounding estate was the latest addition to the World Traveller Hotel Group and, in the process of reopening with its plush fittings and extensive redecoration, it was taking on a team of new staff. All the senior personnel had already been appointed. Gwen was up for one of the last posts advertised as a receptionist.

She was silently swearing at being kept waiting. Turning up five minutes late to her appointment had not been the best start and so, missing her turn, another of the young hopefuls who had been nervously sitting outside in the waiting area was called in before her. She had seen the back of this young man entering the office and closing the door just as she arrived and so for fifteen minutes now Gwen had been cursing to herself.

"Shit, shit, shit," she moaned. "The door's been shut for too long already. Whoever's in there now had better not be getting offered the job I wanted..."

Another five minutes passed before, finally, the manager's door opened again and a smart, neatly combed young man emerged, grinning broadly from ear to ear. Whatever had happened in there, this interviewee seemed pleased with the outcome. He was shaken warmly by the hand by the good-looking, dark-suited individual who followed him out and who escorted him to the stairwell outside. The dark suit then turned and came back to stand in front of Gwen.

"Miss Price?" the manager enquired. Gwen stood up.

"Yes, Mr Hughes," she answered, switching on her best smile.

"You're a little late. What happened?"

"The bus was stuck in traffic for *ages*, Mr Hughes. And then I had a bit of a walk to get here. I'm very sorry." This was a complete fabrication since her mother had driven as fast as she could to get her errant daughter to the hotel on time but Gwen reckoned it sounded as good an excuse as any.

"Never mind, you're here now. Welcome to Camelot." A practised gentleman, the manager held the door and indicated that Gwen should go first. She gave what she thought was a gracious murmur of acceptance and swayed past him, making sure she brushed *very* close by as she passed inside. She took a seat without waiting to be asked, crossed her legs and sat up, looking alert, at the same time ensuring she was showing off her nineteen-year-old figure to maximum advantage. She kept her smile switched on, noting that her interviewer had had a good look at her legs and bust as he rounded the desk and found his seat. Great! First objective achieved.

Much of the interview then passed in a blur. The whole purpose, from Gwen's point of view, was to say little but speak sexily, to hang on to his every word, to push her breasts out, pout her lips and generally offer the promise of an eager and innocent young thing who might do just about *anything* to please her boss. She handed over her CV when asked, standing and bending over the desk and offering a glimpse of her boobs as she did so. She endeavoured to attract his attention to her body and away from the document she was giving him, since much of the experience she had listed there was invented and she didn't want any close questioning of its contents.

It all seemed to work out fine. After twenty minutes of him making polite conversation and occasionally running his eyes up and down her figure, he rose, offered his hand so that she might stand and smilingly indicated that the interview was at an end. Again he held the door open for her to leave. Again she passed by deliberately close to him and, as he followed her through the waiting area outside, Gwen swayed her bottom all the way to the entrance to the stairwell. There she said a sweet goodbye and flashed her eyes back towards him, giving him the cool come-on that she had learned in her numerous exploits over the years was a real man-catcher. Without waiting to see his reaction, she smartly stepped away and down the stairs to the exit. She would get the job, she was certain.

"Well? How did it go? Was everything OK?" Her mother was waiting in the car in the visitor's parking bay, hoping with all her heart that this time her daughter had not blown it. "Did they ask why you were late?"

"Don't be ridiculous, Mother," Gwen snapped back. "Of course I wasn't late and of course it was all OK!"

"Did they offer you the job?" Her mother was hurt by the spiteful reply but did not want to show it.

"They will do." Gwen looked down and started tapping away at her iPhone, indicating she did not want to talk any more. Mother sighed and started the car. She wouldn't get any more out of her daughter now; she just had to wait and see what happened next.

What happened next was Gwen received a phone call two days later at home, asking her to come in the next morning to meet the company's head of human resources. She was to be offered the post of hotel receptionist – one of three such people being appointed. Gwen smiled to herself. Everything *was* OK, then. She immediately called up Paula, one of her friends, to give her the news. They would have to go out and celebrate straight away.

"Well, congratulations, dear," said her mother, overhearing the conversation, "but don't go out for too long – it sounds like you have an important day tomorrow."

"Oh do leave off!" Gwen put the iPhone down and glared at her parent. "Do you have to interfere all the time? No wonder Father left home – you never stop!" She hated her mother listening in on her personal calls; in fact she hated her mother for everything that went wrong in her life. She stormed out of the room, leaving her poor mother sighing again at her daughter's sharp-toothed response.

It was in the local pub, the King Offa, that Gwen and Paula had decided to meet up. They arrived together to find it was packed with students, celebrating noisily after a game of rugby, and all seats were taken. With a queue at the bar, the two girls struggled to make their orders.

"I don't know whether I approve of having these handsome hunks here, or whether I'd prefer them all to go away and leave us some space to sit and talk," said Paula.

"They're making such a devil of a noise that it's hard to think," complained Gwen. "Can't you push through?"

One mountain of a young man turned to look at the two girls who were trying to get past him. A flicker of recognition passed across his features.

"Hi...it's Gwen Price, isn't it?" A smiling but somewhat bloodied and battered face looked down.

Gwen glanced up blankly. "Do I know you?"

"Gareth Jones. Remember me? We were at school together...least we were until you left."

"Gareth? I don't remember you being so ugly...not that you were the prettiest boy in the pack then."

The mountain shifted a little. He groaned. "Charming as ever, Gwen. You really know how to make a chap feel welcome."

"Well you know how it is, Gareth. So many boys like to try it on. Got to make them work for it if they want to get anywhere. You going to buy us drinks then?" She switched on the smile.

"Er, OK." The mountain nodded and bludgeoned his way to the bar, returning moments later with two beers for the girls. Gwen thanked him sweetly.

"Well, I haven't seen you in a while, Gareth," she said, "and you look different now. What you been doing?"

"Engineering: I'm up at university," Gareth replied, moving

his bulk round to prevent the two girls from being jostled. "And playing rugby when I'm not studying. That's how this happened." He flattened his nose which had evidently been broken and reshaped some time ago.

"And it looks like you picked up a few bruises today as well," said Paula. She thought he was a nice, genuine type of guy.

"Aye! That's rugby," he grinned. "What are you two up to these days?"

"I'm working in offices in Newport," said Paula. "Gwen's just been offered a job in this new flash hotel close by."

"Congratulations, Gwen. So you've come here tonight to celebrate?" Gareth smiled at her again. He thought she was a highly attractive female that he'd like to get to know again.

"Sort of...but not with you, I'm afraid!" Gwen retorted. She thought he was a decidedly unattractive male and she wanted to get away. She signalled to her friend that it was time to move. Paula sighed and moved with her.

The mountain with the craggy face raised his eyes to the ceiling in resignation as the two drinks he had bought weaved their way away from him in the crowd, looking for others to share with. "Great evening, girls. Thanks very much!" he called out to their disappearing backs.

* * *

Gwen Price arrived at the Camelot Hotel the next morning, fifteen minutes late and more than a little hung-over. Mrs Elizabeth Morley, head of human relations, was not impressed.

"Good morning, Miss Price," she welcomed Gwen, "I'm glad you have decided to join us. Meet the two other receptionists appointed with you. They and I have been waiting some twenty minutes already for you to arrive. Please see to it that this does not happen again!"

Gwen smiled sweetly and said it would not. She grimaced

internally and thought, *What a cow! Fancy being so unpleasant with your staff on first acquaintance!*

The party all made their introductions to each other. There was Freddy, the one young man who Gwen had seen being interviewed by the manager just before her, and Victoria, a very poised twenty-something young lady that she now met for the first time. Gwen quickly decided she didn't like the look of her. Mrs Morley waited for them all to exchange pleasantries before leading them away for a tour of the hotel.

"We open here in just over a fortnight's time," explained the head of human resources, taking the group first into the ground-floor bar and restaurant. "The company has spared no expense in converting this grand old property into a thoroughly luxurious five-star establishment. You three will eventually work shifts in reception, eight hours at a time, but it is important that you come in every morning at nine am over the next weeks – not only to get to know everyone and everything about this hotel, but also the entire company. World Traveller Hotels is a big international business as I am sure you all know. Do things right here and you can go far. Look at me: I started in one of our smallest, least prestigious hotels in London and now I head up human relations for all our UK operations."

Was this supposed to impress? Gwen had to use all her self-control not to sneer and blow a raspberry.

Elizabeth Morley brought the party out onto the patio outside the restaurant and stopped to show them the extensive lawns and fields rolling away into the Monmouthshire woods beyond, and from there to glimpse the distant Welsh hills where dark clouds were gathering before they would inevitably move east towards them.

"Just look at the majesty of these surroundings. It all contributes to the central message of this distinguished hotel and the work here that we have chosen you three for. We have very carefully selected the team of staff to run this place. Local staff where we can, who we hope will be quite familiar with and at ease with the whole ethos that we wish to promote at this very special hotel. It is important – no, essential – that you fully participate in, and take on board the magical image we are promoting here, derived from the culture of this unique location. A lot has been invested in this fine property, this historic site: the company intend to make this the star attraction of all our British operations. It is going to be our Camelot – fit for a king and his courtiers. If we get this right, it will attract guests from all over the world. It is intended that the whole experience of staying here will be magical, regal, a step into an age of chivalry and honour, where service to the ideal of Camelot is the dream come alive."

The three new members of staff all made approving noises. The faces of two of them were shining – thinking just how incredibly lucky they were to be in on the ground floor of such an exciting, inspiring new venture and how they were determined to do their best to promote this fabulous new enterprise. One, however, was thinking that this all sounded like a lot of hooey but she had read the blurb on the job description and had done her best to echo her enthusiasm for this Arthurian fantasy in her interview. Youthful eagerness, and tastefully close-fitting clothing, had done the rest.

Before moving on, Mrs Elizabeth Morley took the opportunity to look keenly at the three new appointees. "Receptionists are the first people our clients will call; the first they will meet on arrival here. The impression you create with our valued guests is thus of vital importance. You will transmit to them exactly the right image we wish to promote, understand? You have been selected so far because the impression you have given to date has been good. You will now undergo intensive training over a number of weeks to polish your image even more, so that in your every gesture and comment to our future clients you deliver everything that the company wishes to promote and nothing less than that. Is that clear? I am sure you won't disappoint me..."

And if anyone did, Gwen guessed, they wouldn't be employed for very long. She grimaced internally for the second time. *Well I've got so far with this job*, she thought, *I'd better see it through.* It certainly seemed a prestigious appointment, with a salary to match, so she did not want to lose it as quickly as she had lost others before.

The tour continued. A curving path led across a perfectly manicured lawn to old stable blocks detached from the main building. From the outside, the stables looked like two long rows of traditional and well-preserved brick-and-timber units, but inside they had now been tastefully joined together to contain a swimming pool and jacuzzi on one level and, further along in the other block, a gym and exercise room: all brand new and in excellent order, just waiting to be pressed into service. After meeting the pool and gym attendants, and being impressed by all the spotless facilities, the receptionists were eventually steered back into the hotel proper just as a heavy, damp mist breathed its way across the grounds towards them. It was approaching midday but the light had suddenly fallen as the sun disappeared in the whiteness that enwrapped them.

Freddy stopped before re-entering the former country mansion and turned to look around and take it all in. "What atmosphere!" he remarked to Mrs Morley. "You can just imagine the Knights of the Round Table emerging out of those woods below and cantering though the mist towards us, can't you?"

The older woman smiled. "That's the ticket, young man! Keep that up. That is just the sort of thing we want to sell to our guests here."

"Yes," said Victoria. "This place reeks of atmosphere. It will be easy to portray the magical, mystical image you want for this hotel."

Creeps, the two of them, thought Gwen. *If the head of human relations buys into this fawning behaviour, then she's a bigger fool than*

I took her for.

The centuries-old estate did possess a unique character, however. The central property had been knocked down and rebuilt countless times in its long history, evolving in the process from earthworks and wooden palisades to stone battlements to a sprawling country residence and now to a hotel. Part of the ground floor of the main building was still paved with thousand-year-old flagstones; a circular stone staircase stood in one corner and a massive fireplace dominated the banqueting hall. All but the most cynical could hardly remain unimpressed by the restoration. Scholars insist that the exact location of the castle of Camelot is lost in the myths of time but World Traveller Hotels could certainly claim that their latest acquisition had a fair claim to be among the candidates to have hosted King Arthur and his knights.

The three new members of staff were taken next to visit many of the rooms of the hotel and the prize Arthur and Guinevere suites. As before, it was clear that the company had spent a fortune providing the most comfortable surroundings for each paying guest, no matter whether they were taking the smallest room in the hotel or were booking into either of the two senior suites, complete with four-poster king- and queen-size beds and spectacular views of the surrounding countryside. Throughout, World Traveller Hotels had certainly done their best to clothe the rooms, main staircase and walls with drapes, banners, paintings and all sorts of modern evocations of the age of chivalry. There were even suits of armour standing in discreet corners on each floor, never mind that such medieval accoutrements dated from a time several centuries after King Arthur was alleged to have reigned.

Finally the party returned to the reception area where Elizabeth Morley asked them all what they thought of the facilities and whether they thought they would be happy working here. A chorus of appreciation met her request. All said they were delighted and impressed with all they had seen and heard of the hotel and its mission. Gwen vied with the praise of the others and hoped her comments sounded sincere. Mrs Morley looked at each one in turn and nodded with apparent satisfaction that these three new appointees seemed to be making all the right noises. Time would tell how they would make out.

It was time for a break. The head of human resources said how pleased she had been to meet the three of them; she was sure they would all do fine in their new jobs, and then she said goodbye and handed over to the hotel's assistant staff manager Tom Hughes, whom they'd all met before. As the back of Mrs Elizabeth Morley disappeared from view, Tom indicated that they should take time out for some tea and snacks. He led the way into the hotel's lounge.

"Enjoy this while you can," smiled Tom Hughes. "Staff will not be allowed to sit in here when we are open, and you certainly won't have time to relax and take it easy soon. We are going to have a big splash campaign in the local and national media over the next week or so and our first day of operations will be to entertain a legion of journalists who will come in and pore over every inch of the place. And mind you are on top of your game when they arrive – if not, they will be sure to print any criticisms. And if that happens, heads will roll in consequence, you can be certain of that!"

Gwen smiled at the others, giving nothing away. Here was another warning of the high standards that were expected – these people certainly knew how to rub it in on new recruits.

Freddy voiced the same thought. "Are you trying to frighten us?" he asked nervously, "because, if so, I can tell you it's working! Mrs Morley has already said much the same thing."

Tom laughed. "It's not just you who are being frightened. We've all had the same message rammed into us from the general manager at the top, down to the cleaners and gardeners at the bottom; myself included. You'll see – we are all together in this, and as a team we are all pulling together too. Don't be so worried. You will find plenty of help here as you settle in."

"Well that's a relief," said Victoria. "We are going to need all the help we can get at first until we find our feet."

"Talking of gardeners," said Gwen, "we've had a good look around inside the hotel but any chance of seeing a bit more of the grounds outside? Before we get immersed in the details of our job on the front desk, I'd love the opportunity to take some fresh air and have a look at the wider estate." She was doing her best to look enthusiastic. To be sure, a jaunt around the lawns outside in her high heels had no real attraction for her, but it was a chance to get a breather from the high-pressure environment that was being pushed at her, and maybe also the opportunity to flaunt herself at, and maybe gain some favour from her immediate boss.

"Sure. When you've finished up here we'll go out and I'll see if I can find Dai Mervyn for you. He's something of a legend. He came with the property when World Travellers bought this place. They say he's as old as the grounds themselves." Tom laughed again. "Mind, that would put him at several hundreds of years of age!"

Twenty minutes later, as the sun began to win the battle against the thinning mist, the three novices stood outside on the lawns waiting while their host disappeared in the search for the head groundsman. Alone for a few moments, Gwen had no wish to fill the time with false enthusiasm for the job with these future colleagues. *Let those two together get all animated about this fake enterprise,* she thought. *Give me space!*

She wandered off a little to be by herself. Looking around, her idle curiosity was taken by a movement some distance away where fields stretched down to the woods at the westward limit of the estate. A large hound seemed to be running to and fro, seemingly searching out some scent or other. After a pause when it vanished from view into the woods it then reappeared to start galloping towards a tall, slow-moving figure dressed in black or grey. These two came together and made their way across the fields in the general direction of the hotel: an elderly man, as it turned out, and a large, lively Celtic wolfhound that the man seemed to pay no heed to as it leapt and gambolled about him. Tom Hughes suddenly appeared from beside the hotel and directed the man and his dog up to meet Gwen and her two companions.

"Gwen Price, meet Dai Mervyn, our oldest, most experienced and most valued member of staff," Tom waxed expansively. The man in question just snorted.

"Pleased to meet you, Mr Mervyn," said Gwen holding out her hand. She wasn't so sure about his dog: she hated animals that were unpredictable.

"The pleasure's mine," nodded Dai Mervyn, drawing back his dark cloak and taking her hand gently in his wizened paw. He had thin greying hair, a bronze, weathered face with more lines on it than Network Rail and a small, white goatee beard. "Don't mind Morgan, my companion," the groundsman grunted. "He'll be fine when he gets to know you."

That monster doesn't look at all fine just yet, thought Gwen. The big hound had backed off a little and was fixing her with a stony glare, his teeth barely covered in a low growl.

Dai Mervyn ignored this stand-off and moved past Gwen to say hello to the other two who were waiting to meet him. Morgan the wolfhound did not move. He did not shift his gaze either, Gwen noticed with some discomfort.

"I'll leave you with Dai, here, for a while and he can tell you more about this place," said Tom Hughes. "When you're done, come back inside and meet me in reception." He gave a cheery wave and moved off, leaving them all to get to know each other.

The groundsman walked the three new staff around the side of the hotel to the overflow car park that gave a magnificent view over field, valley and distant forest, the big hound following dutifully at a distance.

"I'll not take you down over the meadows," said Dai Mervyn, "seeing as you're all wearing decent clothes and you'll not want to get mud all over you. But you can get a good feel for the estate from up here. You got any questions?"

Away and out of earshot of the hotel management, Gwen was anxious to prick the bubble of this whole Arthurian sales promotion that had been pitched at her. She was too old now for fairy stories and had been biting her lip throughout the tour so far. But this groundsman character was a local gardener or something and clearly had had nothing to do with the hotel company and all its fantastic designs before they'd bought this place. Was he as sceptical of all this as she was?

"What do you think of all this about Camelot they are trying to sell here, Mr Mervyn? Isn't it all a sham? Just a load of rubbish?"

"Aye...it could be..." Dai Mervyn stopped and turned a beady eye upon his young questioner. "What do you think, young lady?"

"Well o' course it is! This place is no more like Camelot than the dump I live in. They're just trying to make money out of stupid tourists."

The head groundsman threw his head back and laughed at how quickly this outrageous young woman was to pour scorn on her new employers.

"You take care, young lady," he grinned at her. "Or you'll not go far with the owners of this place if you persist with that attitude..."

"But come on, Mr Mervyn. You're surely not taken in by all the hype, are you? That's just for the gullible public!"

Dai Mervyn laughed again. "Now, you look here, my girl. Firstly, the guests who will be staying here in due course are not likely to be so stupid as you think they'll be...and secondly, I don't know about the so-called dump you say you live in, but this place has as much right to call itself the site of Camelot as any other."

"Sure. Any place and no place could be Camelot!" came the cynical reply.

The old man looked around at the other two new members of staff. They had said nothing so far and he didn't know whether the three of them were thinking the same or not. He turned back to Gwen.

"You young people think you know it all. Seems there's nothing you can learn now..." He sniffed. "Tis a shame – you live in a world where everything's bought and sold, where appearances are everything and all is superficial and skin deep. And if you can't get what you want straight away, what language – woe betide us! No patience. No one makes any effort now to look any deeper..."

"Well, do tell, Mr Mervyn," piped up Victoria, "if you think there is some basis for the Camelot story here. You must know this place so well and have seen and heard much more than the rest of us. We are not *all* deaf to the lessons of history." She glanced disapprovingly sideways at her colleague.

"Well, there's more to this place than first meets the eye, that's for sure," said the old groundsman. "Over the years, several castles have stood here to defend these rich lands. For example, if you look carefully at the terrain below here you can still see traces of how the farming used to be divided in to long strips in feudal times – this was all centuries before the enclosure movement which gave us the patchwork of fields you see today. There are tracks of medieval jousting lists beyond the stables there, then there are the remnants of the forest to the east where the king and his court used to hunt deer and wild boar. You can also find Roman remains in these parts and even, way before that, there's evidence of stone circles from Neolithic times. So there you have it: a land with a millennia of stories that you people dashing around from here to there today can scarcely guess at."

"And Camelot?" asked Freddy.

"Well, there are lots of places from Cornwall to Carlisle that lay claim to that fabled location, but I'll tell you this: none have a better right to own that myth than this. Arthur was a Celtic king. He fought Saxon invaders and others to establish his rule and I reckon that was hereabouts. You'll find few places on earth more fought over than these borderlands between England and Wales. There're remains of more castles, fortified houses and battlements of one sort and another per square mile in this area than almost anywhere else in the world. Romans, Vikings, Saxons, Celts, Ancient Britons and Normans – they've all been here. What with the River Wye to the east and the Usk to the west, the natural harbour of Newport to the south – invaders can reach here easily by boat and there's been many a battle and much blood spilt defending these lands, I can tell you. And why does the Welsh national flag sport a red dragon across a green field? There's stories told here that originate well before the Church came and people could read and write. King Arthur and his Knights of the Round Table are just one. Aye, Camelot is a mythical place; a spiritual place; an ideal that has captured the imagination of many over the centuries. Too right it could have been here: all the elements that go to make up that story can be found around where we are standing right now..."

The old man's quiet way, his slow musical accent and twinkling eyes caught the imagination of two of his audience. They were ready to believe that Camelot was more than just a fable and had really been here once. Even Morgan the wolfhound had crept closer and had lain mesmerised at the feet of his master as he had unfolded his tale. Gwen, however, was as cynical as ever.

"Well, I don't believe in all this guff – nor Father Christmas neither!" She stood up. "Get off me, you brute!" she brushed aside the wolfhound that had risen up with her.

The hound, being so roughly dismissed, snapped back at its tormentor. Gwen pulled her hand away quickly but not before the dog had drawn blood.

"Ow! He's bitten me!" Gwen cried out more in anger than pain.

"Tis only a scratch, young lady. It'll do you no harm," replied the groundsman. "But you be more careful with Morgan in future. That hound has more about him than you credit him for – he can sense your ill will."

Gwen turned and walked off, shaking her injured hand and swearing aloud. "He'll sense a lot more than ill will if he comes near me again," she blustered. The fields and creatures around here, she decided, were definitely outside her comfort zone. She was no country girl and this hotel was as far from her urban ideal as she wanted to stray. Re-entering the main building, closing the outside door and shutting off the surrounding estate with its elderly keeper and his mangy, long-haired brute of a dog couldn't be done quick enough for her. She had had enough of the fresh air that she said she had wanted.

Tom Hughes breezed over to welcome her back inside. This was more like it, thought Gwen. He was a good-looking executive with an open and friendly manner and was clearly someone of status and influence in her new employment. She switched her smile back on and batted her eyelashes at him.

"Thank you, Mr Hughes," she cooed. "I've seen enough outside. Time to get acquainted with everything here now."

"Fine," said Tom Hughes. He could hardly miss the show of sex and sensuality that simply oozed out of this young recruit as she moved in his direction. This was not exactly the image the company wanted to project, but he'd withhold judgement for the time being. "Let's go get the others and I'll show you your work-station."

The remainder of the day was given over to briefing the three receptionists on the specific details of their post. It was broken by lunch which was provided for all the staff at the same hour – again with a warning that such practice would change as soon as the hotel opened. It nonetheless gave the three newcomers the chance to meet others and begin to get to know the people who they would be working with.

Gwen held herself in and tried to give little away whilst being introduced to the variety of people that staffed this luxury resort – she quickly realised that most had a great deal more experience than she. Despite what she had written on her CV, Gwen's only knowledge of the hotel trade had been a couple of stints serving behind the bar in her local pub. She was a pretty girl, however, and had long ago learnt that a flashing smile and innocuous conversation could compensate for a lack of talent in other respects. It had got her so far, at least, she thought.

Later that evening, it was to the King Offa again that she retired to meet with her friend Paula and recount her first day's impressions of the new job. This time the place was only half full.

"Well? Any decent men there?" Paula settled down with drinks for them both and got straight to the point.

"The head porter kept giving me the eye, as did the assistant chef… good-looking sort, too…but I cut 'em both dead. I'm not interested in their type. Now, the assistant general manager – Tom Hughes – is more like it. He's late twenties, early thirties, I reckon. Smart dresser, got a real way about him and drives a flash Jaguar. I could go for him."

"Married?"

"I guess so, but that don't matter. I'd give him a run for his money!"

"I bet you would too. Has he shown any interest?"

"Not as yet. I'll work on it!"

Paula laughed. "What else can you tell me about the place? You seen inside any of the rooms?"

"That was the first thing they did. Gotta know all about it if we gotta sell it, see. The King Arthur suite is something, I can tell you. Spared no expense in fitting that out – right down to the fancy creams, oils and shampoos in the bath-and-shower suite. All top of the range. I nicked a few, soon as I could. They'll do well in my loo if I can stop my mother from using 'em."

"Oooh, do get me some if you can."

"Should be no problem. They'll have masses of them in the housekeeper's stores and I'll get in there soon as no one's looking. But like everything else in that hotel – money seems to be no object in setting the place up. You should see the main banqueting hall behind the reception desk where I'll be working. Imposing is an understatement. Big stone fireplace; massive oak beams; and they are still working on it: flags and banners are going up overhead with the names and emblems of who they say are the Knights of the Round Table. It's all a load of balls, of course, but that's what I've got to sell. They'll be dressing us up next; I mean the front of house staff, when the media come to the grand opening!"

"Oh, Gwen – you in fancy dress like some lady-in-waiting? That'll be fun"

"No way! A bloody lady-in-waiting? Get me to behave like some brainless bimbo in a fairy tale? They'd better not try. I heard staff talking about it over lunch today. A big joke it was, trying to guess who was going to be dressed up as what. They reckon that even Dai Mervyn will be squeezed into something."

"Dai Mervyn? Is he still there?"

"Yes. Do you know him?"

"My dad does. He works for a construction company that was restoring the country house well before it became this hotel. Dai Mervyn, he'd say – been up on that estate for donkey's years. Knows every wild herb and remedy known to nature; makes his own brew and could drink any of builders under the table. There's respect for you!"

"I don't know about that. He knows the history of the place well enough, though he can't sell me on Camelot any more than the rest of 'em. But he has a dog the size of pony up there – look what he did to me!"

Gwen held up her hand. The scratch at the end of her middle finger had swollen a little in the course of the day.

"You'd better put something on that," said Paula, "looks like it might be infected."

"Nah, I'll live. It's really nothing. Let's get another drink in, it'll be time to go soon. I've got to be back in the hotel bright and early, they're going to show me all the software I'll be using." Gwen didn't have much patience for computers, she knew, and mastering the booking-in process for hotel guests was going to be headache. She couldn't afford to be late tomorrow, she thought ruefully.

Gwen slept badly that night. Dreams of knights on horseback, strange woodsmen and enormous wolfhounds kept racing through her head. That, and a growing throbbing in her hand where she had been bitten, disturbed her sleep. She woke up early and noticed the scratch on her finger was even more swollen and now looking discoloured. She wished she had applied some antiseptic on it earlier. She showered carefully, using the shampoo she had stolen from the hotel, and tried to use her hand as little as possible. She squeezed some antiseptic on her finger after drying off. Better late than never, she reckoned.

Breakfast was hurried. Gwen didn't want her mother noticing anything – she was tired of all the fuss and moralising that never stopped coming from her. It was a wonder she had survived so far. For the umpteenth time, Gwen thought that she'd leave home as soon as she could afford it but she cursed her luck that that was not possible yet. She'd never held down a job long enough, and anyway there were a hundred and one clothes, shoes, electronic playthings and iPhone bills to pay for that prevented her from putting any real money aside.

That was a thought. She'd better raid her mother's purse before leaving. Gwen didn't have more than a few pence to take with her that morning. Her head was still spinning from lack of sleep and a preoccupation with her finger but she focused well enough to lift a couple of banknotes while her mother was upstairs. She shouted goodbye and left the house, walking quickly to catch the bus on the corner. It was ten minutes' walk to the hotel the other end but this time she would not be late.

Half an hour into the briefing on the booking-in system at the Camelot Hotel and Gwen was losing it. Her two colleagues were all attentive, full of questions and clearly following all the instructions of their supervisor, but Gwen was now feeling distinctly dizzy and her hand was hurting more than ever. She took a step back from the others at the desk and tried to clear her head.

"Erm..excuse me for a minute..," she began. She shook her hand and whimpered in pain. "It hurts," she managed to say. Then her breathe came in short rapid gasps, she started to panic, and suddenly it all went black.

Chapter 2

THE LADY GWENDOLYN

This time, the hallucinations did not stop. There were knights in armour charging around on horseback; her mother searching desperately for something in the kitchen; monstrous hounds leaping up with slavering jaws; a shower cubicle, overflowing with bubbly shampoo; the doors of the King Offa swinging open and shut, and all the time the old, grey eyes of Dai Mervyn twinkling mischievously at her.

Gwen moaned and tossed over in bed. What bed? Whose bed? Where was she? Her brain wasn't working properly. It was all dreams still.

There was a girl's voice calling out somewhere but she didn't recognise it. Gwen opened her eyes and gazed around the room but maybe she hadn't opened them at all, since there was nothing there except hallucination. Her head spun. What room was this? Darkness descended and a thundering took over her brain as if horses were still galloping around inside. Consciousness was coming and going in waves.

The girl's voice sounded once more: "Lady Gwendolyn! My lady!" Whoever it was seemed to be far away and very worried. Gwen wondered who it might be and what she was worried about. Suddenly her brain cleared and her eyes flickered open. The room was dark but streaked with a bright band of light that issued from a long, slit window by her bedside. The air was cold but Gwen could feel warm blankets covering her. Where on earth was she?

She sat up at once and a young girl in strange clothes sitting close by jumped back in surprise.

"My lady! Awake at last!"

Gwen looked about her. "What...where...am I?" she

stammered. She didn't recognise anything: not the bed, not the room, nor this strange girl. The last she remembered was standing at the reception desk of the hotel. She supposed she must have fainted and been brought here. But where was here? Gwen looked down at her hand. Her finger was still scratched, swollen and painful...but what was this? What bedclothes was she wearing? Someone must have undressed her and changed her into this long nightdress. Even her underwear had been removed! Outrageous!

"What the bloody hell's been going on!" she demanded loudly and indignantly of anyone in earshot.

The girl at the bedside looked startled at this outburst and was even more alarmed as Gwen swung her legs round and made to stand up. Rising to her feet, Gwen felt incredibly dizzy and she would have liked to have pushed this girl aside – who had quickly recovered and rushed to attend to her – but in the end she was glad for the support. Gwen staggered to the window.

It was a long, narrow stone casement, the sort that bowmen would stand guard at in castles like Raglan that Gwen had once visited. There was no glass. And the walls were so thick! Gwen looked around. This *was* a castle! There could be no mistake – she was standing at the window of a bedroom in a real, live castle! She looked out, angling her head one way, then the other to see as much as she could from the vertical slit. The opening in the massive wall was wide on the inside but offered only the narrowest access from without. It was designed, of course, for archers inside to have a relatively wide field of fire yet to be almost impossible to hit from an outside source.

Gwen had to hold herself up, shaking against the cold stone walls. The girl by her side looked pleadingly up at her, as if she wanted her to return to bed. But Gwen was determined to look out.

Bright sunshine flooded the landscape outside, in contrast to the relative gloom where Gwen was standing, blocking the light from the one limited window into the bedchamber where she had just awoken. She had to move away for a moment and return her eyes to the dark interior to help her spinning vision. What was that outside she had glimpsed? Long strips of land being tended by scores of peasants? Surely not? She turned and looked out again.

I get it, thought Gwen. She must have been brought to this working museum where people dress up like in times gone by and re-enact what it must have been like in Ancient Britain, or something. But she still didn't understand what she was doing here.

Gwen found herself talking out loud: "It's bloody lifelike, I'll give 'em that. Perhaps the hotel has hired all these people for a dress rehearsal before the media come. Christ, they must have pots of money to do all this! Whaddya think, little girl?"

"My lady...my lady...art thou well?" The little girl had a strange way of talking but she was clearly distressed. "Thou hast been delirious these last few days...and still are, methinks..."

Gwen snorted at the silly girl and returned her gaze outside. Her attention was caught by a movement some distance away where the strip fields stretched down to an extensive, greenwood forest in the distance. A large hound seemed to be running to and fro, seemingly searching out some scent or other. After a pause, when it vanished from view into the woods, it then reappeared to start galloping towards a tall, slow-moving figure dressed in black or grey. These two came together and made their way across the fields towards the wall some distance below where Gwen was standing, looking out: an elderly man, as it turned out, and a large, lively Celtic wolfhound that the man seemed to pay no heed to as it leapt and gambolled about him.

Gwen trembled like a feather in the wind and staggered back in a daze. Hadn't she seen precisely this before somehow? Wasn't this *deja vu*? The young girl attending her managed to get Gwen to lie back down again on the bed. It wasn't difficult. Her consciousness was coming and going again.

Moments later a dark, hooded shape loomed up from the interior.

"How fares the lady, my loyal Kate?" It seemed to be a voice vaguely familiar.

"She awoke, sire, and stood awhile...but is yet delirious and still suffers convulsions, I fear," the girl responded.

"Leave us, Kate. Thou hast done thy duty and must rest thyself now."

"Aye, sire"

Gwen had a notion that this newcomer had come to sit beside her as the young girl withdrew from earshot. This wasn't good enough. Damn it all – she had to make an effort to come round now. She'd never let any strange men within a hundred yards of her at any time in her past and there was no way anyone was going to do so now while she was still hung-over. She propped herself up on an elbow and turned a face towards her visitor.

"Have I been drinking," she asked, "or am I stoned on drugs?"

The man laughed. His hooded face was difficult to make out in the dark shadows. "Neither, my lady. Thou hast been in fever these last three days."

The voice was familiar but the message shook Gwen rigid.

"*Three days*? That can't be. I gotta get out of here..." She sat bolt upright and fought down the queasiness. "Who brought me here? Does my mother know? What's going on? And put the bloody light on, can't you. I'm not staying in this dingy hole any longer."

"My my! Such a tirade! And which of these questions should I answer first?"

"None! First of all, you tell me who the hell you are and what you're doing hanging around my bedside, you...you weirdo..."

"My dear Lady Gwendolyn, thou hast awoken with such spirit. Methinks your character is much influenced by your fever."

"Shut that, old man. Just show me your face and tell me who you are."

The man stood and turned to one side. There was a metallic scraping sound, a spark and a candle flamed into life. The man put back his hood and Gwen could easily now see his features as he bent over to place the lighted candle on a small bedside table.

"Good God! Mr Mervyn!"

He looked at her quizzically. "Merlyn, milady, at thy service. It seems thou hast not lost complete command of your faculties"

Gwen ignored that response. "But what are you doing here? What am I doing here? Is this some sort of re-enactment of ancient times? And who took my clothes off!" Her sense of outrage came back to her. She swung her legs round to fiercely interrogate her visitor – though this time she did not risk attempting to stand.

The man called Merlyn sat down in front of her with a wry smile. "Again, such a torrent of questions. Do not be in such a hurry, my fair lady. Thou hast lost only three days and have the rest of thy life still to live."

God, this is so irritating, thought Gwen. *Old Dai Mervyn still lives in another age where time moves as slowly as he does!*

"Well, would you mind making *some* attempt to tell me what has been happening to me whilst I've been out cold?" she asked, pointedly. "If it's not too much bother, like"

Another wry smile. "Thou hast a sharp tongue after thy long sleep, my lady. Take care whom thee cuts with that! Since thou art so insistent, let me inform thee that after thy collapse, thy faithful maid Kate and others of her station carried thee here, undressed and made thee ready to receive me. As the court physician I came straight-way to give thee medicine to reduce the fever and convulsions that had most noxiously consumed thee. And here thou art now – almost recovered, though I dare say there hast been some wondrous transformation in thy spirit and vocabulary..."

Gwen tried to puzzle out what on earth he was talking about.

"Look, can you knock off the attempt at old-fashioned language? All these thees and thous! You don't have to resort to re-enactment talk now. And how far am I from where I blacked out in reception? Is this room at the top of the spiral staircase I saw? I never knew there were such remains of a castle left standing in the hotel..."

"Thy mind is racing again, my lady. Slow down! 'Tis fair strange thy manner of speaking and clearly the fever has not left thee, so take care. Indeed – thee 'blacked out', as thou says, in the hall below and from thence were carried up the staircase yonder to thy bedchamber here. I suggest thou rest a while longer now until thy illness has receded further and thy memory returns."

"Sod that, Dai Mervyn! I gotta get dressed and get out of here. Where's the loo? I have to go first..."

Merlyn rolled his eyes at his recalcitrant patient and, holding one hand on Gwen's shoulder to delay her from standing, he called out for the maid.

"Kate! Kate! Come hither. Thy mistress needs thee!"

Poor Kate rushed in within the minute, clearly concerned. She could not have been far away.

Gwen struggled to rise from the bed, her head still complaining, her voice more agitated still.

"Where's the toilet, Kate? Dai Mervyn, leggo of me!"

Gwen was fighting the strange storms in her head as well as the man and girl in this room that were trying to prevent her from standing up and then keeling over. She understood that they were trying to help her but they did not understand that she badly needed to exert some sort of control over her life. She was not going to be prevented from rising and trying to shake off this awful headache and the hallucinations that went with it.

But first things first: "Kate! The toilet!"

The young girl finally got the message. She helped Gwen stagger out of the bedchamber and the older man let her go.

In a few minutes, Gwen was back. "God, it's bloody primitive out there! Sitting over a hole in the stone floor is taking re-enactment a bit too far! Now where's my clothes?"

Gwen did appear to understand that this Kate of hers was a tireless worker. She dove into a large chest at the back of the bedchamber and re-emerged with long robes. Dai Mervyn retreated from the room to allow Gwen some privacy, but more problems kept coming.

"No, Kate, I don't want to go join everyone else in all this museum garb. I want the clothes I had on last, before I blacked out. And my bra and knickers. Where are they?"

Kate did not appear to understand.

"My lady – these are all the things thou used last. I undressed thee myself amidst thy swoon! But Lo! Here art other clothes if thou desires a different set..?"

Gwen stumbled over to the chest of clothes and rummaged inside, even though bending over made her head spin more than ever. Damn everything, there was nothing but these rough garments that looked, bright colours notwithstanding, as if they had been copied from history books or lifted off a film set. No underwear, no hotel uniform, not even jeans and a tee shirt. Gwen complained loudly.

There was no heating in the cold, dark air of the bedchamber and Kate was clearly anxious to help her, so in the end Gwen gave up cursing and resisting and was glad to draw on robes that covered her from neck to foot. Next she was offered leather sandals. Surprise, surprise, they fitted her perfectly and anyway Gwen reckoned they would be a whole lot easier to wear on these rough stone floors than the high heels she had had on last.

It was time to get outside. She didn't know which way to go, which way was where and the interior of this part of the castle or hotel or whatever it was had no indications, no little green notices showing escape routes in case of fire or other emergencies. An opening to a circular staircase beckoned. Gwen suddenly got it into her head that she should go up into the fresh air and have a good look around from some vantage point or other. Yes, that would be best. Kate was by her side again, holding onto her hand in case she might stagger, and Dai Mervyn had also reappeared. Curious that Gwen should feel his presence so reassuring in some way. She guessed that that was because the old man clearly felt at ease in these surroundings that were so strange and unsettling to her.

A stone stairway led up and round and up, up again to where sunlight flooded in. Gwen's fever still had a hold on her but she struggled upwards towards the light and a fresh breeze feeling certain that once she got out into the open she would feel a whole lot better. The view would be invigorating, she was sure.

"WHAT? Good...good God Almighty!" Gwen stopped in her tracks in astonishment. She had arrived at the top of the castle's central keep, looking over the battlements...and the landscape that confronted her was totally, utterly unrecognisable. There were strip fields, and extensive forests, rolling away on all sides but not a sign of any roads, houses, distant towns, church spires and all the comforting sights of the Monmouthshire that she knew. Looking down she saw a courtyard below her, enclosed by a solid curtain wall of the castle, and much activity about the gatehouse as various people, children, horses, cattle and dogs were coming and going amongst market stalls and numerous thatched single-storey wooden and mud huts that clustered about inside and outside the castle. It was all very real. Not a film set, nor a living museum.

"Where the Christ am I? What...what country *is* this?"

"This is Camelot, my lady," said Kate, simply. "Your home in Cymru; Cambria; Wales!" She tried different words to get through to her mistress who clearly was still suffering hallucinations and reverting to foreign gobbledegook. "Hast thou no memory?"

Gwen looked round at Kate and Merlyn, her face looking

desolate.

"I want to go home…" She burst into tears and sunk to her knees as deep, uncomprehending blackness descended upon her.

Eight more hours of sleep found Gwen stirring again and then slowly, cautiously, opening her eyes. Peeking out, she saw the same dark, dimly lit bedchamber as before with, again, someone sitting patiently beside her.

She groaned: "Shit!"

Only a tiny sound and she shut her eyes tight again, as if blocking out all that she had glimpsed in the hope that it would disappear. But it didn't.

"My lady?" The same girl's voice.

This was no good: she couldn't hide away from whatever was out there. Gwen resolved to get a grip on herself and all that surrounded her. She opened her eyes again and then sat up. No dizziness. That at least was an improvement.

"Hello, Kate. Is Dai Mervyn about?"

Kate grimaced and nodded. "Merlyn!" she shouted.

Gwen looked down at herself. Once again she was in bedclothes.

"Kate – did you undress me again and put me to bed?"

Kate nodded silently, half in fear of what would happen next with her unpredictable mistress.

Gwen sighed. "Thank you. Good girl. You won't need to do that again, I'm better now." Gwen's shoulder-length, black hair had been combed. She shook it, feeling altogether recovered. But she looked around her bedchamber as she had done before and felt a little frightened. This was all so *weird!*

Merlyn entered.

Gwen looked at him. "Are you Dai Mervyn or not?" she demanded to know.

"I've had many names o'er the years, my lady. But Merlyn is what thou called me before and what I expect thee to call me again." Merlyn looked at her. Her face was clear, her eyes had lost the glaze that was there a short while ago. The fever seemed to have abated but the spirited behaviour had not. "But from whence dost thy strange vocabulary come, my fair young lady?"

"Seems to me that *yours* is the strange language, Merlyn, my man. Am I really in Camelot? Really, *really*?"

"Of course, my lady. Thou hast passed here some nineteen winters, by all accounts. Thou dost not recall?"

"Not a sausage"

Kate shivered at her mistress's evident ignorance, though she had no idea of what a 'sossage' meant.

"By Our Lady, this is serious. Thy fever has had a result without precedent."

"Unprecedented is an understatement! You don't know the half of it – I've been catapulted back over a thousand years in time. Maybe I'm dreaming..." Gwen wondered aloud.

Merlyn stretched across and held Gwen's hand. He squeezed the finger that was swollen.

"Ouch! I'm not dreaming. Your bloody wolfhound did that!"

"My Lady Gwendolyn, at least thou dost remember something. But what is this with thy strange tongue? Methinks it is some Saxon or Danish corruption? How come this sudden change?"

"Not easy to explain! But you tell me: this...this Lady Gwendolyn – I look the same? I mean – is that who you take me for?"

Kate was distraught. "My lady, thou art my own dear mistress. Thou hast lain here for days unconscious with a fever such would burn the forests down. I have done my duty and cared for thee, bathed thy temple, combed thy hair and prayed that you would recover. Now thou art awake and as fair and lovely as ever...but there is some devil inside of thee that frightens me to my very soul." She put her face in her hands and wept. "My lady, what has happened to you...come back to me..."

Merlyn nodded sombrely. "There is some undoubted strange demon inside of thee, Lady Gwendolyn."

Gwen looked at the two of them. "Bugger!" she said quietly.

Kate sobbed loudly as if stung.

"Have faith, my dear Kate," said Merlyn. "There is still some magic of my own that I can apply. We will get your mistress back to you, never fear!"

Gwen looked at the scene in front of her and shook her head in wonderment. *I just hope he's got some really powerful magic up his sleeve somewhere,* she thought. *These two may be upset at the woman they've lost. That's nothing. I've lost a whole bloody world!*

"I need to get up, Kate. Nothing achieved by staying here. It's been days and days already and nothing's sorted out yet. We'll see if I can return to normality..." (*That's a forlorn hope,* thought Gwen. *I've no idea what is normal here in Camelot!*)

Kate nodded and busied about as before in dressing her mistress as Merlyn, again, diplomatically retired. Then Gwen took a deep breath and sallied forth. What should she do and where should she go? If she had truly travelled back to the time of Camelot, unbelievable as it still seemed to her, then she had to come out of her bed and confront it. Not a little courage was called for. She looked nervously at Merlyn, waiting in the passageway outside.

"God, it's bloody cold, dark and draughty in here. Take me downstairs, Merlyn. And let's meet whoever I should..."

Merlyn got the message. A frightened young woman who had lost her memory needed to return to people and places that might help her recover.

"Fear not, milady. Kate and I will help thee all the way. See – here is the way down to the main banqueting hall where thee fell bedazed a while ago."

A wide stone stairway led to a great hall, dominated at the far end by a long, oaken high table in front of a massive fireplace. The floor of the hall was now crowded with a large number of knights and their ladies, squires, attendants and various servants. Drinks were flowing and an air of celebration was evident.

"What's going on?" asked Gwen nervously as they reached the foot of the stairs.

"They are all awaiting the arrival of King Arthur and Queen Guinevere," replied Merlyn. "It's a celebration of the outcome of a successful royal hunt. Dost thou recognise anything or anyone here?"

"Yes," said Gwen, with surprise. "I recognise that fireplace, although this room is very different now. As for everything else: nothing...but...but maybe that big man over there looks familiar in some way." She picked out a tall, heavy-set man with a broken nose.

The large man called out.

"Ho there! Here comes Merlyn with the prettiest picture in all of Camelot. Thou hast worked thy magic again, you sorcerer!"

"Come, milady. Let me introduce thee to this knight, his squire and others gathered here," he whispered, urging Gwen forward. Kate dutifully followed behind.

The men nearby all stood back as Gwen approached and, nervous as she was, she noted they all bowed respectfully to her. That helped her confidence.

"The Lady Gwendolyn, is stronger, as you can see noble sire, but I regret that she is not yet fully recovered. Her mind is still confused with fever." Merlyn stopped and looked at Gwen. "Milady, let me present Sir Gareth and with him, Brangwyn, his squire, and attendants..."

Gwen looked at the knight. "I think...I think...I recognise him..." she whispered to her companion. Her eyes met those of the large man who immediately sank down on one knee before her.

"Thou favours me with a glance, fair lady. I am thus honoured."

Gwen grinned. She could quite get to like this – big men

falling all over her.

"Haven't I seen you before someplace?" she asked.

"If thou hast noticed me before I am twice honoured," he replied

The knight remained kneeling, his head bowed, averting his eyes. Three others who had been conversing with him all retreated respectfully a couple of paces back from this conversation.

"Oh, do get up and let me have a good look at you. I gotta be sure," she said. The knight duly stood up, his face somewhat bewildered. Gwen sensed Merlyn stiffening beside her, clearly disapproving of her blunt remark, but *Sod it!* Gwen thought, *I can't pretend to be someone I'm not.*

With the knight standing immense in front of her, Gwen could have a closer look at his features – blank and expressionless as they were at the moment.

"Bloody hell," she couldn't stop herself from exclaiming. "It's Gareth the ugly rugby player!"

"Noble knight," Merlyn quickly interjected. "I warned thee that the Lady Gwendolyn is still afflicted by the fever..."

Sir Gareth nodded, bowing to Gwen. "The lady's comments indeed fall unkindly to my ears. I wish her a full and speedy recovery." He returned to gaze at Gwen, looking her up and down.

Gwen had seen that look before – interested men, giving her the once-over – many times in the last few years and it evoked in her the same reaction as always.

She pouted: "I may have been ill, sunshine, but I'm still more than a match for men like you, so don't get any bright ideas!"

Sir Gareth looked utterly bemused. He clearly had no idea what this outburst meant but the tone of this reply directed at him was unmistakeable. He stepped back. "With thy lady's permission..." He bowed once more, and stepped away, waving his squire and attendants back as he withdrew.

Merlyn was annoyed. "Poorly done, milady! Such a courteous advance should not be so ill-treated by one such as thee. Look at yon noble knight. He is fair confused at such savage treatment from one he thought so gentle and refined."

"He'll feel a lot more confused next time he treats me like some soft pushover with marshmallow for brains!"

"Forgive me, my lady, but truly thou dost possess brains of the softness of which thou speaks. Where dost thee think thou resides? With barbarians, or hordes from the East? Or at Camelot? If it is in this fair citadel then thou should understand the ways of gentlefolk here. Yon noble knight is horrified now but should thee repeat the comportment thou hast just displayed then in time he will become convinced that there is witches' blood within thee."

Gwen was losing patience with this. "Don't be ridiculous!" she snorted. "The Gwendolyn you knew might have been accustomed to men bowing and scraping in front of her, but I'll choose the man I want to talk to, thank you very much. Speaking of which – who's that hunk over there? That's more like it. Now *he* can stick his sword in me any time he likes! What a dish!" She was looking at a knight at the head of a number of others, waiting above beside the high table.

Kate had been listening to all that had been going on, standing close to her mistress but now she could remain silent no longer. She burst into tears. "My lady. No! There is an evil darkness within thee yet..." She fell back into the throng behind, her face aghast.

Merlyn spoke severely. "Thy illness still casts a long shadow o'er thy mind, Lady Gwendolyn. Thou art still a maiden yet speak of Sir Lancelot like women of a common courtyard. Clearly thy memory is much clouded still. Thou knowest not of the danger thy invokes with such language..."

"What are you on about, Merlyn? If that is Lancelot over there, then I'm only saying he's a nice piece of work. That knight can share a night with me any time he wants!"

"Hast thou truly forgotten *everything* here? Milady: thou art the queen's most trusted lady-in-waiting and must know that all the court is abuzz with rumours about Lancelot and how he is moonstruck by the queen. His behaviour threatens the very fabric of Camelot. Any hint of infidelity on the part of the queen will bring down the walls of this city. The code of chivalry that all knights and ladies are pledged to uphold will be broken. In such a delicate situation, sentiments such as thine – seemingly encouraging forbidden liaisons – thus become subversive, dangerous, even treasonable. It threatens not only thine own life, but of that of others too…"

"Bloody hell, Merlyn! Can't I say anything without you shrinking in horror? I gotta say what I think, haven't I? I've never been some feeble female that can't say boo to a goose…"

"Milady, think on these things: There are many here that are not so forgiving as I for such behaviour as thine. Before you swooned away you were the fairest, most gentle maiden in Camelot and now have awoken as some fiery harridan from the depths of hell. If thou dost not moderate thy language it will not be long before Sir Gareth, for example, becomes convinced that thy once fair soul has been consumed by devils, demons, or dragons. And he is sworn to fight and defeat such evil. He will have no choice but to run thee through with his sword. Or slice thy head from thy shoulders. I do not jest. All other knights will praise him for such resolution."

It was Gwen's turn to look horrified. She stared at the serious face of her guide and knew he was in deadly earnest.

"But that is *barbaric*!"

"Nay, milady. He will be saving Camelot from evil. And if nothing else, think also of poor Kate, thy maid "

"What do you mean?"

"Thy most loyal and trusted servant is sworn to thee. She has pledged her very life to thee. She would place herself in front of any sword that threatens you. She knows, of course, that if thou art condemned to death then so, too, is she and thus would gladly sacrifice her own life before thine was taken from thee."

"Oh shit, shit, shit!" Gwen sank to the floor in agony, feeling as if knives were already sticking in her. How in heaven's name was she ever going to survive in this place?

Chapter 3

CAMELOT

There was a blare of trumpets outside the banqueting hall. Everyone's attention in the gathering was directed to the entrance and Gwen had no option other than to rise to her feet, her faithful maid Kate returning to her side as she did so.

Two heralds entered the hall and sounded their trumpets once more. Then, in strode the king and queen – Gwen realised it could be none other, given the deference of everyone gathered about her. The queen came first, moving graciously, holding her head high and she appeared to be some ten to fifteen years Gwen's senior. The king waited back for his wife to reach the high table where she stood, turned and waited. Then in he came, carrying himself with an air of absolute authority, dignified, bearded, kindly of expression and some five to ten years older than the queen. As the entire audience bobbed and weaved in their presence, Gwen became aware that her head and shoulders rose above everyone else's. Rather belatedly, she realised she ought to bow down herself…but not before someone had noticed her standing there, her head proud of the others.

"The Lady Gwendolyn, back amongst us!" cried Queen Guinevere. "Do approach us, fair lady!"

The queen clapped in pleasure at seeing her friend amongst the gathering and at once everyone awaiting the royal couple took up this lead and a general applause echoed around the hall. Knights and all their attendants drew back like biblical waters and a path opened up in front of Gwen from the rear of the hall up to the high table. Gwen looked in desperation for Merlyn and Kate to accompany her.

"Go on," urged Merlyn quietly. "Fear not, we shall be with thee."

"What the fuck do I say to a king and queen? I've never done this before?" Gwen was terrified of losing her head. The only thing she could think of was what transpired in Alice in Wonderland.

"The fog tells thee to curtsey prettily, to say little and to agree with whatever they say," Merlyn advised, misinterpreting Gwen's foreign vocabulary. "I'll explain thy difficulty, trouble thee not."

"And here comes my trusted physician!" cried the king, on seeing their movement down the hall. "What say ye, Merlyn? Has the Lady Gwendolyn now recovered fully from her stupor?"

"Not fully, my king." Merlyn bowed. "The Lady Gwendolyn has just this moment risen from her bed to greet thy return, but I fear that dark clouds yet confuse her mind."

Merlyn turned to Gwen and indicated with a flash of his eyes that she should sink down low before their majesties.

"My dearest and most treasured friend," said the queen, her face showing concern, "art thou still faint? Is there still some evil in the air? What has caused thy most unwelcome seizure?"

Gwen gulped. She kept her eyes on the floor as she bobbed down as far as she could. She tried to mimic Merlyn's style of speaking: "I know not, my queen," but she sounded, she thought, like she was some extra in Star Wars.

"Come join us at the table," commanded King Arthur. "I ask that two of my dear companions sacrifice their place for our chosen guests..." He looked amongst the assembled knights to see who would volunteer. Sir Lancelot and Sir Gareth took the hint. "I thank you, sires for your gracious generosity." The king nodded his satisfaction.

King and queen took the centre of the high table; Merlyn sat beside Arthur; Gwen – heart in her mouth – sat beside Guinevere. Kate sat on the floor behind her with other attendants. There was a general bustling about the hall now as the assembled company all found their individual places on the long lines of tables that stretched back on either side. Servants who had been waiting for this moment then appeared with goblets of drink and platters of various delicacies to set before the court, starting, as hierarchy dictated, from the centre of the high table and working their way outwards and then down to the low tables. Gwen had enough sense to wait and see what those beside her did first – there were no forks in evidence but she touched neither knife nor food and drink until she saw how the royal couple and Merlyn attacked the fare set before them. She noticed that everyone else did the same. OK. Good start.

The queen took a draught from her goblet and turned to Gwen. "So tell me, dear Gwen, hast Merlyn been good to thee whilst thou hast suffered so?"

Gwen almost choked. She had lifted her own drink to her lips but it was less the strange, fermented honey-flavoured concoction that she tasted, more the queen's style of address that provoked her reaction. No one had yet called her Gwen before in this new world she was now inhabiting. It was an unexpected familiarity that brought tears to her eyes.

"My...my queen..." she stammered.

"There, there, my dear. Do not take on so. I see in thy face, so pale and drawn, that thou art still unwell. Merlyn – what hast thee been doing to my faithful ward that she is still so ill-disposed?"

"Your Majesty, I and the Lady Gwendolyn's loyal servant have been at her bedside every hour these last four days, ministering to her. My most efficacious remedies have been applied. The lady has thus recovered well enough to insist on returning to thy service...but I fear there is still some malicious influence at work within her blood that has yet to yield to my good offices. If I might dare to advise thee, fair queen, it is that the Lady Gwendolyn should return to her bedchamber as soon as thou sees fit to relieve her of her duties this evening."

Guinevere nodded. "But of course, Merlyn. I thank thee." She turned to Gwen again. "You may leave the table, my dear, soonest thou hast supped thy fill. Do not wait for my lord, the king, to dismiss thee."

Gwen gulped again. She felt all the colour had drained from her face so she didn't feel the need to act faint at all. "I thank thee," she repeated. "Too kind, my queen..." She noted as she said this that the queen, probably in her mid-thirties, had teeth discoloured and of an appearance that would not be tolerated in a lady twice her age in modern Monmouthshire...wherever that place now existed, thought Gwen, wistfully.

The meal got underway. Gwen had stabbed at some pieces of fruit – pears and plums that had been delicately cut and presented first – then came a plate piled high with meat, a type of pork that was of a particularly strong flavour, accompanied by green vegetables. No rice nor potatoes, Gwen noted. Where did rice come from? China? And didn't spuds come over from the Americas, with Sir Walter Raleigh or someone? Wasn't that some time after King Arthur? Gwen racked her brain trying to remember her history and geography lessons. She wished now she had paid more attention in school.

A type of bread, very nutty and filling, came with the main meal and Gwen couldn't manage much. Washing it all down with the honey drink, however, began to make her head feel light and dizzy again. *But I know that feeling,* thought Gwen. *This is no fever – just alcohol doing its work!* She stopped taking any more. There was no way she wanted to loosen her tongue whilst she still felt in dangerous company.

Queen Guinevere was experiencing some trouble eating. She laid a hand on her husband's arm and begged that he draw Merlyn's attention.

"Merlyn, our noble and most trusted physician, I fear that not only the Lady Gwendolyn has need of thy services. Later tonight, wouldst thou send to my chamber some remedy for a sore tooth? It pains me much to eat this evening!"

"I would be honoured, my queen. Soonest I have entrusted thy lady-in-waiting to her faithful servant I wilst straight-way look to my medicines on thy behalf. Tis good as done."

There was an opening here for Gwen to make a retreat. This had been the most nervous meal she had taken in her life and, with her stomach in knots, she could eat no more. She looked back at Kate, seated on the floor behind her and using her fingers to consume whatever titbits had been offered her way. Ravenous though she was, as soon as Kate felt Gwen's eyes upon her she stopped, mid chew, frozen and awaiting her command. Gwen shifted her chair back a little and was delighted that the queen had noticed the subtle movement.

"How art thee, my fair and favourite companion? Thou hast said barely a word beside me all this time? Art thou feeling poorly?"

Gwen did her best to look feeble and washed out – not difficult but not something she had ever needed to do before. "My queen, I am. Indeed I am...may I, could I..?" She tried to make it obvious that she wanted to leave.

"Sire..." Merlyn whispered to the king, "if I might accompany the Lady Gwendolyn to her rooms I shall then be able to attend to the queen's wishes all the more swiftly..."

"By all means, my friend. Go to; go to!" The king waved his hand, granting the required permission.

Merlyn rose from his chair, bowed and stood to help Gwen do the same. All the knights in the hall stopped eating and rose as one as Gwen left the table. A nudge in her side bade her to bow her head to the company that was graciously standing respectfully, awaiting her departure. Another nudge bade her to curtsey to the king and queen who had remained seated. Then Gwen and Merlyn backed away, with Kate disappearing first before them.

Merlyn steered them quickly out of the hall so that the assembled banqueters could return to their seats. Gwen was pleased just to get out of sight of them all – she could then afford to relax a little. Merlyn mentioned, as they found their way along stone corridors on the ground floor, that they had to take a different route back and up to her bedchamber and they could not go up the stairway out of the hall the same way as they had entered, since that would imply turning their backs on the high table – an unforgiveable indiscretion before the king.

Gwen complained. She'd never much concerned herself about others' sensibilities before and she resented such emphasis on all these pettifogging customs and conventions. In addition to putting up with this bizarre ritual, she had just stomached the strangest, semi-indigestible food she'd ever consumed; endured the most primitive and uncomfortable surroundings, been frightened of saying something that would lead to her losing her head and now she was being taken back to a dark, damp and draughty bedchamber where she was sure there was going to be no welcoming television set or iPhone or any company other than what appeared to be a silly, thirteen-year-old servant girl.

Gwen came to a halt halfway along a long passageway after she had put some distance between herself and the banqueting hall behind her. She pulled Merlyn round to look at her. Kate dutifully stopped close by.

"Now look, Merlyn, or Dai Mervyn as I know you. I think you'd better get one thing clear before we go any further. I've *not* lost my memory, as you put it. That's a convenient story for the people here, so I've gone along with it so far, get me? But maybe you didn't hear me before when I told you... the truth is – however difficult it might be for you to believe – I actually come from a different *time* to this. Same place – I think – but years and years in the future. Understand?"

Merlyn looked patient, disbelieving, waiting for this charade to finish. Kate, as before, just looked worried about her mistress's mental health.

Gwen could feel her temper rising. "Look, I tell you what I remember: I got up in the morning in my mother's house. I nicked a couple of quid for the bus fare and whatever, and then I came to this hotel where I've just started work, OK? Then my bloody hand started hurting more than ever," she held up her sore finger to demonstrate, "and then I blacked out. I woke up above here somewhere with you lot for company." She waved her hand at Merlyn and Kate.

"Before all that, here's more news for you, old man: buses go on roads! These are hard, tarmac surfaces where horseless machines run along them, fast and efficient-like, going here and there. And airplanes cross the skies, carrying people up in the air, really, really fast, gettit? And if you get toothache, like the queen seems to have, you go to the dentist who gives you an injection and he puts your tooth to sleep before drilling and filling it, using some amazing electric drill that would just about blow your mind, I reckon. We don't have candles in the future, either. We just flick a switch and the light goes on. And hot water comes from taps. And if you want to pee or crap you don't sit on some primeval pan but flush it all away down the loo with no one else doing the dirty work. Am I making sense to you, Merlyn? I guess not 'cos I've seen things you can't even dream of..." Gwen paused, running out of breath, though not running out of fire, frustration and fear about where she was and when it was all going to end. The sooner the better she hoped.

Merlyn looked at her.

"Thou art indeed the strangest creature that I have ever come across in my long and eventful life – there is no doubt of that, milady. The transformation of my Lady Gwendolyn can only have come about by some devilment that I fear is beyond my understanding. The hallucinations of which thou speak are indeed fabulous creations, full of what I can only call demons, dragons and the darkest forces from a troubled mind. Thy spirit is indeed in danger, my lady..." Merlyn shook his head sadly. Kate meanwhile was weeping uncontrollably and could not stop a quiet, desolate moaning, her poor face looking up at the two of them streaked with dirt and tears.

Gwen was not stupid. She could see that what was beyond the understanding of people in this age would soon be labelled witchcraft. And that led only to one awful outcome, she was sure. But she would not give up yet. Calmer and more thoughtful now, she took a different tack.

"Merlyn, let's say that in my sleep I visited a different place and time. A strong magic got hold of me, OK? But what I learned there was that people, in that time and place, revered the name of Merlyn! You're famous there. They tell tales of you being the most amazing magician ever. They tell tales of Camelot and how you made things happen here that no one has ever been able to do, before or since. You cured the sick, protected the strong and defeated all evil. Let's see what we can do about that. The queen has got a toothache, right? Does she clean her teeth morning and night? I bet she doesn't. I don't suppose you use toothpaste here, do you? If you do, you wouldn't get half as much trouble. I learnt that in primary school! That's at least some magic I can suggest that will help you, and the queen and stop you all thinking I'm crazy…"

"Milady, thy head is spinning faster and faster…" Merlyn warned.

Gwen stopped. *Yeah*, she thought. *I gotta get used to a different pace of life here…*

"OK, I got it," she said. "I'll promise to control the hallucinations and devilment, as you call it, but you've got to promise to try one or two things that I've seen in my visions of the future, OK?"

Merlyn and Kate looked at one another. The doubt and fear was plain to see on their faces.

"C'mon, you two. Let's take this slowly, one step at a time…" Gwen thought hard, *Paula's dad said that Dai Mervyn knew all about the herbs and remedies you can gather from the wild. Start with toothpaste*, she thought. *I wonder if he could make up toothpaste?*

"Merlyn, can you make a paste out of something that really foams up and cleans the inside of your mouth? Nothing dangerous, like. Maybe with a minty flavour? You know – you wash the inside of your mouth and then spit it out, like washing soap off you... You do use soap here, don't you?" Gwen stopped again. *Christ*, she thought. *I wonder if they even know what soap is...?*

"And what use would such a paste be, my dear lady, if thou spits it out? It neither satisfies hunger nor thirst but may instead just frustrate thy appetite."

"Oh c'mon, Merlyn. I'm sure you must wonder what causes tooth decay, bad breath and ruins a person's smile? You've surely seen the state of the queen's teeth. If you gave a woman's smile and beauty back to her, you would soon be hailed as the finest beautician of the age..." Gwen grinned, showing a set of fine, white, undamaged, teenage teeth. Merlyn, sceptical as he was, could clearly see what she was aiming at.

"And if you can make such a paste, what about a toothbrush?" Gwen asked. "Can you get a very small, fine brush made, its head no bigger than a fingertip? You use it with the paste to clean each and every tooth. Every morning after breakfast, and every night before bed. Do that every day and the queen's teeth will look and feel healthier."

Merlyn looked at Gwen quizzically. It was a novel idea and it made sense after all the nonsense she had spouted.

Gwen could see she was getting somewhere. "Then, when her teeth are thoroughly clean," she continued, "you could examine them in more detail and see which one was the problem. Numb that one with cocaine or whatever you've got and see if you can fix it. How's that?"

Still Gwen wasn't finished. Whilst Merlyn was silent, thinking through what she had just told him, out came another remark: "Here's something else my mother taught me: Cleanliness is next to godliness, she said. See my finger? I didn't clean it straight away. That's where the demons got in. Any injury, Merlyn, any injury at all – you gotta clean it properly. With clean hands. No good if the queen has servants with unwashed hands waiting on her. That's what they say in the future, see, what my vision showed me. Even if you can't see them demons, they are still there. Hands have to be *spotless* if they are cleaning wounds or serving food, or whatever. Cleanliness is next to godliness. Gettit?"

Merlyn snorted. He was loathe to take advice from a young woman he thought to be half crazy. Kate, however, was more amenable to persuasion. It was at least an improvement on the wild stories her mistress had earlier been recounting. Gwen smiled at her.

"Kate, you and I have got to go to work on Merlyn here. We want to make him famous don't we? We want him to impress the queen and make her beautiful, don't we? Merlyn, you gotta do this. If not, I'll turn into a witch..."

"NO, my lady!" Kate almost shrieked in alarm.

"All right, all right!" Merlyn gave way. "Enough, my lady. I'll agree to thy contract if it saves thy life and that of thy loyal and true servant. Fear not, Kate, we will see this idea of your mistress through. The remedy I promised the queen shall be the paste thou suggesteth. I'll see to it this moment. A brush such as thou dost recommend I shall have to search for – I yet may find one amongst the tools and implements I possess." Gwen's face suddenly grew worried. "Yes – have no fear, I shall boil it in water to kill any demons that you say may venture amongst the bristles. And I shall instruct the queen's good servants how this medicine should be applied. We shall see then what transpires. Does that meet with thy approval? Wilt thou thus cease from frightening thy maid and all others with tales of horseless machines and men that fly through the air? Of lights that thou can command at thy bidding? Answer me that."

"It's a deal, good Merlyn. No more strange tales. But I'll save my ideas for improving toilets until another day. There's some simple engineering there that will not frighten anyone, I promise!" Gwen laughed.

The three of them resumed their journey through the castle's lower passageway. As they passed the courtyard, Merlyn called a large wolfhound over to him. A big, grey, long-haired dog that stood almost as high as Kate came bounding over. It stopped on encountering Gwen, however. A low growl issued from its muzzle.

"Keep that monster away from me, Merlyn," called Gwen. "He's the one that bit me before, vicious mutt that he is!" Her whole hand began throbbing with the memory.

"Strange indeed, my lady." The older man marvelled at his hound's reaction, "Morgan here was a devoted admirer of thine before. But clearly he senses thou art different today."

"Too right I'm different. Just get him away!"

Merlyn took the hint. He made his farewells and said he was going to his workshop where he would begin preparing the remedies that he would take to the queen. He directed his gaze to Gwen's companion.

"Dear Kate, thou most loyal and true servant: I entrust the Lady Gwendolyn to thy care now. Take her back to her rooms and keep her away from any interference, and away from any kind of trouble. I will return in due course and serve her a sleeping draught. But until then she is in thy hands." With that, the old man and his dog departed across the inner bailey and disappeared through an archway on the other side.

Gwen grinned to herself. She was not going to go off to bed like some meek and mild sheep just yet. It was still early afternoon; there was no one of the king's court in sight; she was feeling fine, her spirits were up and there was yet much in this Camelot that she wanted to explore.

"C'mon, Kate," she ordered, "show me around this place before I return to my rooms. Let's start with what's over there…"

Gwen marched determinedly in the direction of what looked to her like large kitchens. Kate, fearful as always, hurried after her. The two arrived at the wide open doorway of a scene of much heat and activity. People were busying about stoking large fires, boiling up caldrons of water, sharpening vicious-looking knives, and slicing up various animals – from small rabbits to larger chickens and geese, there were deer, and even wicked-looking wild boar. All were in the process of being transferred on wide platters into or out of huge stone ovens.

"What's all this, Kate? Haven't we just eaten? The king and his knights haven't ordered more, have they?"

"The court always eats first, my lady. But Camelot is home to a great army of craftsmen, merchants, soldiers, servants, attendants and all manner of folk that support the nobility. And the king has just returned from a most successful foray in the forest. The food that is left over from the banquet is thus devoted to the all the rest of us that do not dine with the king. His majesty is very generous, as thou canst see."

Gwen took a few paces forward into the first of three, large interconnected kitchens. The nearest workers immediately stopped what they were doing and bowed respectfully. Gwen was immediately attracted to a large plate of juicy-looking black-berries, strawberries and other fruits of the forest that had been prepared and was standing to one side of the nearest woman dressed in a long, plain white apron.

"Oooh, I fancy a taste of some of that," Gwen exclaimed. It was something that indeed looked welcome and familiar – albeit was not smothered in ice cream that she was accustomed to on visits to Newport shopping mall.

The aproned woman noticed the direction of Gwen's interest and bobbed down in front of her, inviting her to take what she wanted.

"Can I scoff some of that?" Gwen asked Kate discreetly. Her appetite had now returned, having earlier been shrunken by nerves and the sight of strange, heavy and less appetizing dishes on the king's table.

"My lady, thou art the queen's favourite and all here know this. You may take whatever thou wishes and none would dare to object."

Kate feared to mention, and Gwen neither thought nor cared that the more she ate herself, the less there would be for the army of castle workers for whom all this food was reserved – and hierarchy ensured that the most valued and important ate first, the youngest, least skilled and poorest came last. Thus the berries and sweetmeats that Gwen consumed would never reach the fingers of the poorest children of the castle.

Gwen nonetheless took a great handful of the dessert that had been prepared and nodded her thanks to the kitchen workers as she set about devouring her haul.

"Umm, thanks, something…er…palatable at last…" she murmured through a full mouth as she wandered away. She looked around. "Where can I wash my hands now?" she wondered.

Kate directed her to a well in the centre of the courtyard. A bucket half full of water sat waiting there. As Gwen stooped to rinse off the juice that stained her hands, a great stomping of horses' hooves echoed around inside the castle walls. A knight and his squire had emerged from the stables and were preparing to leave. As the gatekeepers hurried to haul back the great oaken doors and open the way for the two horsemen to depart, the knight drew his horse up close to where Gwen and Kate stood by the well. He raised his helmet.

"My Lady Gwendolyn, I humbly salute thee!" Sir Gareth bowed low in the saddle.

"Milady! Return his salute!" Kate whispered.

Gwen waved her hand and forced a smile up at the broken-nosed horseman. *I s'pose I gotta go along with this,* she thought. The knight and his horse, stamping and snorting, backed off a little and then, with another wave of his helmet, Sir Gareth said goodbye, kicked his steed and they cantered across the courtyard, past the gatehouse and away, Squire Brangwyn following. A cloud of dust was thrown up behind them as they disappeared.

Gwen waved the dust way from her face, complaining bitterly. She then picked her way back across the courtyard to the stone passageway by which she had entered, tiptoeing carefully across the mud and gravel, desperate to avoid the horse manure that was splattered about in various places.

"Bloody hell! What filth, what a mess those two leave behind. Ugly is not the word for it from that man!" Gwen reached the safety of the passageway and stepped onto clean, swept flagstones but still kept up her moaning. "What next, Kate? Return to a dark, cold bedchamber? What I'd give for decent carpets, comfy chairs and hot showers now. God, please get me out of here!"

Kate dutifully led her away and via a circuitous route they reached a stone staircase and eventually climbed up to reach Gwen's quarters.

Gwen sat on her bed and looked about her. Her heart began to sink. "No light; no glass in the window; no shower and toilet in a bathroom outside. What am I going to do, Kate? This place is going to drive me nuts! No decent clothes to wear. No means to contact home. Four days already and my mother must be wondering where I am. My friends too. Dirt and ugliness all over and if I say anything I'm likely to be branded a witch!" She looked at her servant girl and put her head in her hands.

"My lady, wouldst thou allow me to speak?" Kate asked.

Gwen looked up. "Go ahead"

"My lady, I believe what thou says. Thou art not a witch but a lost soul. I have held my tongue all this time since thou awoke; I have heard thee speak of visions that are indeed far beyond my ken. Thou speakest now of thy mother as if she is alive – yet she was taken from thee, killed by Saxon invaders, even before I was born. I have heard thee speak of medical remedies that are entirely new to me. I do believe that thou cometh from a different time and place, by what magic I cannot guess. I *do* believe thee. But it is none of the things of which thou speakest that convince me. It is instead in thy manner, thy very soul. Thou seest that which lies only upon the surface but thou cannot see beneath. Thy noble knight Sir Gareth, thou speakest of him as if he is some wart upon the skin of Camelot, yet thou cannot see his heart – so fair, so true, so gracious, so generous and kind that many a maiden here does wish that he would tarry by her side. Yet he sees only thee and he would lay his life to defend thy honour...but thou dost not see this. Thou seest nothing. My lady, thou art *not* my lady. The Lady Gwendolyn that I know sees all this of which I speak, and yet more. She has taught me well. Thou inhabits her body, but thou hast come from a different place. Not Camelot. Thou has said so and I believe thee."

Gwen stared, astonished at this outpouring. A thirteen-year-old girl was trying to teach her a lesson?

"My lady, I remain thy loyal and faithful servant. I will serve thee as well as I can, as well as I must. But open thine eyes and thy heart to this fair citadel. I beg thee! There is no dirt and ugliness here. This is Camelot! A place that many across this kingdom, and across others too, speak of with awe. To reside here is to be blessed. The Knights of the Round Table pledge their lives to defend the most noble of ideals – to never cheat or lie; to uphold the law; to never to do battle for mercenary gain, or against a noble and honourable opponent; to fight and defeat evil with all their might; to grant mercy to those defeated and to seek in every endeavour to serve and never dishonour a lady...and thus earn the respect of their fellow knights. My lady – thou, or rather the Lady Gwendolyn that *I* know, art a treasured part of that ideal. The Lady Gwendolyn is the fairest, most gentle and most honoured maiden that lives here. There are many knights that might worship her...but they would not recognise the words that thou hast uttered these last hours. How canst thee talk of not being able to survive, or of wishing to leave? Clearly thou knowest not of the love here, without which we are all destined to wither away. There is a depth of love, warmth, affection and respect here that I believe thou cannot see in the shallow world from whenst thee came. Embrace it or truly thou wilst die."

Gwen was struck dumb. She just goggled at her servant.

"Forgive me, my lady." Kate lowered her eyes. "Thou may dismiss me; send me away; banish me from thy presence and from Camelot too for speaking thus, if that is thy wish..." Tears were again flowing from the young face.

Gwen did none of those things. "Stay, Kate. Just give me a minute..."

Gwen lay back and tried to make sense of it all. She was free now of fever, of dizziness, even of the alcohol from the recent meal that might have clouded her mind. She was living in a different world now, like it or not. *Make the best of it, 'cos there's nothing else to be done.* And her body? Was she the same person, inhabiting the same body? There was the cut on her finger – just the same as before. But...but this wasn't the same body now – somehow she knew it. Her brain was still the same. Her personality? Unchanged, no matter how badly it was suited to this entirely different culture that now surrounded her – Kate had made that patently clear. But her body was *not* the one she had lived in before. She knew it. What was it that Kate said, and Merlyn had said before? That she was a fair and gentle young maiden? A *maiden*?

"Oh, fuck it!" said Gwen quietly to herself. "I'm still a virgin!"

Chapter 4

THE HOSPITAL

In his early-seventies, hale and hearty and proud of it, Dai Mervyn had never before been to Newport General Hospital. As a result, he got lost wandering about inside, looking for the ward he'd been directed to, but after twenty minutes of confusion, eventually he found the place. A small ward of four beds, with one in particular curtained off. And there was Gwen Price, still unconscious, and her worried, ashen-faced mother sitting beside her.

"Ceri Griffiths? Gwen's mother? How do – I'm Dai Mervyn."

"Mr Mervyn? That's kind of you indeed to come."

"Call me Dai, please. No – it's the least I can do. My dog that bit her, see. It didn't seem like anything at the time but they tell me now that next morning she hyperventilated in reception, then fainted and concussed herself. Stone floors, see. Must have given herself quite a blow. Has she woken up yet?"

The question brought Ceri Griffiths close to tears. "No. Three days it's been. The doctors have run brain scans and told me there's no damage...but she still hasn't come round and no one knows when she will. A coma is hard to predict, they say."

"Aye." Dai Mervyn just stood beside the bed. There wasn't much else he could do. The two adults kept themselves company for a while and then Dai went off to see if he could get a couple of teas. He came back within a few minutes to see Ceri Griffiths standing, leaning over the bed.

"Gwen, Gwen, can you hear me?" A mixture of relief, hope and concern were all surging within her. "Gwen, it's your mother, dear. Please wake up!" Dai put the teas down on a small bedside cabinet and watched a growing movement in the bed beside him.

The patient was stirring. Eyes opened and just as quickly shut again. A faint moan issued from her lips. Gwen's mother was desperate to see signs of life returning to her daughter after such a long time when she had not moved so much as an eyelid.

"Gwen, I'm here, my love. It's your mother. Please wake up…"

It looked like the patient was trying to oblige. Her eyes flickered once more.

It was a cold, brilliant, white light. A light that was alien, artificial and frightening for one unaccustomed to it. Lady Gwendolyn kept her eyes tight shut and put a hand up over them.

"Kate," she called out, her voice weak and unsteady.

"Gwen! It's your mother; how are you, dear?"

Lady Gwendolyn was blank. Her expression registered confusion, then fear and, with her hand shading her eyes, she looked first at one silhouette, then the other standing over her. She whimpered in shock, bewilderment and fright.

"Kate! Where art thou?" she called out again.

"I'll ring for the nurse," said Dai Mervyn, reaching across to the buzzer above the bed.

"Merlyn!" whispered the patient. "What medicament hast thou given me?" She reached up and grasped his hand; her grip surprisingly strong with panic.

"Steady on, young lady," replied Dai Mervyn. "You've had a nasty fall. Take it easy now."

"Where…where am I?" The blinding light was totally disorientating.

"In hospital, my love. You've been in a coma for days. I've been worried sick about you."

Lady Gwendolyn looked up at the mature woman who was smiling down at her. There was something faintly familiar about her but she couldn't place what it was.

"Who are you?" she questioned weakly.

"I'm your *mother*, Gwen. Goodness, what a long sleep you

have had – you're dreadfully dizzy still."

The reaction this remark provoked in the patient was alarming. Her eyes opened wide in amazement and fright. She looked first at one adult, then the other. She held on tight still to Dai Mervyn.

"Is this a dream? Am I in heaven? Merlyn – art thou still with me? Tell me what magic is this?" Lady Gwendolyn was in some considerable distress.

Dai Mervyn was quite taken by this poor girl, trembling before him, her eyes beseeching him to reply.

"Take a hold of your mother, Gwen. Not me. She's been waiting here for days for you to wake up. Look at her."

The Lady Gwendolyn returned her gaze to the woman looking down on her; the woman with features which awakened long-buried memories, and with such love and worry clearly registering in her expression. But Gwendolyn could not speak to her. Instead, a tiny sound started in her throat, then grew and grew and could not be stopped until finally she was howling hysterically.

A nurse came hurrying in to the bedside. "The duty doctor is on his way," she said. "Don't worry, we'll calm her down."

* * *

A white coat, an unfamiliar face, an injection and the Lady Gwendolyn was once more unconscious. The doctor said that she had been given a quick knock-out, but that there was no danger involved; only that she would now sleep peacefully overnight and the two waiting by her bedside might just as well get some sleep themselves and come back in the morning. There was nothing more that could be achieved by staying with her. Ceri Griffiths, emotionally exhausted and lacking in sleep herself, took his advice but, of course, she was still extremely worried.

"She didn't recognise me, Dai," she said as the two walked

away. "Just what will she be like when she next comes round?"

"Well she did, and she didn't, Ms Griffiths," replied Dai Mervyn. "She seems to have made some sort of connection with you, and with me too – which is surprising. But I reckon that that knock on the head has scrambled a lot up for her and she is still struggling to put it all back together again. If I may, Ms Griffiths, I'd like to come back again to see her tomorrow – only if that's OK with you, of course. I don't want to interfere, like, but you know there was something there in her reaction this afternoon that really got to me…"

"That's fine with me, Dai. And do call me Ceri. To be honest, it'll be a comfort to me travelling to the hospital and back with someone to talk to – someone to take my mind off all the worries I have."

"Well thank you. That's very kind of you, considering everything," Dai replied.

As he walked with Ceri Griffiths to her car, Dai Mervyn found himself examining his own feelings. He gratefully accepted the offer of a lift back home – in his case, a tiny cottage that was now part of the Camelot Hotel estate – but he decided he wanted to share his thoughts with the mother of this poor girl he felt in some way responsible for.

"Funny it is, Ceri," he said. "But when I first met your daughter a couple of days ago I thought she was a strong-minded lass but there was nothing more to it than that. A bit too spirited, if not actually rebellious, know what I mean? But just now, seeing her expression and her reaction to you and me in hospital, I see an entirely different side to her. Takes me back more years than I want to remember to the daughter who I lost…"

Ceri started the car and took it out into the slow-moving traffic that was flowing past the hospital. She glanced quickly across to her passenger who was lost in thought beside her. She wondered about him. She'd heard about this man – somewhat of a recluse up in that cottage of his – but she never knew he had lost a daughter of his own.

"I didn't know you had family once, Dai."

"Aye. Fine girl she was, like your'n. Her mother and I never got on though. We separated and so young Bethan she'd come and stay with me on weekends. I lived for those days when we'd go out walking together through the woods and across the fields. Then she was taken from me. Car hit her when she was on her bicycle, it did. She never woke up. I couldn't get over it – not for years. It still haunts me. And I've never been able to move away from those woods, either. I never will. They'll have to bury me on that estate, they will – near the pathways we used to walk together. But I don't want to go on about it. Only that…seeing your daughter, lying there in that bed, her young face looking up at me…brought it all back, see. She was calling out to me, she was, did you notice? My, that hasn't happened to me for almost forty years…proper got to me it did."

Ceri had left the main city of Newport now and was winding her way through country roads relatively empty of traffic. She could afford to glance at the older man's face and see the emotion that resided there.

"Thank you for telling me that, Dai," she said. "And knowing what you've just said, it'll be good to have you with me tomorrow when I hope that Gwen wakes up again. You'll understand what I'll be going through, won't you?"

"I will that, Ceri. I certainly will."

* * *

Approaching the nurses' desk on the ward the following morning, Ceri Griffiths' heart was in her mouth.

"How's Gwen?" she asked.

The nurse looked up. "You are Gwen's mother? And is this Mr Merlyn?"

"Mervyn, Dai Mervyn I am"

"I see." The nurse nodded, said no more but looked round to call over the duty doctor to speak to them both. Ominous.

"Your daughter woke up very early today, Ms Griffiths. We've had to move her to a room by herself, at the bottom of the corridor outside, on the right." The doctor looked keenly at her. "Gwen Price's mother, yes? And you, sir, a friend of the family?"

"Aye, Dai Mervyn's the name."

"Well she's been asking for you both, on and off since before six o'clock…"

"How is she, Doctor? Is it OK to visit her now?" Ceri Griffiths couldn't wait to get to her daughter's bedside.

The doctor paused; he looked down. Ominous again.

"Your daughter woke up very distressed, Ms Griffiths. Like I said, we had to move her to a separate room."

"I have to see her!"

"Not just yet, I'm afraid. I called over the consultant psychiatrist to see her as soon as was possible this morning and he's with her at the moment. When he comes out, we'll have to hear what he recommends."

"A psychiatrist?" The shock took Ceri Griffiths completely by surprise, turning her legs to jelly. "What…what on earth's the matter?" Dai Mervyn took a step closer to his companion and rested a hand on her arm. This did not sound good.

"Ms Griffiths, you daughter is at present a very frightened young woman. I have to warn you that she has shown all the symptoms of returning to her childhood. Her language, her behaviour, it all seems to be typical of a small child, not a nineteen-year-old. She seems perfectly physically well, but her emotional state is that of one who is terrified of the light, of all sounds, of everyone who approaches her. She's been crying like a babe. To prevent any disturbance to other patients in the ward we transferred her bed to a private room, but that movement itself provoked even more alarm. So we have sedated her, not enough to knock her out since in her state we considered that inadvisable now, and I called in the psychiatrist to examine her. People coming out of comas can be expected to have trouble reawakening, but after a relatively brief period of unconsciousness on your daughter's part, her reaction since awakening has been extraordinary. Something quite unprecedented."

All colour drained from Ceri Griffiths' face. "I must see her! Please, Doctor…very frightened you say she is?"

"Frightened to the point of burying her head in bed and not wanting to emerge. She has been calling for Mr Merlyn, and yourself, and for someone called Kate. Perhaps if you both come with me now, I'll see what the psychiatrist says." The doctor led the way down the corridor some twenty-five yards to a private room. He gently knocked on the door and waited.

A minute or two passed, then the door opened quietly and out of the darkened room came a senior, besuited consultant: Mr Jerome Cohen. He was introduced to the two who were anxiously waiting outside.

"Ms Griffiths? Mr Merlyn? Pleased to meet you. " He saw the worry on Ceri Griffiths' face and her desperate need to enter the room and see her daughter, but he forestalled her for the moment.

"Ms Griffiths, your daughter is in shock. She is in a world she cannot understand. Her concussion has left her with no physical bruising to the brain; no damage at all that we have been able to detect; to all intents and purposes she is perfectly fit. But her emotional state is in turmoil. She is frightened by the slightest sounds and cannot bear the light. I think it is important that she sees you both – clearly she cannot rest until she does so – but I must warn you to be as gentle as you can when you speak to her. No demands, no surprises, nothing that might excite her unduly. If you do not mind, I will come in with you and stay at the back to observe her behaviour. This young lady is portraying behaviour that is…different…to say the least and I need to understand her emotional state a little better before I can be sure of any correct diagnosis of her condition."

If the dear Mr Cohen wanted Gwen's mother to act as reassuringly as possible to the patient and not to excite her unduly then this briefing was hardly preparing Ceri Griffiths to be a calming influence. She was now almost frantic with worry. But she looked at Dai Mervyn, took a deep breath, and they both went in. The consultant followed and, good as his word, he stayed back, aside from the bed and out of the eye-line of the patient as she looked at her two visitors.

"Merlyn! At last! Why hast thou not come before? And my dear Kate? How come she has deserted me? And... and...truly...is this my mother yet come to see me again?" The Lady Gwendolyn drew herself up in the bed and wept tears of relief, at last seeing someone she recognised.

"Gwen, my Gwen..." Ceri Griffiths was so full of emotion after all she had heard that she hardly knew how to react. She placed an arm around her daughter's shoulder, held her close and kissed her tear-stained cheek. "I love you so...please don't be frightened."

Lady Gwendolyn looked at this woman caressing her, this woman she could hardly believe was her mother returned to her, and tears fell in silent streams down her face. She looked up at Dai Mervyn.

"Merlyn, our most trusted physician, is this thy magic that thou hast conjured forth – to bring my mother back to me? Indeed I am transported to a strange and foreign place where miracles surround me. And this is the greatest miracle of them all." She turned to her mother again.

"I see in thy heart that thou art truly my parent. No one else could treat me thus, though I know not how this is possible. Thou were taken from me, killed by Saxons, when I was but a child, not seven winters old. I saw thy lifeless body and cried over it like an infant. But here thou art with me alive once more, this very day. In thine eyes, in the line of thy face, I see my mother again. Older, 'tis true, but thy heart and mine do not lie. I am thy daughter!" The Lady Gwendolyn lifted her arms and the two women embraced, tears springing forth from them both.

Gwen's mother looked across at Dai Mervyn. Had she heard right? Was her daughter really saying that she thought her mother was dead? Killed by Saxons? One thing she was sure of, and overjoyed for, was that her daughter had thrown herself into her arms and returned the love that was offered her in a way that had not happened for years. Ceri did not know whether or not her daughter's emotional state was in turmoil, but now, for certain, her mother's was!

Dai Mervyn was feeling more than a little uncomfortable. He was witness to a remarkable family reunion and felt as if he was intruding – like an actor in a play who could not think of his lines. He shifted on his feet.

"Shall I wait outside while you two get acquainted with one another again?" he asked.

"NO, Merlyn!" Fear lent urgency to Lady Gwendolyn's command. "Thou must *not* leave me again! 'Tis only thee, I suspect, that can explain all that has happened here. So many, most disturbing visions and strange persons have passed this morn that are beyond my ken. I am thus scared witless without thee. Pray tell me, dear friend, who are the many emotionless people who live in this citadel? I am a stranger to them as they are to me, yet they approach with such foreign ways and customs – neither warlike nor welcoming; neither friend nor foe. Most unsettling. And the light! How dost it change so much? So fearfully strong and bright, yet it comes and goes like no candle can shine. Merlyn – there are so many mysteries here. Art thou comfortable with all this? Tell me if my fears have reason or not."

Dai Mervyn glanced at the psychiatrist, sitting silently in the corner, and looked at Gwen's mother as well. How was he to react to this strange request? The poor girl was certainly not on the same planet as the rest of them; in shock, maybe;

undoubtedly under the mistaken impression that he knew her, and she him, better than was in fact the case. They'd only met once before yet she spoke as if they were old friends, if not actual family.

"Gwen, you've woken up in hospital. It's a place where the people here are dedicated to help thee get better. It's not that they are emotionless. It's just that they are trying to understand what's made you so ill, and how best they can help you. If they get emotionally involved with thee, they can't see straight enough to find a cure, see?"

He found himself talking to Gwen like a little girl that needed fatherly reassurance. Even his language was reverting to that he'd once used with his own daughter. He was being drawn into a role that was making significant emotional inroads on him – let alone the effect it had on her.

"As for the light, well they've had to darken it in here for you, my love. Switch off the lights in this room, see, but they left 'em on outside in the corridor, so the doctors and nurses can go about their business, OK?"

"Switch lights? Doctors and nurses?" Lady Gwendolyn shook her head, not understanding a thing of this.

"Gwen, you've been to the doctors before, haven't you?" Gwen's mother reminded her. "Remember how they poke you about to see what hurts and what doesn't? They're not being unfriendly or unemotional – they are just trying to sort you out. Don't worry, love."

Lady Gwendolyn nodded. She supposed that it did make some sort of sense, though she'd never seen such behaviour before – nor had Merlyn ever been so distant with the many injured folk he had treated over the years in Camelot. Camelot! The emotional atmosphere in that place called to her.

"Now I have awoke, wilst thou take me back to Camelot? I accept what thou tellest me about this place, but I yearn for the warmth and friendship of my home!"

"Aye, Gwen. That we'll do for thee as soon as they tell us you're better. OK? But we'll have to talk to the doctors here about that first." Dai Mervyn looked questioningly at Mr Cohen. Perhaps they could all talk outside for a moment?

The consultant silently withdrew, signalling to the other two that they should do so as well.

Ceri leaned over and kissed her daughter. "We're just going outside for a minute, dear. To talk to the doctors, my love. We're not going to leave you, OK? We're coming back."

Dai Mervyn agreed. "Just you hold on here awhile? Alright? There's tidy for you." He felt as if he could kiss Gwen as well, so much was the effect this was having on him. He was glad to get outside the room to try and get a hold on himself.

Mr Jerome Cohen closed the door quietly on Gwen as soon as all three were outside. He looked at both Ceri Griffiths and Dai Mervyn to gauge their reactions. The two were considerably moved by the experience.

"My poor girl," said her mother. "She...she doesn't fully understand what has happened to her. There's obviously some dreamlike fantasy about me dying in the past...but, my God, she's beautiful with me. Beautiful. I've not had her like that with me for *years*."

"Dunno about your daughter coming back to you, so much, Ceri, but I tell you – she's doing that to *me*," said Dai Mervyn. "Quite, quite, remarkable!"

Mr Cohen nodded. He was trying to put all his many thoughts together over this uniquely puzzling case.

"Ms Griffiths, Mr Merlyn, your own reactions to this experience are perfectly normal. I have to consider how far the behaviour of the patient – which has provoked your own emotions – can itself be considered 'normal'. Physically, she is well. I can detect no dizziness. Her vision is clear. Her intellectual faculties do not seem to be incapacitated in any way. Her short-term memory is equally fine. She can recall what has happened to her here, in hospital, with no difficulty. Her emotional state has changed *significantly* in the short time she has been awake. She has been frightened to the point of almost fainting away in fear, but now – thanks to your influence – she has quickly, remarkably quickly, returned to equanimity. It appears now that she is not emotionally unstable to the point of being a danger to herself or others. It is too soon to be certain but early fears of chronic mental illness appear unjustified. Her emotional variability seems not to be due to some imagined, internal mental conflict but instead has been brought upon by an external environment that appears to be entirely new and strange to her."

He stopped.

"And that is the crux of the problem for me. The situation Gwen Price is confronting is a world of which she seems to have little prior knowledge. Her language is strangely old-fashioned for us; by the same token, our language, the concepts we refer to, is strange and foreign to her. Lights that switch on and off, for example. Perfect sense to us; nonsense to her. So Gwen is struggling to come to terms with a new reality for her. No wonder she is emotional! The loss of her mother was clearly very real to her at one time in her past, Ms Griffiths. Imagine coming to terms with her new, live mother now. Her emotional state is therefore quite normal, given the size of the adjustment she is required to make. The issue is *why* is she faced with this great emotional adjustment? You've been alive and living with her all along, if I'm not mistaken?"

Ceri Griffiths nodded. "Is…is she schizophrenic, Doctor?" She hated using the term. It frightened her, but she had to ask.

"Schizophrenic? The term covers a wide range of conditions. This is far from being a typical case of schizophrenia. Her language is important: an external symptom of her internal world. It is certainly not childish language. It's construction and use is mature, consistent and not in any way confused or muddled. It is the product of a sound mind. I return to the paradox – a sound mind but confronted with a reality that is entirely strange to her. No, not entirely strange – you two, particularly *you*, Sir, are reassuringly familiar to her. But who is Kate, I should ask? Before you came, she was repeatedly calling for this person."

"The only Kate she has ever known," Ceri said, "was a cloth doll she had when she was a child. She named it herself. Went to bed holding it every night, she did."

"Until what age, may I ask?"

"I've been trying to think. Around six or seven, I suppose."

"Around the time she alleged her mother died," Mr Cohen confirmed. "That fits. Another question, if I might insist: your own surname indicates you separated from Gwen's father some time ago. How long ago, please?"

"Gwen was nine when we finally separated. But things had been stormy between us for some years leading up to the final break."

"Does she still see her father regularly?"

"When she wants to. I don't think she's got a major problem there. But they are not that close; nor is Gwen with me, to be honest. She's always been an independent girl, strong-willed and not one to give, nor willing to receive, much love and affection. 'Til just now, that is." Ceri's eyes filled with water just thinking of it.

"Hmm. Thank you, Ms Griffiths."

"Mr Cohen," Dai Mervyn butted-in to the conversation, "what about taking Gwen home? Can we? Does she really need to stay here in hospital, 'specially since it frightens her?" He was pushing for a decision in their favour.

Mr Cohen smiled; the heavy hint was not needed. "Mr Merlyn, I need to see her again. That is imperative. I need to see what sort of progress she makes over the next few days, and even longer into the future. Gwen is a unique case in my experience of almost forty years of clinical psychiatry. Absolutely unique. But take her home? The journey itself will confront her with a range of experiences that may well seem new and frightening for her. But I have just said she has a sound mind and confronting her new reality will have to take place whatever and wherever she is. Given the emotional support that only you can provide, perhaps it is best that she goes home with you. The more she is in a familiar emotional environment, the better." He saw the leap of relief to the two beside him. "Go back into Gwen now and let me get things arranged here. There are a number of things we have to sort out before she can go but I think that by lunchtime, that is twelve o'clock, midday, we can get everything finished. The nurse will come and sign her out around then. Gwen will have to continue seeing me as an out-patient, of course. We will fix up appointments for her and let you know before you leave. Well, that's all for now – I will indeed be seeing you again in due course. Good day to you both."

Ceri Griffiths was overcome with conflicting emotions: delighted that she could take Gwen home with her; worried about Gwen's confused state of mind and what it all meant; delighted that her daughter sought the love and support of her mother. Dai Mervyn looked across at Ceri and could feel some of the turmoil that was going on within her. He smiled kindly at her.

"C'mon!" he said, opening the door. They both went back in to see Gwen.

"Good news, Gwen," her mother couldn't wait to tell her. "We are going to take you home soon. First, let's get you up, showered and dressed. Dai – can you find out where I can take her?"

"No problem, Ceri. There's a shower room and toilet right next door." Dai Mervyn held the door for the two women to leave.

The next half an hour was entertaining and yet even more emotionally impactful for Ceri. It was like taking a little child through a host of wondrous new experiences that were totally unexpected. Her daughter seemed never before to have seen doors that opened and shut so silently; the floor's surface for her bare feet was so smooth and fascinating to touch; and such a mundane and prosaic necessity as going to the toilet was converted into a surprising and diverting experience involving this miraculous fountain with water gushing with a roar from hidden places! Gwen's hospital robe was discarded in the shower room, but she then had to run her hands over the glass of the shower cubicle to understand what this amazing transparent shield was...and the mirror over the basin? *Was that me in there with my mother?* Lady Gwendolyn hugged her mother with eyes wide open in astonishment and then did it again, watching herself do so in the mirror, laughing and crying with joy and wonder. Her mother could not stop her own tears, sharing such intimacy with her new daughter. Most entertaining of all was turning those strange tap things and seeing hot water spray forth out of the wall. Lady Gwendolyn shrieked in surprise and pleasure as she turned herself around and around under the shower. She waved to her mother from under the cascade, smothered herself in shampoo and played with the bubbles as they coursed down her own body, smiling and giggling in the sheer magic of it all. Her mother just watched, scarcely able to believe the transformation in her daughter that she was witnessing.

Dai Mervyn all this time was waiting outside, listening to the shrieks of laughter and amazement and could only guess what was going on inside that room. Eventually mother and daughter emerged, hanging on to one another and Gwen wrapped in towels and grinning from ear to ear. So much fun to be had in simple ablutions. Dai couldn't stop himself from joining in with their laughter and general merriment.

By the time that the Lady Gwendolyn had to get dressed she had come to realise that the miracles would never stop. She allowed her mother to produce the strangest clothes she had ever worn, realising that these garments, particularly those that clothed her legs, would make her look a lot like all those other strange emotionless people she had seen earlier. A functionary came and went, speaking to her mother and Merlyn and she understood that there was now no restriction on them all leaving this citadel together. She had to walk slowly along the passageway, however, staring one way and the other at a myriad of persons and objects that were utterly foreign to her. They came to magic doors that glided open. She looked at Merlyn in alarm.

"Stop!" she cried. "This is too much! Into what sort of torture chamber dost thou take me, Merlyn?"

Merlyn and her mother just laughed. They reassured her it would be fine. All stepped into this strange metal box, lights flickered, the box shook and she felt for a moment as if she was falling. Then it stopped, the doors glided open and the scene outside had changed: she had magically been transported down to a different level where scores of people seemed to be hurrying to and fro. Gwendolyn was for a moment frozen rigid. So much activity! She allowed herself to be walked out through large transparent shields and into the open air. She stopped again. Everything was totally bewildering. Smooth stone surfaces stretched away in every direction. People with blank, hard expressions hurried past not even looking at her. There was a large area dotted with strange, evil-smelling, variously-coloured horseless chariots. Merlyn led the way across this area, seemingly undisturbed, and she held tight to her mother's hand wondering where this was all going to lead. It was all so unimaginably exotic. Camelot seemed an entirely different world away.

"This is my battered old Land Rover, Gwen," Merlyn said to her. "I insisted on bringing your mother here today. So you get in the back with your mother, I'll drive you home."

Climbing aboard was at first a startling experience, especially when the engine came alive. But the movement, the noise, the speed and the rapidly changing view of street corners, traffic lights, shop-fronts, bridges over and under, and monstrous buildings, buildings and more buildings became altogether too much. It was overwhelming; alien; frightening. The Lady Gwendolyn had to bury her head in her mother's lap and cover her ears. The city was a terrifying place.

Chapter 5

THE HOTEL

The car stopped and Dai Mervyn switched off the engine.

"You're home!" he called.

Lady Gwendolyn lifted her head at last from her mother's lap and could risk a look at her surroundings. A small village road was outside; lined with a terrace of slate-roofed, brick houses, each with a small garden in front. They had stopped by number 5, Raglan Road, which had a small wooden gate and a privet hedge.

"But this is not Camelot," she trembled.

"It's our home, my love, where we both live. You don't remember it?"

"I remember living at Camelot, where I was taken as a child after...after I lost you, Mother...and where I have lived these last dozen years – with Kate, with Merlyn, with all the Court of King Arthur and my beloved queen. Merlyn – thou knowest all this. Tell my mother so and take us there forthwith in thy chariot!"

This was something of a problem for Dai Mervyn. He'd got used to her calling him by the wrong name; he understood that she was living in the past and was frightened by the present, and that he and her mother were the only contacts that could bring these two worlds of hers together, but how could he take her to visit this Camelot that existed only in her mind?

"Gwen, my precious young lady, the Camelot I can take you to is a lot different to what you imagine, I reckon..."

"Different? How so? Dost thou not live there anymore?" Gwendolyn thought over all that she had recently experienced and the entirely foreign appearance of just about everything she had seen since she awoke. Had Camelot too undergone some violent and alien transformation? Her heart sank. She feared the worst. But if so she still had to see it.

"Aye, my precious. I still live there...but you do not!"

"No matter! Whatever Camelot has become, I must see it. I must." She looked pleadingly at her mother. "I fell and became unconscious there. That fair citadel is everything I have come to know and value in life. If it too has changed as all else, then I must return and see what has become of it."

"Go on, Dai," Ceri Griffiths said. "We can come back here later, but the hotel was where she collapsed so maybe something there will jog her memory."

Dai started the Land Rover. "I'll drive slowly so not to frighten her too much. There's little traffic on the way now."

It was a fifteen-minute drive normally but they took half an hour over it, pointing out the woods and fields as they drove up into rural Monmouthshire. Gwendolyn took it all in – different but not so as to be completely beyond her understanding this time. The gravelled, curving drive rose up into the Camelot Hotel grounds and was there something vaguely familiar about the lie of the land?

Dai Mervyn stopped the car, got out and held the door open for his two passengers. As he did so, a great bounding Celtic wolfhound appeared and came bouncing over, barking a welcome.

"Morgan! 'Tis Morgan my faithful and devoted friend!" the Lady Gwendolyn squealed in delight. "Come here and say hello to me. You bad animal – see how you savaged my poor finger the last time I saw you!"

She held out her hand to the dog, her voice warm and affectionate, far from castigating him for his past deed. The wolfhound came straight to her and nuzzled her outstretched palm, his tail wagging furiously.

"Well would you believe it!" marvelled the old groundsman. "These two know each other. And I swear Morgan has never given this sort of welcome before to anyone but me. Most visitors stay well back from him, as did Gwen when she was here last."

Ceri Griffiths was just glad that there was something, some creature here that her daughter could relate to and relax with. "Well, Dai, this is an unexpected find. At least it makes Gwen happy. Let's go and see what else is here."

They entered the hotel. Reception was staffed by Victoria and Freddy, both still learning their roles and both surprised by the appearance of Dai Mervyn and especially Gwen Price, who they had last seen being taken to hospital unconscious.

"Mr Mervyn, good afternoon, sir. And Gwen! You are back out of hospital...how are you?" Freddy was polite and well-mannered as always.

The Lady Gwendolyn smiled and curtsied prettily but she did not recognise this person who seemed to know her. She looked up at her mother to answer for her.

"My daughter has just been released from Newport General, but she has not yet fully recovered from her coma. Her memory in particular has been affected so please do not take offence if she does not seem to know you."

Freddy and Victoria looked at one another. Then they both looked at Gwen and could see no flicker of recognition in her face.

"We're very sorry to hear that. Is there anything we can do for you, and for Gwen?" asked Victoria.

"Good of you to ask but leave it to us," said Dai Mervyn. "I'll be showing her around this place and we will see if there is anything here which she begins to recognise. Just tell Tom Hughes, can you, that we are here? Thanks." He led his guests away through to the large banqueting hall behind the reception desk.

Lady Gwendolyn stopped mid-stride. Her hand went up to her mouth. "Is...is this the banqueting hall where I fell?" She looked down at the stone floor, then up and around on all sides. "But 'tis much different now. My, how it is changed! See how smooth the flagstones are! Those walls are too close – I do not recognise them, but there are parts of the fireplace that I seem to know – though much looks as if it has been rebuilt. The staircase! 'Tis the same!" She ran over excitedly, then stopped, examining the stone stairs. "This leads to my bedchamber...but see how worn are these steps! How can that be?"

She tentatively began to climb but came to a door, opened it and entered the next floor. Disappointment marked all her features.

"What is it, Gwen?" Her mother and Dai Mervyn had followed right behind her.

Lady Gwendolyn looked lost. Her face turned back to her mother and then looked at Dai Mervyn. Tears filled her eyes.

"'Tis all gone! I know nothing of this here. The stairway should continue higher and higher but there is no more. The castle walls? Where are they? Mine own quarters? Gone! Gone with all who lived here bar thee, Merlyn. What tragedy has befallen this place? What could have happened here?"

"Gwen, it's nothing but the passage of time. The Camelot that you dream of was long, long ago. This place contains the barest relics of that time. You have seen the world we live in now – it is all very different from the place that lives in your mind." He tried to say it as gently as he could.

"But it was here, large and solid as stone and filled with life and love and honour and chivalry and everything good and worth striving for... It cannot all have fallen! Merlyn, please tell me its spirit still survives..."

"Well the stories live on – of that there is no doubt. How much of its spirit still survives I cannot say. You must judge that yourself. Come away from here, young lady, see the world around you now and tell us what you think of it – tell us how much of what is in your dreams you still recognise today."

"Come away, where to?" Her voice was trembling; her dreams were shaken to their core.

"We will walk a little first – take Morgan back to my cottage – and then you must go with your mother, Gwen, to the home you've forgotten all about. C'mon, my precious, back down out of here." He led her along the first floor of the hotel, past guest rooms she did not recognise, to another staircase at the north end of the building and then down and out into the surrounding grounds.

Gwen's mother stopped and looked at the majestic spread of fields that rolled away downslope until they met woods some distance away. To the north and west could be seen the brooding hulk of Black Mountain, where clouds as usual seemed to be building above it.

"Take a look around here, Gwen. Is it familiar?" It was an impressive view on a clear afternoon and Ceri hoped that, even if she did not recognise anything, the beauty of these surroundings might nonetheless lift her spirits.

"There is something here that speaks to me, Mother. As all else I have seen, there is much that has changed – the farmland is now lush and green and devoid of people working their strips. The forest is much reduced. But the distant mountain, yes, I recognise. The air smells different but the wind...the wind...it tells of the same stories that I know. The very skies...they welcome me as always with a familiar face. Oh, but, Mother, there is much sadness within me that I cannot contain!"

"I know, I know, my love. But you must try to come to terms with all that seems so new to you. Let's catch up with Dai Mervyn now. Look, Morgan is with him! Come on!" Ceri walked her daughter as quickly as she could along the footpath that crossed over to the nearest field.

The lawns around the hotel finished in a line of hedgerows that gave on to fields that may have been farmed many years ago but were now grassy recreation grounds and, lower down, meadows that fell away to a stream that marked the beginning of woodland. There was a gathering of people in a far corner of the recreation ground and as the three visitors and dog reached the first hedgerow a team of hoop-jerseyed young men came trotting over from the hotel and passed in front of them en route to where the crowd had gathered.

"A rugby team," called back Dai Mervyn. "Look, the other team are already over there, warming up."

Lady Gwendolyn looked round with interest. "Is this a tournament?" she asked. "I want to see!"

As they arrived at the touchline, the two teams of players were separated in rival groups at either end of the pitch. Various cries emanated from each team as they psyched themselves up for the imminent battle, and shouts of encouragement were aired from the number of supporters that were lined up alongside. The Lady Gwendolyn did not understand the significance of the lines on the playing field, nor the tall white goalposts at either end but, when the whistle blew and the ball went up and two teams of men ran and hurled themselves at each other, she didn't need to know any more. No armour or weapons seemed to be at hand, she noted, so this must be a trial of just strength, speed and aggression. Different, but familiar enough to anyone accustomed to seeing men training for battle.

The atmosphere was infectious. Great cries from the spectating crowd went up if any player of either side broke through the opposing defence and ran some distance before being tackled and brought crashing to the ground. Lady Gwendolyn was caught up with the enthusiasm – clapping and cheering particularly when one mountain of a man put his head down and charged full tilt at a ruck of others trying to stop him. She turned to look at Dai Mervyn, her eyes shining with excitement.

"How brave he is! How noble a sacrifice!" She watched as the grounded warrior tried to get the ball back to teammates following, despite being trampled upon by the opposition.

"What is this sport, Merlyn?" she asked. "Is this some sort of military training?"

"It's a rugby game, Gwen. The University of Wales hires this pitch from the hotel on occasions. Teams from rival colleges come here often and they bring plenty of their friends along to provide moral support. Look, they're forming a scrum!"

Two groups of eight men linked arms, hunkered down and, from Lady Gwendolyn's perspective, they took the form of battering rams intent on demolishing each other. Crash! Irresistible force was pitched against unmoveable object. Great cries from the onlookers rent the air: "Heave!" "Harder!" "Go on!" etc. The Lady Gwendolyn was mesmerised by the contest.

Suddenly the scrum broke, the ball was away, players were running and then the action switched direction and quickly came back towards the touchline. The mountain man seen before gathered the ball from a fallen comrade and, again, lowered his head and thundered forward like some angry bull. Bang! Past one. Crunch! He shrugged off another tackle; then desperation and determination from the opposition led to three men smashing him to the floor just yards from the line where Lady Gwendolyn was standing, leaping and cheering him on.

The ball was somehow sent back, a teammate collected it and flung it to another and again the action swiftly moved off with twenty-nine warriors cantering away across field following the play, leaving behind the line of spectators...and one man groaning and crumpled motionless in the dirt.

With her heart in her mouth, Lady Gwendolyn watched as the injured soldier slowly came back to life, struggled onto his knees and crouched bent over, shaking his head. He crawled on all fours towards the line. A tracksuited individual appeared from somewhere with a bucket of water and a sponge. The poor rugby player, first having been beaten into the mud and almost knocked unconscious now had to contend with another man grabbing hold of him and dousing him in cold water. The unfortunate victim shook his head once more, water splashing everywhere.

Lady Gwendolyn could not stand-by watching this any longer. She ran forward and caught hold of the face of this mountain, looking deep into his eyes, ignoring his broken nose.

"Thou art truly a brave and noble knight! Such strength, courage and sacrifice! Thou art an inspiration..." carried away with the emotion of it all, Lady Gwendolyn suddenly stopped mid flow. "Why! 'tis *Sir Gareth*" she exclaimed. "Of course – the most gallant, loyal and faithful of them all! Thou hast won my heart, Sir Knight, and thou shalt take it with thee into battle..."

Gareth Jones, second-row forward in University College Swansea's first XV rugby team was still shaking his head in the attempt to gather his senses. He didn't know what this girl was talking about ...but then he recognised her. "Gwen! It's Gwen, isn't it?" He smiled in recognition before turning to run off and rejoin the game. He waved back, grinning as he trotted away – then his broken features refocused on what was going on with his teammates and so he galloped off once more to the melee in the distance.

The two teams were equally matched; the game was finely poised with neither side gaining the upper hand. As play progressed, Lady Gwendolyn was hopping up and down in excitement and Morgan the wolfhound, normally a silent animal, picked up on these sentiments and became increasingly active himself, barking enthusiastically as the rugby players charged to and fro. The antics of these two became quite noticeable. Knowing now that her favourite was participating in this contest of the mighty, the Lady Gwendolyn was completely consumed in watching him and trying to understand what was going on. Her cries of support and encouragement became more agitated if she saw him fall or if another seemed to strike him. Being rugby, of course, and him being one of the biggest in the pack, Gareth Jones was frequently in the thick of it, tackling others and being struck himself.

"Watch out! Ho there! A foul blow, sire! How darest thee

stoop so low!" The Lady Gwendolyn was reeling as if she felt every blow herself. Morgan reacted similarly – leaping, twisting and running up and down the line, barking, growling and howling in turns. Dai Mervyn had never seen his dog react so before. Likewise, Ceri Griffiths wondered at the intensity of emotion coming from her daughter: so thoroughly caught up in a rugby game that she had never before shown the slightest interest in.

When half time came, Lady Gwendolyn turned to her companions full of questions: What was going on now? Had they finished? Were the bravest knights awarded prizes? It took a little time to explain that the teams would change ends, the game would soon restart and there were no individual prizes – the team that had won the most, erm, territory by the end of the game were declared victors. Dai Mervyn understood perfectly that he was not going to get Gwen, and therefore Morgan, to leave this match until it was all over. He looked at Ceri. She had come to the same conclusion.

The next half went much the same as the first. A lot of the play took place in the middle of the pitch as neither team could dominate. The final result when it came meant nothing to Lady Gwendolyn, she was only concerned with how her Sir Gareth had fared. He walked slowly off the pitch with all others of his team, though he remembered to look for one particular female fan. In amongst the spectators, she waved, smiled and held out one arm, as if proffering her heart. He smiled and waved back – her generosity of spirit was not lost on him.

Nor was it lost on her companions. Ceri was beginning to wonder if this really was her daughter; the change in her personality was so dramatic. Her fear and ignorance of people and events in the hospital and on the journey home; her childish delight in showering; her instant friendship with Dai Mervyn; her devotion to and desperate need for her mother, and now her interest in rugby and no hesitation in showing her affection for one particular player – none of this was like her daughter before her coma. She had transformed from a being a cold, materialistic, self-centred and frankly not-very-friendly human being into a warm, naïve and highly emotional young woman who evoked feelings of love and affection from everyone so far who had come into contact with her. Even Morgan the wolfhound was attracted to her. Ceri couldn't explain it. She just hoped that as Gwen became increasingly accustomed to the world she had forgotten then this loving persona that seemed to have emerged from her subconscious would still remain. For some reason she feared that it would not.

It was time to walk on. Morgan knew his way to Dai Mervyn's cottage and Ceri watched as Gwen walked happily with him, talking to him all the time, telling him how she had enjoyed watching these valiant knights battle it out on the rugby field. Morgan clearly thrived on the attention she was giving him; he lifted his head frequently to be caressed, his tail wagging as he did so. Ceri nudged Dai Mervyn as they followed after the girl and the dog that was half her size as if to say – 'Look! Have you ever seen anything like it?'

As they neared the stream and the edge of the woods, Dai Mervyn heard a voice cry out. It was Tom Hughes.

"Wait up, Dai!" he called.

Half walking, half sliding down the meadow as it steepened towards the stream bed, Tom Hughes caught up with the party and introduced himself.

"Ceri Griffiths? Gwen's mother? I'm pleased to meet you. I'm Tom Hughes, assistant manager here." He looked at the back of Gwen and her accompanying wolfhound disappearing across a small footbridge and into the wood. "I'm delighted to see Gwen back with us. Is she fully recovered now? I heard that she had fainted and was knocked unconscious, we were all so worried…"

Tom did his best to be polite, concerned and welcoming. He was effusive in his greeting of Ceri Griffiths because most of all he wanted to make sure that she and Gwen were happy with the way everything had turned out. After the accident, he had been given a thorough briefing from Elizabeth Morley, head of human relations, to ensure that Gwen and her mother had no complaints about everything the hotel had done for them. Providing as much first aid as they could, calling the emergency services, contacting the hospital to ensure that anything that could be done for Gwen was done – Tom had to do as much as possible to cover his employers and ascertain if mother and daughter considered Camelot Hotel and the World Traveller Group were in any way liable for what had befallen Gwen.

Dai Mervyn just sniffed at seeing Tom Hughes' desperation at trying to please. He could guess what was going on. Ceri, however, did not catch this. She was just anxious to explain her daughter's current situation and did not want the hotel removing the offer of employment from her, or causing any other difficulty.

"Thank you for your concern, Mr Hughes. Gwen is much better now, thank you, but she has only just been discharged from hospital and she is not fully back to being herself yet. In particular, she seems to have lost part of her memory, so we are here now to see if walking over your estate helps jog things back into place for her. Dai Mervyn here has been particularly helpful."

"I'm very pleased that Dai has been of assistance." Tom looked up at Dai and thanked him on behalf of the Hotel Group. Dai just sniffed again. "But I do hope that Gwen makes a complete recovery. We are all very concerned about her," he added nervously.

"Thank you, Mr Hughes. I'll call Gwen back and you can judge for yourself how she is," said her mother. "You did interview her originally and offer her the job here, didn't you?"

Tom nodded as Ceri cried out to her daughter to return. A few minutes passed before Gwen, smiling happily, and Morgan the wolfhound, came back across the footbridge to meet the three waiting for them.

"It's all very different now, Mother, but there is a feeling about this place that resonates with me. Thank you so much, Merlyn, for bringing us here. I love it all...and Morgan has just showed me where thee and he live!"

"Gwen, come and say hello to Tom Hughes. He is the assistant manager here who interviewed you before offering you work in the hotel. Do you remember?"

"Oh..." The Lady Gwendolyn knew nothing of interviews and offers and what work in a hotel meant. But she understood that she was in some way beholden to this older man who her mother addressed as if he was some sort of authority. Even Merlyn was silent in his presence. She curtseyed down in front of him.

"I'm honoured to meet you, sire," she said, bobbing low and averting her eyes.

Ceri apologised for her daughter and whispered that clearly Gwen did not remember him as yet. However, her memory would come back in due course, she assured him.

The Lady Gwendolyn rose and hovered demurely, respect-fully at a distance, smiling sweetly at this unknown individual to whom she had just been introduced.

Tom Hughes expressed his genuine concern that Gwen had still not fully recovered from her fall. He silently hoped that she did get better soon with no lasting ill-effects and the Hotel Group would not be sued. At the same time as all these concerns crowded his mind, he was nonetheless impressed by what saw. The rather forward, flirtatious and overconfident young woman he had met, and had since wondered if she was really appro-priate for the post he had offered her, now showed what a well-mannered and courteous lady she could be. A beautiful, unclouded, innocent face looked at him. And such a ladylike bearing! He was thinking that with a full recovery she could be a real asset to an enterprise seeking to cultivate an Arthurian atmosphere in a modern-day Camelot.

"Gwen," he addressed her directly, "we would like you to come back to Camelot as soon as you are able. In just over a week's time we will have a staff briefing on the spirit of Camelot that we are committed to promote in the hotel – we have an outside expert invited to come and speak to us – and following that there is the grand opening to which all the nation's major media will be attending. If you are feeling better by then, those are two important dates for which we would love to have you with us... Of course," here he paused to look at Gwen's mother, "this all depends on how well you recover." Then he turned to Dai Mervyn. "And, Dai, of course you know about all this. I'll leave it with you and Gwen's mother to see if our young receptionist here is up to it. You'll need to be at the briefing in any case."

"Aye," said Dai Mervyn, non-committedly.

The Lady Gwendolyn curtsied once more. "Nothing, sire, would give me greater pleasure than to recapture the spirit of Camelot. That is why I am here and what I am looking for today: 'tis an ideal that means everything to me."

Tom Hughes saw the simple sincerity in her eyes. *She really means it,* he thought. *Where did this miracle come from? Not at all like so many too-clever-by-half people her age who seem to know it all and can't be trusted even to welcome my own grandmother.*

"Well, I'm delighted to hear you say that, Gwen. With that attitude, I think that the sooner you can come back to us, the better!" He smiled broadly, thanked Ceri Griffiths and Dai Mervyn and said his goodbyes. Tom Hughes turned and made his way back up the meadow, away from the stream and off to the hotel, only pausing for a moment to look back and wave to Gwen.

"Well, if he is your employer," said Ceri to both Dai and Gwen, "he doesn't seem a bad sort."

"Not so bad," echoed the old groundsman. "He's cheerful enough now. We'll see how he turns out when the hotel is open and the pressure is on. I've seen plenty young fellas like him in my time – coming in with lots of ideas and schemes before they hit a brick wall."

Ceri nodded. She understood. But the idea of promoting Camelot in the hotel she hoped would work out – it seemed like something that would help Gwen readjust; would help her bring together her imaginary world with that of today.

Dai left mother and daughter alone for a moment while he took Morgan into his cottage; then he returned and led them back across the grounds to go around to the side of the hotel and to find his beaten-up old Land Rover.

As he guided mother and daughter back up to the hotel, he sighed. These last couple of days, coming to know this young lady who was living in the past, who seemed to think he was out of Camelot himself, this had all been an intensely emotional journey – one that was totally unexpected and a journey that he never thought he would ever take again. Chaperoning Gwen out of hospital and now over the grounds where he had once walked his own daughter – decades ago when she too was young and impressionable – was like walking in a dream. It was a dream he had treasured and, indeed, wallowed in for years and years...and now here he was taking part in it. Was that wrong? To want your dreams to come true? Who is to say what is right and what is best? If living in the past made you happy, why not? Was he a stupid old fool for wanting to roll back the years and revisit a time gone by? He looked at Gwen, the girl who said she came from Camelot, and wondered.

Dai Mervyn walked on, over land he had worked and loved and got to know for over half a century; land that had seen the passage of civilisations grow and decline and grow again over millennia; land where dreams had come alive and where thousands of ghosts still walked, including that of his daughter. But he eventually arrived back at the car park, back at his Land Rover where he escorted his guests into the rear of his motor, got into the front and started it up. The noise of twenty-first-century machinery bursting into life shook him out of his reverie.

"Gwen, anytime you want to come back and see me, that's fine, OK? But for now: I'm taking you and your mother home."

Chapter 6

STORM CLOUDS

It was late summer, the days were still long and Camelot had been baking in a heat wave for a fortnight. There was not the slightest breath of wind and the air inside the castle, even behind insulating stone walls that were eight foot thick, had grown warm, heavy and humid. Over to the west, storm clouds were building up and a break in the weather was coming soon but for the time being Gwen Price was finding it difficult to sleep during the short, oppressive nights.

It had been a week since Gwen had woken up in the past, in unknown company, alone and shipwrecked in time, and she was now fed up with it. This farce had gone on long enough. She missed her friends – kindred spirits with whom she could share her thoughts and moan about all the creature comforts that did not exist here. Cold water, primitive toilets, awful clothes, no lights and thus having to go to bed at sunset and wake at sunrise – it was all far too uncomfortable to endure. Paula would be sure to understand. Where was her iPhone; her tablet computer; her music; her fashionable clothes? Gwen even missed her mother and the home she provided for her. This Kate was a sort of substitute – equally moralising! – but she was too immature and, unlike her mother, had no real idea of who Gwen was.

Gwen was an independent spirit who was accustomed to being in control of her life and of the people who she chose to be with. But here in Camelot none of that was possible. It drove her crazy at first. Now it was beginning to drive her into depression. She was moody, bad-tempered and increasingly resentful of the role she was being asked to play. She was not at all like the person everyone mistook her for...but she hardly dared to revert to her normal self for any sustained period of time for fear of being branded a witch. What a primitive, superstitious and savage society to be stuck in! And what a stupid and unliberated set of women she had to mix with too. She had had her fill of accompanying the queen in visiting the poor and handing out food parcels and other goodies; of watching the knights in combat practice and applauding their exploits; of sitting around with other ladies-in-waiting and joining in their tiny-minded chatter. She hated Camelot and wanted to go home.

Goody-goody Kate was beginning to irritate her. She was an uncomplaining, unwavering helper, maid and servant who, after her initial outburst had never again uttered a word of criticism, but her silence and fearful expressions at times were eloquent indications of her disapproval and lack of sympathy whenever Gwen could hold back the outbursts of frustration no longer. Why was it so bloody disagreeable living here? Going to the toilet was disgusting. Thank God that it was Kate's job to carry the water and wash away Gwen's toilet whenever she had to squat down in that smelly little room that served for the purpose. Ugh! A revolting way to have to carry on. Someone really ought to design a better way to answer the call of nature in a castle than to put up with such a primitive facilities. And why couldn't Kate see that?

Talking of which, that smelly little room still wasn't clean enough. It was late, getting dark and in the humid air the stink from that hole was unsupportable. She shouted for Kate.

"Kate! For goodness sake please bring a lot more water and flush this awful toilet out. I can't sleep with that stink. It's a wonder you didn't notice yourself!"

Kate appeared, spluttering and sneezing. "Yes, my lady..."

"Oh, bloody hell, don't sneeze all over me! What's the matter with you?"

"I'm very sorry, my lady. I don't know what the matter is...my head is aching, I feel very tired, I can't stop sneezing, my nose is running..."

"No wonder you can't smell the stink in there. Go on – off you go and get some water and sluice that place out again. Quick, before I throw up and give you more to do..."

"Yes, my lady."

Kate curtsied and disappeared, stumbling away and looking in a dreadful state.

She's probably going down with a cold or the flu, thought Gwen. *That's all I need now!* She closed the oaken door to her bedchamber and walked over to peer out of the slit window before going to bed. The twilight sky was still clear enough to see what sort of weather was in store for the morrow: clouds loomed heavily in the west, so there was a good chance of a storm to break the torrid heat. A flickering of lightning over the mountains far in the distance gave Gwen hope.

She changed out of her long robes and into her nightwear, still with all sorts of issues coursing through her mind. It was too hot to sleep, the stupid bed was lumpy and uncomfortable and clearly people here didn't know what a proper spring mattress was. There was simply so much people had to learn here about how to live properly that Gwen didn't know where to start. Well, at least the queen's teeth were looking better. She didn't have such a yellow and off-putting smile now. Gwen was pleased that her suggestion to Merlyn to make up some form of toothpaste had been a success. Maybe she ought to tell him next about spring mattresses?

Lightning suddenly flashed around her bedchamber. No thunder yet, so Gwen waited: the storm must still be some way off. A distant rumble came moments later, like the passage of lots of heavy lorries. *Not that any fools here would know what they were,* she thought. What was it? How many seconds did you have to count between lightning flash and thunder clap to work out the distance? Gwen vaguely knew it was about sound travelling slower than light but had forgotten what the time relation was. She was never an attentive student in school. Not like that Gareth

Jones – too clever by half, he was.

Gwen lay there listening to see if she could hear Kate returning with buckets of water for the toilet. Yes – there she was, coughing and sneezing outside her door. She'd told Kate some time ago to leave at least one full bucket there over night, just in case Gwen woke up and wanted to pee. She had better remember!

Another flash of lightning…and moments later a *Crump!* of thunder. The storm was rapidly coming closer, though no rain as yet. There was a clattering outside Gwen's door. It sounded like Kate had quickly finished her work, dropped the buckets and scuttled away. Gwen wondered if she was frightened of thunder and lightning. Some people were. And the silly girl was young after all.

The air abruptly became oppressively hot and humid – uncomfortably so. Gwen began to feel the dust in the air and the hair on her head come alive. Frightening – she knew straight away that the air was becoming electrified – so at least she had some idea of what was going on. The electric storm was right on top of them. Then from outside somewhere she could hear a lot of shouting and people running about. Since there was no possibility of sleep, and there was still no rain, Gwen took the decision to leave her room and go out and see what was happening. She did not get far. There were guards, those originally detailed to be on look-out on the battlements above, leaping and tripping down the spiral stairs and running for cover as fast as they could. Some were shouting in fear. Light all around was flashing blue and purple and the air seemed to be alive. Gwen was sure she heard a sort of buzzing. She had to admit it was eerie; she'd never seen lightning effects like these before – no bolts from the blue, no thunderous crashes – just a silent flickering and flashing and it was most unsettling.

Then: KABOOM! There came the most almighty crash and everything around seemed to explode. A tremendous lightning strike illuminated everything – the castle's passageways and interior, various terrified faces of men who had attempted to take cover, the darkest recesses of the spiral stairs, and metal studs in some of the doors twinkling like torches – the strike dazzled and lit up everywhere like an immense strobe light. Time stopped. There seemed to be a shimmering of multiple strikes but it could only have been all within a split-second.

And then the castle moved. Great stone blocks somewhere came crashing down. Now Gwen *was* frightened. Pitch blackness resumed as soon as the lightning had discharged its enormous electric load and in the total darkness she could hear part of the castle was collapsing. Screams, not shouts of alarm, came in waves through the thick air. There was someone crying, sobbing uncontrollably. And still Gwen could hear the crash of falling masonry. She ran for the safety of her room. That is, she hoped her room was safe but really it was only the familiarity of her quarters that attracted her. If this place was going to fall apart who was to tell which corners of the castle were going to be safer than others?

Gwen realised that now the rain was falling in torrents. In her room it was still watertight, so the stone above her must be undamaged, she realised with a leap of relief. Outside in the passageways and spiral stairs, however, water was cascading down so the rain was getting in somewhere above. Bang! More thunder and lightning – though this time there was no deep, rumbling sound of stone blocks tumbling away from a castle wall or tower. Gwen prayed that there would be no further direct hits. Meanwhile, the relentless noise of the rain obliterated the sound of whatever screams, cries and personal calamities were transpiring elsewhere. Crash! Another heart-shaking clap of thunder, though this time the sound seemed to have occurred *after* the lightning flash. Gwen got into bed and pulled the blankets over her head. Now it wasn't so oppressively hot and humid. Colder air was blowing and, despite the fearful thunder and lightning, Gwen could sense the release of energy in the atmosphere. If the storm kept moving, if no more direct lightning strikes occurred, she would be safe.

Thunder continued to roll every few seconds, but every few seconds it became more distant, more dislocated from the flash that accompanied it. Gwen's room was secure. She looked around it: reassuringly dim, dark and dry. That was all she needed to know. The air was colder and fresher and the rain could fall all night outside so far as she was concerned. This time, she would sleep.

* * *

Early the next morning, there came a thundering on the door that could not be ignored: "Castle inspection, by order of the king! Any damage here?"

Roused from strange dreams of her mother, searching in a thunderstorm, Gwen staggered to the door and opened it. "No, no everything is OK in here," she said sleepily to the herald waiting outside. She went back in but instead of returning to bed, she thought better of it. If the castle walls and/or towers had been breached by the storm, she wanted to see where and how much damage was involved.

Gwen called for Kate to help her get ready for going out, but there was no reply. She waited a few moments, almost finished dressing herself alone, then called out again. Still no answer. *Sod it!* Gwen finished getting herself ready on her own and prepared to leave. Kate could jolly well stay in bed and stew there for a while, for all Gwen cared.

The rain had long since finished but the spiral staircase leading up from her level was still damp and slippery from the thunderstorm. When Gwen reached to the top of the keep she met a number of people already there, blocking the exit from the staircase, who were surveying the damage that had occurred during the night.

A knight called back to her. "Careful, my lady! Don't push! There is much stonework now missing here!"

One or two faces Gwen recognised from last night: they were a couple of the guards who had cowered downstairs away from the lightning and who had now returned to their station, or what remained of it. One corner of the battlements and a section of one side on this top floor had disappeared, as had part of the stone floor. A long castle room below was open to the sky. It was fortunately not a residential quarter but a guard room, which now had part of one wall missing plus had gained a number of stone blocks that had fallen in from above. All across the top of the keep, concentrated around the area that was missing, there was evidence of scorched stone – blackened by the intense heat of the lightning blast. Over the side, peering carefully, a large amount of similarly blackened stonework could be seen lying jumbled around in the courtyard below. A couple of thatch-roofed market stalls had been demolished by this avalanche of stone but fortunately, since the damage had all occurred in the dead of night, it seemed there were no serious injuries down there.

Gwen had joined a company that included a number of guardsmen, plus two knights and their respective squires. There were no women apart from herself. The general conversation that took place amongst them was disturbed by the arrival of Merlyn, who had clambered up from below behind Gwen and, like the rest of them, had come to assess the extent of the damage.

"Look at this!" said one guard. "Hast thou ever seen anything like it?"

"'Twas a dragon. Only a dragon could do all this," claimed another.

"I saw it a long way away. It was breathing fire in the distance over the mountains there," replied the first guard. "Then it attacked us!"

Merlyn nodded. "The heat and noise was tremendous,

certainly," he agreed.

One of the squires spoke next. "I was up here and my sword started to glow in a blue light. And it made a sort of *buzzing* sound! The most amazing thing you ever saw! Some evil magic was certainly about. I threw it down and ran...and thank God I did because next the dragon blasted us all with his fiery breath!"

"Aye!" cried one of the guards. "I saw all that! Thy sword, even the armour and thy helmet started to glow. Awful! Terrible! Thou werst being possessed by evil! I ran away from thee and down the stairs as fast as I could. But thee...thou escapest just in time before the dragon struck..."

Gwen began to lose patience with all this nonsense. "This was a lightning strike – what are you talking about? There're no such things as dragons!"

A grim silence followed this remark. Gwen realised she was challenging a popular superstition so she thought she'd better back it up.

"I recognise some of you from last night, during the storm. We all saw the same, didn't we – lots of lightning and thunder, right? There was no dragon attacking us!"

"Aye, milady, but where did the thunder and lightning come from?" one of the knights, Sir Gareth, politely spoke up. "Such evil power as to do all this. It was a dragon. We all know that!"

Gwen was aghast at the primitive fears and beliefs of these people. "But lightning comes from the clouds...it's...it's a massive electric shock." She realised she did not know how it all worked. Did clouds discharge their electricity by bumping into high buildings? She couldn't explain it, other than she knew that dragons didn't produce it. Dragons did not exist!

The men around her smiled at her patronisingly. Sir Gareth spoke again, courteously as befitting a knight speaking to a lady.

"Milady, clouds are delicate, translucent creations of air and water with no weight or power – just mists that float with the wind. I have ridden through them many times. There is no heat and fire and enormous power within them. Clouds, milady, cannot do this. But they can hide evil creatures that are intent on doing us harm. Look at what this dragon did!"

"It was an electric shock that did this. Did anyone *see* a dragon?" Gwen was getting annoyed.

"I saw no lecktrickshock. What sort of evil spirit is that? What does it look like?" said one man.

"Was it hiding in the clouds?" asked another.

"No...the shock, the lightning strike, is conjured from out of the clouds themselves. Not from some mythical beast," Gwen repeated

No one was convinced.

"Milady, clouds are not evil spirits," repeated Sir Gareth gently.

One of the guards was less polite with this outspoken lady who was trespassing on his male-reserved territory.

"If it sounds like a dragon; if it flies across the mountain tops like a dragon; if it spits fire, flames and fury like a dragon, then what is it? A unicorn? A cloud? A lectrickshock? Pah! Only someone who wants to lose his life goes out and tries to see it. What I want to know is – why did it come here? Who summoned it? Whose magic brought it here?"

Merlyn spoke now. "None of us know the ways of dragons. None of us in Camelot know the dark, black minds of malevolent spirits. But we all know that evil is the enemy of the good. So long as Camelot stands proud against the forces of evil we will always need to maintain the strongest defences against such attacks that will, that must, continue against us."

The second knight present, Sir Kay, spoke next. "Merlyn speaks true. Now I say this: our King Arthur will in time summon a meeting of the Knights of the Round Table. He will want to discuss what happened here last night; how the damage can be repaired; how our defences can be strengthened; how perhaps we might go out and strike against the forces of evil rather than wait for the next attack. If any of thee have any knowledge of what transpired here thou shouldst tell the knight that commands thee so that he may address the Round Table. In the meantime, we must away now, and rest, and await his royal summons."

There was a general agreement to let this finish now. The company dispersed, although one or two of the guards who had been frightened out of their wits last night were not assuaged. One source of discontent was, as one continued to question under his breath as he walked away: "What brought that dragon here?" Another source of disquiet was a lady appearing in their midst, openly doubting their claims, overstepping her jurisdiction and intruding on theirs – unsettling, inexcusable, unladylike. Merlyn took all this in, descending the spiral staircase last of all with a serious, thoughtful expression.

Gwen returned to her bedchamber and found it undisturbed. Kate had not been in to tidy it up in her absence. What on earth was going on with that girl? She went immediately to the small room next door to give her maid a good shaking. What she found was poor Kate burning with fever, buried under her bedclothes and given to shaking uncontrollably every few seconds. She was very ill indeed.

"Oh bugger!" Gwen swore. Now what? She supposed she had better get Merlyn. Gwen left Kate where she was and started off bad-temperedly down to the ground floor to find the physician's workshop. That was all she needed: her servant girl incapacitated and bed-ridden – who was going to run after her now, clean out the toilet and do all the chores that were necessary? She was bored, fed up and tired enough of Camelot already without Kate falling sick and being unable to do her duties. Why now? Why did Kate have to get ill now?

Gwen found Merlyn hidden behind a whole battery of pots and utensils in his workshop, cooking up some foul-smelling concoction on a wooden bench.

"Hi Merlyn!" she called out. "Can you come and see what's the matter with Kate? She hasn't moved out of her bed this morning and looks pretty sick to me..."

Merlyn raised his head. "Another one? I am at this very moment preparing a medicament for Her Majesty the Queen who is feeling distinctly unwell. She tells me also that there are two of her ladies-in-waiting who appear to be sickening as well. And now Kate? Tell me, milady, of what malady doth she appear to be suffering?"

"I don't know! Perhaps it's a cold or the flu? She's been coughing and spluttering for a number of days now. Come and see for yourself!" Gwen was altogether too grumpy and annoyed with everything to do Merlyn's job for him.

"I will indeed come and see thy loyal and long-suffering young companion as soon as I have finished here. From what thou tellest me, all seem to be afflicted similarly. It indicates a sudden outbreak of some poisonous influence. Worrying!"

Merlyn decanted some of the liquid he had been boiling up into a small goblet. He crushed some mint leaves into it and stirred it all with a wooden spoon. "Come!" he said to Gwen. "I'll quickly go with thee before I take this to the queen."

A few moments later he entered the room where Kate lay; he knelt down beside her and gently raised her into a sitting position. She whimpered as he felt her forehead.

"So cold!" she complained weakly. "I'm so cold."

"Thou shouldst have come to me before, dear Kate," scolded Merlyn. "Thy fever would not appear so strong now without some earlier symptoms. What hast thou suffered these last few days? Tell me."

"I have been coughing and sneezing, and my throat hurts, and now I am so tired and everything aches..."

"Sounds like the flu to me!" snorted Gwen, who had been standing behind, watching Merlyn at work. She had little patience with people who were not well.

"The Flew?" Merlyn grimaced. Here was yet another occasion where this new Lady Gwendolyn seemed to know it all. He fought down his reaction to ignore this offending manner she persisted in maintaining. He was an old, experienced physician and weaver of supposedly magic spells, but he still prized his capacity to learn from even the most unlikely of sources. This awkward, contrary young woman who possessed the unique capacity to discomfort others was certainly an unlikely source.

"And what course, pray, do you expect this illness to run?"

"Dunno, Merlyn. It looks a bad dose to me. Last time I had something like that was a year ago, in the winter. I stayed in bed for a week and my mother gave me plenty of liquid to drink. I had honey or something like it for my sore throat. I felt bloody awful but it went away in the end."

Merlyn raised his eyes heavenward. Lady Gwendolyn's mother had died over a dozen years ago, so he did not know what she was talking about. But he now recognised that that was normal. Nobody in Camelot knew what she was talking about half the time. But there was, as before, a glimmer of something useful in all the smoke and confusion that came out of her mouth. "Kate," Merlyn asked, "hast thy body lost much liquid? Hast thy nose been flowing freely?"

Kate nodded.

"Thou shouldst rest. Drink this warming fluid that I have prepared for the queen. I will take her another. Thou shouldst stay in bed and we will find someone to care for thee. Thou hast taken aboard some evil influence but with love, care and attention we shall overcome that which has invaded thy body and make thee better. Now, keep warm!"

Merlyn helped Kate drink the concoction in the goblet he proffered, then he laid her back down and pulled the blankets and a woollen sheepskin over her to stop her shivering.

He kissed Kate's cheek, stood up and signalled to Gwen to come with him outside.

"Milady," he confided in her outside the door, "I must go straight-way to see the queen and deliver to her much the same medicine...but thou must understand that, given the destruction caused in the storm, and now this illness of a number of people in the castle, every servant and attendant in Camelot has much to do. So who canst care for Kate on a regular basis? Only thee. Care for her, milady, in the same manner that she has cared for thee. That is thy duty now." Mervyn stared pointedly into Gwen's eyes.

"Oh shit!" responded Gwen. "Shit, shit, shit! Can't you find *someone*, somewhere to come and look after her. I can't do it!" She was never cut out to be a nurse, it was the last thing she wanted to do.

"Milady, thy young ward has devoted her life to thee. Does she not deserve some little effort on thy part to repay her kindness with a little care and consideration of thine own? Thou must, if her illness is not to deteriorate. And consider: thou hast said thyself that thou knowest of this ailment that has stricken her. Thou art the only one who dost know this!"

"No, Merlyn. I can't! I really can't!"

"And if thou dost not care for her, and Kate's condition is to worsen, who wilst serve thee in the future? None other, I can assure thee of that. None will pledge their lives for the new Lady Gwendolyn with this attitude thou hast shown all of recent. If thou canst perform this service for thine own devoted companion when she is in need of this most of all, then beware! Thine own future wilst be the poorer for it. I leave thee now to attend the queen. Thinkest on these things, my lady..."

Merlyn disappeared on the errand of mercy to the queen that he had promised. Gwen was left alone. She went slowly back to her bedchamber and shut the door before she let out a shriek of annoyance, frustration and defiance at the whole world she was trapped in. She had no choice, she knew it. If she wanted Kate to run around after her again in the future then Gwen had to perform the same service for her maid now. She swore again.

* * *

A bell sounded. It was the castle bell to summon all knights to the Round Table. Everything stopped – all duties were put on hold. The only duty that remained was to ensure that all knights – within the castle or away outside – were informed that they should return to Camelot this instant. Within the hour the king would convene a meeting of his chosen counsellors and any that were absent must be excused by Royal Command or be accused of dishonouring the highest ideal of Camelot, and thus be stripped of their knighthood.

Only knights were allowed to enter the Round Room. Not even the queen was allowed in. She, her most favoured ladies-in-waiting, and others by invitation could observe from the gallery, though a strict chivalric code prevented their participation in any of the discussion and decision-making that took place.

And so, on the hour, twelve knights were seated around the Round Table: thirteen including the king himself: Sir Bedivere; Sir Blamore; Sir Bleoberis; Sir Bors; Sir Galahad; Sir Gareth; Sir Gawain; Sir Geoffrey; Sir Geraint; Sir Hector; Sir Kay; Sir Percival, the only one missing was Sir Lancelot – away on a quest with the permission of the king. The fourteenth present was Merlyn: not a knight, but his presence as counsellor to the king and the court was considered indispensable and he had been granted an especial right to attendance many years ago.

The gallery was crowded as always. Although the queen and two of her ladies-in-waiting were absent, many others had begged permission to be present in their place. The king's herald-in-chief, the Black Rod, had the power to decide who should receive that honour. Those he had chosen were the two squires of the senior knights, Sir Lancelot and Sir Bedivere.

King Arthur opened the proceedings.

"Fellow Knights of the Round Table: you are all welcome. We are come together because I believe we are all aware of what has recently threatened Camelot. Out task is to determine exactly how serious this evil is that threatens us, if indeed we decide that there *is* evil at our gates or even amongst us. Sir Bors has requested to speak first. As is our custom, there is no head to the Round Table. All are equal amongst us and all are entitled to speak – only that he who speaks must first be passed the Camelot mace. Sir Bors!"

The ceremonial mace was handed round the table to Sir Bors, who grasped it and rose to his feet.

"Fellow knights, at this moment there are several work parties being organised to repair the stonework that has been breached by the dragon's attack. My squire has been appointed to lead those parties and to delegate the work amongst the castle staff. The head stonemason will be in charge of how the walls and tower will be rebuilt. There is much to be done. It will take several weeks for the work to be completed and the castle's defences then returned to their original state. But my question is – is this enough?"

Sir Gareth raised his hand to request the mace. He rose to speak – a large man, modest and rarely given to speak at the Round Table, so his desire to address his colleagues now drew instant attention.

"My dear and honourable friends, you all know that I am content to let others speak for me at most of our meetings, but on this occasion I must confess there are matters afoot that sorely trouble me and it is thus incumbent upon myself to draw these matters to the attention of all. I am reluctant to say this…indeed it pains my very soul…but I fear there is a malevolent influence about us in Camelot that has caused not only the dragon's attack but also – and far worse – this evil has caused an outbreak of some severe illness that is at this very moment weakening the health of our beloved queen and a number of her ladies-in-waiting!"

Cries of horror greeted this remark. Several knights struck the table with their fists; one pushed back his chair and was about to draw his sword. An attack upon the ladies of Camelot was something all knights were sworn to repel, with their lives if necessary. Sir Gareth waited for the reaction to his remarks to subside before raising the mace to indicate he wished to continue.

"Noble knights, we pledge ourselves each year at the Feast of Pentecost to serve Camelot and, amongst our other commitments, to never dishonour a lady of the court. Sir Kay, thou knowest mine own devotion to one lady of Camelot in particular so thou will know'st how much it tortures me to say this...but...but there is some evil spirit that has invaded the fair person of Lady Gwendolyn and – through her – is broadcasting its influence throughout this citadel. I have earlier mentioned my fears to King Arthur and he instructs me to inform you all of this."

Horror was replaced by incredulity in the faces of all around the Table. Lady Gwendolyn was known to be the fairest, most honourable maiden and closest confidant of Queen Guinevere. Evil to be harboured within the most trusted lady and one so close to the seat of power within Camelot? How could this be? A storm of outrage and disbelief broke out amongst all those present.

The king stood up and commanded silence. "Continue, Sir Gareth. Thou strikest at the very heart of Camelot. Explain this allegation thou makest!"

"My king, my honourable fellow knights and colleagues, why do I speak thus? My fears were first awakened on the day after the fair Lady Gwendolyn rose from her fever to greet the return of the king and queen from the royal hunt. The language that emanated from her throat that day was not that of the fair maiden I knew she to be. Men and womenfolk of the castle kitchens later confirmed to me that her behaviour that day was somehow very different to what they had seen before. No matter! Such eccentricities can be explained away by the after-effects of the noxious fever that had consumed her for three days. Our noble and trusted physician, Merlyn, warned us of this. But...but what has transpired since? The assault of an evil dragon that has breached our outer defences and, worse, the outbreak of some foul plague that has attacked us from within and has brought down some of our most treasured and beloved ladyfolk – both these forces of evil can be traced to the same source!"

Here Sir Gareth paused to draw breath. It had the desired effect on his colleagues: every eye around the table was riveted on his. Not a sound was uttered.

"Let me begin with the dead of last night and the dragon's attack – who came out straight-way at the height of the attack, attempting to ascend to the top of the keep? *A lady!* What was a lady attempting to do there? I believe, noble sires, that she came out to summon the dragon to her! And then again, this morning...Sir Kay, thou canst confirm what she said to those that assembled atop the keep this morning..."

The mace was passed across to Sir Kay.

"Aye, Sir Gareth. Again, this very morn, there was the Lady Gwendolyn alone who joined the guards, myself and Sir Gareth at the top of the keep. She attempted to deny that a dragon had caused the thunder and lightning. Fire came from out of the clouds, merely the clouds, she said, claiming there had been no dragon hiding there. Sir Gareth questioned her most respectfully, most honourably, sire, I attest to that. But the Lady Gwendolyn insisted there was no dragon that had attacked the castle, but that fire and flames came from out of the clouds. Noble knights, my fellows – there is more energy that comes from a babe in arms than exists in the body of clouds! The Lady Gwendolyn was spreading falsehoods!"

At this point, King Arthur stood and requested the mace be passed over.

"Noble knights, my chosen few, I have to say that the

evidence of the plague is even more alarming," he began. "Honoured Knights of the Round Table – we can take up arms to defend Camelot from the fiercest attacks from without. We have repelled sieges from barbarians, Danes and Saxons many times over the years. We will stand as one to prevent even the most mighty of dragons from entering this most revered and treasured citadel. But to stop the spread of some malevolent spirit from invading the bodies of our ladyfolk? I am certain that every last one of us here would lay his life on the line to prevent this. Yet my beloved Guinevere, the fair queen herself, at this moment lies sick as we gather at the Round Table today! Sir Gareth came to see me before this morn with the dreadful news that this sickness is spreading and it can only be a plague spread by the most evil of influences. I have thus commanded the bell to be rung and for us all to assemble. Tell us more, Sir Gareth!"

"Where did this plague originate?" Sir Gareth asked. "Who was struck down first? It was the loyal and faithful maid to Lady Gwendolyn who was the first and is the most affected by this sickness. She lays now bed-ridden and her condition worsens by the hour. Who next? Two of Lady Gwendolyn's companion ladies-in-waiting with whom she has shared much time recently have since become afflicted, and then – to the dismay of us all – the plague has struck our beloved queen and consort to the king. But who will fall next? Are we to await the attack of evil on the very head and heart of Camelot? The king? Can we afford to wait or should we first strike as quickly as possible to remove this malevolent spirit before it destroys our leader, our king, the very foundation stone of everything we have created here? Fellow knights: the survival of Camelot is threatened."

"No!" Uproar followed. Knights rose to their feet; swords flashed in the air. "Death to all evil!" was a cry that echoed around the chamber of the Round Room. And to what evil should all these swords be pointed? None other than the evil that resided within the Lady Gwendolyn.

Chapter 7

THE MISCHIEVOUS DEMON

King Arthur called for order once more. "Noble colleagues, honourable friends, I thank each and every one of thee for thy loyal support. But stay your passions for a moment. Sir Gareth has spoken most eloquently, most fearfully, and indeed doth most sadly recount his utmost despair for the soul of the Lady Gwendolyn. But there is one amongst us who has counselled the fair lady for years as if he were her father and has ministered to her on a daily basis since her recent fever. He knows the fair lady better than all of us and I desire to hear his opinion. His wisdom and recommendation has always served the Round Table well in the past and I do not doubt Merlyn has no little insight with which to enlighten us on this occasion too. Merlyn – the mace!"

Merlyn rose slowly to take the mace. He shook his head in sadness, held still for a moment, then slowly began to air his thoughts.

"There is much that Sir Gareth has said that is true. I personally formed the same opinion as my noble friend before the bell summoned me to this table: that the source of the troubles that have been visited upon Camelot can only have come from Lady Gwendolyn. All the evidence, I regret to say, leads me to this conclusion that I share with the noble knight." Merlyn stopped. He looked about the Round Table, took a deep breath and continued, emphasising each individual point with a tap of his fingers on the table.

"Honourable Knights of the Round Table, I have served yourselves for decades, and before yourselves, many of your fathers. I have been face to face with evil on a number of occasions. The king himself knowest I speak true. But hear this: I do *not* believe that the good Lady Gwendolyn has become consumed with evil. No! Rather that, somehow, in the fever that brought her close to death, some form of mischievous demon has seized hold of her. I believe, however, that the goodness that we all know was her true character before her illness is still within her but at present is dormant, unable to assert itself, whilst the demon is in ascendance in her soul. How so a mischievous spirit, and not pure evil? Because in the exercise of malevolence that this spirit propagates lie also the seeds of some contrasting remedy. As Sir Gareth so astutely surmised on his first encounter with the lady after her fever, her language was strange, even offensive, as if designed to spread discord amongst us. But at the same time as this, almost as if t'were by accident, she suggested a potent new medicine to cure the queen's toothache and improve the health of her smile. And again, this very morn, she seemed firstly unaware that her own influence was at fault for the sickness that has befallen her maid, Kate, as well as to our beloved queen and, almost in the same breath as pointing out to me the plague that is afoot, she has suggested a remedy that will contain it. There is a mischievous demon within her, therefore, that is playing with her, and though her, with us all..."

Sir Kay rose to request the mace and contest the words of the old magician.

"The dragon, wise Merlyn! The dragon! The Lady Gwendolyn, or if thou speakest true, the mischievous demon within her has clearly summoned the dragon to attack Camelot. Has this demon let slip some form of weakness by which one may beat off the next assault, or in some way draw out the dragon's teeth and fire?" Sir Kay passed the mace back across the table so that Merlyn might reply.

"I thank thee, Sir Kay, for that intervention for truly thy suggestion is the key test of my supposition. I will speak more of this in a moment. As yet, in truth, I have not spoken to the Lady Gwendolyn about the dragon. I have spoken little with her, except to discuss the sickness that has overcome her loyal and faithful servant. I have in fact insisted that the good lady should stay by her maid's bedside and care for her in the same way that she herself has been served. For that reason, Lady Gwendolyn has not visited the gallery above, as is her right as the queen's closest confidant. She is in her maid's chambers – evidence in my view that evil has not yet been successful in completely consuming her soul. The mischievous spirit within her has a malevolent side – of that I do not doubt – but it is contested still within her ladyship by her own innate goodness. And noble knights – is that not true of *all* of us? Search thine own conscience, each one of thee. Is it not true that for each and every one of us, there resides deep down within us a voice that would have us act dishonourably on occasions? Do we not all, at times, have to fight base emotions within ourselves in order that good may triumph? It would be easy to be good; indeed there would be no honour in being good if we were each born without the capacity for evil. It is because we *choose* to fight against our own demons that we thereby achieve honour. And so I ask that we give to Lady Gwendolyn that same choice as we give ourselves. If she chooses to be good, then she and Camelot are saved. If the demon within her is triumphant, however, and she cannot contain the evil within her soul, then it must be for some chosen knight amongst us to end her life and that of the malevolent spirit that has overpowered her. Sir Kay – you ask about the dragon. Noble sire, allow me to ask the Lady Gwendolyn about this dragon. I shall ask in a most innocent and innocuous way what does the lady think about dragons and their formidable powers. If I am right, the mischievous spirit within her will reveal some clue as to how we might successfully draw the dragon's teeth and fire, as you ask. That will prove my hypothesis correct. And if so, from thereon it will be for us to devise a quest to give my lady opportunity to come to terms with her own mischievous demon and in doing so, allow good to ultimately triumph against evil. The demon will be exorcised by the lady's own efforts. What sayest thou, Sir Kay? Dost thou agree? And, Sir Gareth? My honourable Knights of the Round Table, how dost this argument sound? My king, how dost thee command?"

It was a long speech. A longish silence followed, as all thought through Merlyn's words. Then one knight applauded – it was Sir Gareth. Others soon followed and applause soon rang round the chamber. Finally, King Arthur called for the mace. He rose from the table.

"Wise Merlyn, thou art a true and faithful servant of Camelot. Thy wisdom shames us all. We who would rush out unthinkingly to confront evil may do more harm than good. Thy counsel – that we each have to confront our own demons – is undoubtedly true. That we should grant this same choice to the fair Lady Gwendolyn must also be true. For near two decades she has been the very epitome of goodness at Camelot and in so doing has captured the hearts of many, including that of mine own dear queen. So how can we not deny the fact that she deserves her own right to contest the mischievous spirit within her and thus attain honour, like everyone else present here, myself included? I propose we follow Merlyn's recommendation, therefore. Are there any here who would wish to differ? Or otherwise wish to express a contrary opinion?"

None did.

"It is thus decided. Merlyn, our most valiant and valued friend, it is hereby entrusted to you to test the fair Lady Gwendolyn and to inform us all of what transpires as a result. Let none who hear these words, at this Round Table or above in the gallery, betray what has happened here this afternoon. Let none speak with the Lady Gwendolyn until Merlyn has first given her the choice between good and evil of which he has spoken. Let none, by accident or design, frustrate this most important venture that Merlyn is about to undertake. This, by order of the Round Table, the highest order of chivalric code within Camelot and abroad in the entire country. I, King Arthur, on behalf of the Round Table, order it so."

The meeting ended.

* * *

Kate, the queen and indeed the entire court that shared the castle of Camelot had no defence against a flu virus that came straight from the twenty-first century. Fortunately, Gwen was a strong, healthy girl and had arrived in the fifth century with no virulent strain of this debilitating and sometimes fatal sickness incubating within her. But what was a mere cold to someone from the future could nonetheless be a serious, life-threatening sickness to those who had no experience of such an ailment from a different age. Kate was very ill, therefore, and needed constant attention. Gwen, with no previous experience nor interest in caring for others, was both bemused and intensely annoyed at the being required to perform nursing duties. But she had to do it. Kate was too ill even to rise and visit the toilet next door so Gwen, though she resisted until the last moment, had to go fetch a pan from the kitchens, return to Kate's bedside, encourage her toilet and then had to dispose of it and sluice it away down the hole in the next door toilet room. Ugh! She was not at all happy with her new role.

Gwen had no hesitation in telling Merlyn all this when he next visited. She was angry at him for making her perform such tasks and insisted yet again that someone other than she should be called upon to do this dirty work. Merlyn simply ignored her. He had other things on his mind.

When Gwen's tirade against toilets, primitive technologies and the lack of castle staff had worn itself out, Merlyn turned the conversation towards dragons and the attack on the castle the night before. Gwen was as dismissive as ever.

"Why don't you people get it?" she enquired impatiently.

"There are no such things as dragons, nor fire-breathing demons – just like there is no Loch Ness Monster nor Father Christmas! Has anyone honestly *seen* a dragon? Except in their dreams, that is."

"No dragons? Then how dost thee account for the serious damage inflicted upon the castle?" Merlyn asked.

Gwen groaned. "It was thunder and lightning! Don't ask me how clouds produce all that 'cos I dunno. OK? Clever bastards like Gareth Jones would know and could explain it, but not me. One thing I *do* know, however, is that without a lightning conductor, any tall building is vulnerable to being damaged by a lightning strike, should an electric storm hit. Clever Gareth once told me that."

"Would this clever bar steward Gareth Jones know how to protect Camelot, therefore?"

"Sure! I just said, Merlyn – if we had a lightning conductor then *that* would protect us."

"How so, milady?"

"It's...it's like a great sword or metal spike that pokes up into the sky on the roof. It is connected to a thick metal rod or cable that runs all the way down the building from the very top, in more or less a straight line, to the very bottom and then deep into the earth. Lightning is sort of attracted to the top of this sword and away from the building itself; the electric current then passes all the way down the metal rod and harmlessly into the ground. Only if the cable is broken then the electricity enters the building. Kaboom! Not good! Gettit? You gotta construct the lightning rod all the way from top to bottom in an unbroken line. And if the lightning comes, don't touch the rod! You'll get electrocuted! Zillions of volts will fry your insides!"

Merlyn nodded sagely. Another rare story. He thought it through...if he understood right, the dragon's fire would go down the metal and not into the building. Again, he could see some sense in this. Blacksmiths heating up metal to forge swords or, more commonly, to produce horseshoes know all about the superior power of metal to conduct heat away from a fire. Why shouldn't that idea work on a grand scale – taking a dragon's fire down and away from the battlements and into the earth below where it would be swallowed up and defeated? The idea was quite ingenious.

"My lady, thine ideas and arguments are as always quite fascinating. If I may be so bold, I will say that ideas such as these – if they work – will save thy life, as well as the lives of others…"

"What do you mean, Merlyn, save my life? Have I been accused of spreading evil, like you warned me? Have I? Tell me I haven't, *please!*"

"I regret, my lady, that indeed thou hast been so accused."

"Oh, Merlyn! You don't think I'm evil do you? Do you? You will defend me against these stupid accusations, won't you? Tell me you would! What *do* you think of me?"

"Milady, I did indeed warn thee that since thy fever, thy words and deeds strike many here as strange and unbecoming a lady. How come such a gracious and fair young maiden has become so radically different, challenging, even threatening in her comportment? How come she seeks to defend dragons? How come some strange and alien affliction has laid low not only thy servant and ladies thou hast recently met with, but has even attacked the queen and thus struck at the very heart of Camelot?"

"But I'm not evil! I'm different, that's all. So I know things and believe things that must seem strange to people here, I suppose you are right. As for this affliction you accuse me of…well that might be true, now you come to mention it. It is like going back to work after a holiday – people bring all sorts of viruses with them. I could've brought some virus with me….but it's just a cold, isn't it? Or maybe the flu? That will pass in time, I'm sure of it. Christ I hope it does, 'cos if not I can see I'm gonna be in big trouble…"

"Milady, thou art already in big trouble"

"But haven't you defended me, Merlyn? Don't tell me you believe I am some evil influence?"

"My Lady Gwendolyn, I do not believe that thou art evil. But thou hast undoubtedly and suddenly become a strange and challenging influence amongst us. That cannot be denied. Some rare magic has infected thee, has brought thee hence from another time and place, thou hast said. Such magic neither thee nor I can explain. But whatever is this place that thou knowest, it must be an aggressive, hostile and unfriendly world for that is the temperament thou bring'st with thee."

Gwen protested angrily at this accusation. "That's not fair, Merlyn! You've no right to insult me or my home like that. It's much more sophisticated and advanced than this hole I'm now stuck in!"

"Milady, thou reveal'st the aggression of which I speak. Thou complainest mightily about Camelot and insist that this other place of which thou speakest is in some way advanced, or superior. Thine own comportment contradicts thee. There is little noble, honest and true in much of what thou dost practise. Thou demandest that others should serve thee, but do not wish to serve others; thou hast taken food from the kitchens with no thought for those thou denies in so doing; thou speakest roughly with knights and attendants alike. These are not the ways of some advanced and civilised society. The illness that thou hast brought with thee is but a symbol of a more subtle but even more deadly influence that thou bring'st: a mean and ungenerous spirit which, if it were to spread, would eat away at the very essence of Camelot. Lady Gwendolyn, until this magic that has hold of thee dost let go of thy character, thou must change thy ways. Fight down the demon within thee that complains at everything and corrupts thy vision. Learn to see and value the goodness around thee."

This sounded like more moralising – similar to what Kate had said earlier; similar indeed to what Gwen's own mother had been going on and on about for years and years until Gwen had closed her ears against it and pushed her mother away. This was the same old tune and Gwen didn't want to hear any more of it.

Merlyn could see the resentful expression on Gwen's face and understood that she could not take much more. Her capacity to learn was exhausted. Time to lay his message on the line.

"Milady, thou hast three pathways to choose from. First: give nothing; insist on your own superiority; fight against Camelot and take the consequences. Second: begin to serve others and honour Camelot for fear of what may befall thee if thou dost not. Third: devote thyself to the service and welfare of others for *their* sake, and not for thine own. Which pathway dost thou choose? Which path dost thou think is the way of Camelot?"

Gwen was no fool. If she fought against the customs and traditions of Camelot there would be only one outcome. She would be banished, or imprisoned, or worse. She'd heard about what people did to witches in feudal times and didn't want any of that. No thank you! Being sent away from Camelot would be a less painful fate, but what would she do, where would she go, how would she survive in a world of barbarians outside the gates? Whatever else she might moan about, Camelot was at least safe and she was housed and fed here.

Gwen had to accept that she had done very little to earn her keep so far. She had lived off the goodwill earned by the person whose body she just happened to be inhabiting...and that goodwill was clearly evaporating. She could not keep demanding that everyone else should change their ways to suit her, even if she was always right and they were all wrong. And maybe, it began to occur to her, just maybe they were not always in the wrong. Maybe she wasn't always right, after all? OK, she knew that dragons didn't exist really but they were as good as anything else she could think of for explaining lightning and thunder.

Merlyn watched Gwen's face. He'd got through. He could see her thinking seriously about her situation. He had one more throw of the dice left to win the contest between them.

"We agreed on a contract, milady, dost thou remember? Thou wouldst contain thy devilment if I would try some of thine ideas garnered by thy magical insight. I have upheld my part of this bargain: the medicines thou hast recommended I have delivered. I shall shortly take thy suggestion for containing dragon's fire to the king. But where is thy commitment to refrain from undermining the spirit of this fair citadel? Thou dost possess thine own unique magic. Use it to serve Camelot – suggesting new medicaments, caring for the poor, protecting the castle from dragons – and use it not to criticise others and to serve only thyself. Show us all that thou may be different... but thou art not an evil influence."

Gwen looked up. Merlyn was right. This world she had entered was not going to change to suit her so she would have to change herself or be condemned to misery, or witchery or worse. It was no good pining for the world she had lost – she had to make the best of this Camelot she had found herself in. Isn't that what all travellers did? She remembered that was what some teacher had told her once when she was away on a school camping trip, moaning about how foreign and uncomfortable it all was.

"OK, Merlyn," she finally gave way. "You're the man. I'll do as you say. Both you and Kate have said what a wonderful ideal is Camelot. I'll *try* and see it. I won't hanker after the internet, my clothes, my iPhone, cars, hamburgers and chips, or any other of the luxuries I miss here. I'll really try, OK? I'll look after Kate 'til she's well again and not complain. But...but there's a fourth pathway that you did not mention... my way back home. If ever I find it, or if you find it for me, that is the one I really want to take, understand?"

"Of course, milady. It may well be that thou will find it thyself at the end of the third pathway that lies in front of thee. It is my contention that the mischievous spirit that has arisen within thee has come to test thee. If thou defeatest this selfish, sharp-tongued, mean-spirited demon that is fighting to overcome thy soul, if thou can triumph over its influence, then perhaps thou wilst be able to find thine own way back home to thy true self and all will be well...but thou must work at it! Welcome to Camelot..."

For the first time in a week, Gwen smiled. That sounded good. Maybe that's what this was all about – some sort of test of her character. If so, she was determined to win.

"So it's a deal, then. Go take my suggestion for a lightning conductor to the king. Save me, please, from them all branding me as some sort of evil witch. Protect me, Merlyn! I'll go, meanwhile, and look after Kate and maybe think up some other ways to serve the interests of Camelot. I'll not become some timid little lady with brains like water and be told what to do all the time...but OK...OK..." Gwen could see the look of concern on Merlyn's face. "I'll try my very, very best not to upset the applecart and challenge *all* the customs of this castle." She grinned. *Only some of them,* she thought, *those that won't put my head in the stocks!*

Chapter 8

THE SPIRIT OF CAMELOT

The Lady Gwendolyn had passed a most fascinating, most challenging, most unsettling week. She was at home with her mother – something that might normally be considered unremarkable, except that her mother was someone who was very new to her; she did not know this 'home', and that every day the twenty-first century brought fresh surprises and inexplicable happenings.

It was a world full of things, gadgets, possessions and surprisingly devoid of warmth, that is: real, live, person-to-person contact. There were amazingly lifelike pictures and miniatures of people everywhere in this home, some of them moving on a truly baffling, flickering screen. There were also people's voices that came through the ether when a bell or buzzer sounded, but very few actually came to visit in person.

The home her mother introduced her to contained her own bedchamber...but this too was entirely novel. There were these lifelike miniatures of herself on the walls – at different ages, evidently. This was fascinating. Lady Gwendolyn did not realise they were of herself until her mother told her so. Are those really me. She had asked. Did I look like that? She had no idea. But who painted these, she questioned. They were not painted, apparently but they came out from this machine called a camera. Oh! The Lady Gwendolyn learned that just about everything came out of one machine or other.

There were machines for washing clothes. There were machines for cooking. There was a machine for cleaning the house that had a long tail connected to the wall and which roared around picking up dirt. There were machines for heating and controlling some form of fire. There was a machine for making things cold. (The kitchen was just full of machines!) There were machines that made music. Machines that held all these flickering pictures. Machines to dry your hair. Machines – horseless chariots she had already seen – to travel in. Machines that you controlled with lots of buttons and could bring words and pictures out of the ether. But there was no Kate. When Mother was not around, there was only cold, emotionless machines.

Her mother showed her lots of pictures, of places near and far, some she had apparently visited, many others she had not. There were buildings, beaches, mountains and machines of all varieties. There were shopping catalogues full of glamorous and shiny things that she never knew she needed; there were travel brochures full of smiling people in places she could never have imagined – cities that towered into the sky, boats that were like cities on the sea. It was a world full of things.

Twenty-first century Britain was also full of people – far more than there were some fifteen centuries earlier – but although they were everywhere, relations between these modern folk were generally fleeting, families were smaller, cooler and people inevitably more independent. If you needed help you did not ask a friend or relation but went to see a professional. The Lady Gwendolyn had difficulty coming to terms with this. She did not enjoy her return visit to the hospital to see the consultant Jerome Cohen, for example. But she learned quickly that if she did not overexcite his academic interest she would not have to see him very often. She could then be freer to look for people who did *not* wear white coats and could instead try and find those who were generally concerned about her as a person and not as some medical case to be examined, poked around and investigated.

One evening there was a ding-dong sound that meant a visitor had called. Mother said that Lady Gwendolyn's friend, Paula, had come to see her. It was suggested they go to the bedchamber to have a talk together. The Lady Gwendolyn was rather shy but she did so want to meet another person, whoever it was; in this case – a friend she did not know.

Conversation was stilted at first as both became aware of how little they really knew of each other. Lady Gwendolyn assured her friend that she was quite well after her period of unconsciousness, only her memory had been erased and she felt she was living in a strange new world, whose institutions, customs and practices were entirely foreign to her. Paula had some difficulty in believing this.

"Do you mean to say you don't remember who I am?" she asked.

"Truly, I do not," Lady Gwendolyn bashfully replied. "I've never seen thee before."

Paula's eyes grew round in wonder. "Wow! I've heard of this but never thought it would really happen to a friend of mine. Don't you remember going to the King Offa with me, Gwen?"

"No. What's the King Offa?"

"A pub." No sign of recognition, "Our local!" Still nothing. "Where we go for a drink in the evenings some times when you want to get away from your mother..."

"I don't want to get away from my mother. I've only just found her."

"You *what*?"

Lady Gwendolyn had come to realise that the story of who she really was and the only life she had known and now lost was far too difficult for people in this world to understand. She couldn't explain it herself, after all. And there was simply too much to learn in this bewildering, frightening new reality so it was easiest to say that she had lost her memory and that way maybe people would help her come to terms with it all.

"I've only just realised what my mother is like. She...she's...lovely!"

"Well good for you. How about that? I always thought you were a bit extreme in her regard, but that's your affair, not mine. Anyway, since you don't remember going to the King Offa, how about if we go there now? Just to spend an hour or so? So that you will remember it next time! Yes?"

"Yes, I want to see it. There's so much here I do not know. But help me, Paula – thou hast to understand everything here is so difficult, so different, even frightening for me..."

Paula nodded but at the same time she could not help but wonder at the transformation of her friend. Gwen had always been the dominant one – a bit too dominant and radical at times. Indeed Paula had often felt intimidated in her company, though she had never let on. Now here was her independent, outspoken and almost too forceful friend acting shy, lacking in self-confidence and needing her support. Could this really be Gwen? Of course it was, but clearly her concussion and hospitalisation had really battered her self-esteem. Paula was going to have to be the dominant one now – at least for the time being. It was going to be a new relationship: she rather liked that idea.

"Don't worry, Gwen, you'll be fine. It's only a short bus ride away – you've done it lots of times. C'mon, let's go!"

"I have to ask my mother if she doesn't mind that we're going out..."

Paula smiled. That was a first – *asking* her mother. She realised that there were likely to be lots of other firsts from now on – this memory-loss thing was going to mean a whole new way of doing things for both of them.

Catching a bus was a new experience. It was a horseless wagon with a number of people inside, none of whom talked to each other and some of whom fiddled away at these little black tiles that were connected by threads to their ears. They must be mini-machines of some sort. The Lady Gwendolyn was accustomed now to the amazing range of materials that things were made from; she had seen noisy, smelly chariots before; that pathways were hard and smooth and movement was very rapid; she had marvelled at the fact that horses idled away in fields and did not seem to be used for any sort of work; but time and again she could not get used to people not greeting and interacting with each other. This really was not a very sociable world.

The King Offa was an inn or tavern of sorts. Paula had already learned in the bus journey that Gwen had no idea of money, so the bus fare and the half-pint of beer she paid for. She enjoyed watching Gwen examine her glass and gently sip its contents as if this was the first time she had ever seen alcohol. So many firsts!

"So you don't recognise any of this, Gwen?"

"No...but we've been here before?"

"Yes – the very evening before you went to hospital. Amazing!"

"So dost thou know any of the people assembled here?"

The pub was half empty: some men at the bar, two couples sat with their drinks at separate tables across the lounge from them. There was a television screen suspended from the wall in one corner, though no one was paying any attention to it. In the room next door there were a number of people moving about.

"No...I recognise a couple of faces here but I can't say I know them."

"And that screen in the corner – what is it for?"

"People can watch if they want. It's quite popular when there's football on – lots of people come in then. Now, it's just a load of adverts."

The Lady Gwendolyn had watched the television before with her mother. She understood that it showed lots of different programmes, though to her many looked the same. On this occasion there was a painted young lady absolutely thrilled about this paste you put on your teeth, and a doctor in a white coat (she knew about them) saying how this paste was really magical. The lady had lots of very white teeth so it must be. Then there were fast-moving pictures of people being very sad about their bodies and some machines that made them very happy. People didn't seem to mind showing off their bodies at all: Lady Gwendolyn was quite shocked at first by this but nobody else seemed to be. Lots of other moving pictures and scenes followed she really did not understand but the overall message in all of this was that these possessions in some way or another made your life better. People seemed to be defined in terms of the possessions they had. Funny that there was lots of agitated discussion going on in this screen, though looking around inside the tavern, people did not seem to be talking to one another quite so animatedly – maybe they were missing all those things on the screen?

Lady Gwendolyn did not miss them. She was just anxious to talk to Paula and find out more about all that she did not understand.

"The people here, Paula – do they stay in this inn or do they just come to meet here?"

"I think they've got a couple of rooms for visitors to stay, but it is not a hotel – this is mostly just a pub where people come to drink and eat. The nearest hotel is the one you've just started in – the Camelot. You are going back to work there aren't you?"

"It's…it's very different to what I thought it would be. But that is the one place I really do want to get to know. There is this Tom Hughes who wants me to go back there next week and I cannot think now of anything else other than returning to Camelot."

Paula remembered a past conversation: "Tom Hughes? Isn't he the one you fancy, Gwen?"

"Fancy??"

"You know, don't you quite go for him? You wanted to get him into bed, didn't you?"

"NO!" The Lady Gwendolyn was horrified. That anyone should think that was extremely embarrassing and the whole notion shocked her. She blushed to her roots.

"Paula…I do not know this man. He seems quite courteous… but I could never…would never…it…it is unthinkable…"

Paula got the message. Gwen did not actually need to say

anything because her whole being physically recoiled in abhorrence at the suggestion. This was indeed a very different Gwen – as if completely innocent of the ways of the modern world.

"Sorry, Gwen, I didn't want to shock you."

The Lady Gwendolyn felt waves of emotion rising within her at the thought that Paula could consider her behaving so dishonourably. Barbarian women might undoubtedly be so unrestrained but ladies of Camelot could never entertain such unchivalrous notions. Given the strained relations in the case of Queen Guinevere and Lancelot, in particular, any actions or words by members of the Court of King Arthur thought to condone illicit liaisons could be considered treasonable. The entire code of ethics that Camelot was built upon would be threatened. The Lady Gwendolyn shuddered at the idea.

How could any of this be explained in the world she was now inhabiting? The fact that Lady Gwendolyn had been asked, quite openly, about her carnal desires indicated to her that indulging in such practice here must be quite common. Was this then a barbarian world; that the notion of chivalry was forgotten; that the spirit of Camelot was dead? And all this again raised the disturbing and unanswerable question of what was she doing here, anyway. People who say they know her, people like Paula who says she is her friend…they must have known a very different person. What was that person like? Lady Gwendolyn hugged herself. All of a sudden, she felt very uneasy in her own skin, as if she were unclean.

"I am sorry, Paula," she eventually managed to say to her friend, "but everything is so new to me here. It takes a lot of getting used to…"

"I can see that," agreed Paula. It was like taking a little girl out into the world. Gwen seemed so immature, so lost, so much in need of someone to protect her.

A change of subject was called for. Paula began to feel quite sorry for her bewildered friend so she started talking about her own job as a secretary in a big insurance firm in Newport. This wasn't really making much sense to her friend she could see, so Paula was just beginning to wonder what on earth they could talk about usefully when the door to the King Offa opened and in walked a big man to rescue the situation. It was Gareth Jones.

"Hello, Gareth," Paula called out, "you back from uni already?"

The mountain turned round and saw two girls smiling at him. They seemed more welcoming than the last time he was in here so he moved across to greet them.

"Yes, I've just finished my exams. Can I join you?"

Lady Gwendolyn beamed at him. "It would please us greatly to have such a valiant warrior grace us with his presence." She would have curtsied as honour dictated but she was seated already and anyway she had seen that ladies did not do that in this world. So she bowed her head and lowered her eyes at the table instead.

Gareth hesitated; he was caught in two minds by this remark. Such a corny and anachronistic turn of phrase! Was this a cynical, deliberately sarcastic invitation by someone who was setting him up just to put him down and make a fool of him – like before when she'd got him to buy them drinks? A glance at Gwen's face as she looked back up – open and sincere in expression – persuaded him to take the risk. Paula, meanwhile, was stunned into silence by her friend's completely out-of-character reply

Gareth pulled a seat round to sit opposite across the table to the two girls. The Lady Gwendolyn's eyes were now shining at him.

"Sir Gareth, didst thou suffer much after that battle at...at rugby whenst I saw thee last?"

Gareth looked down. He looked across at Paula and then back at Gwen. Was she for real or was this an elaborate ruse to set him up? Paula was not grinning as if she was in on some practical joke. Gwen looked at him kindly, as if genuinely concerned. He played along.

"Did I suffer? Not really. I've got used to that now," he replied guardedly

"But I saw three men set upon thee at the same time. Is that fair?"

Gareth remembered she had spoken to him on the touchline and was as friendly and supportive of him then as she seemed to be now. He smiled.

"It's fair if they tackle you properly. On that occasion there was no foul play...but it's not always like that. I'm big, see, so there's many a time when people try to bring me down by playing dirty. I get that from women too..." He looked pointedly at Paula and back at Gwen. Paula got what he meant straight away, he could tell from her expression, but it went straight over Gwen's head.

"Those who act so dishonourably win only condemnation and lose their soul," she replied seriously. "They're destined never to inspire or attain greatness. They will never enter Camelot."

Gareth laughed. "Funny you should say that 'cos I've just come back from there. Thanks to you, I knew they were taking on new staff, so I applied for a summer job. I got lucky: your assistant manager there has just appointed me!"

The Lady Gwendolyn clapped her hands in delight. "Oh, well done, Sir Gareth!"

Paula grinned. She was watching an exchange that she could scarcely believe. Her friend couldn't get away from this man quickly enough the last time they were here in the King Offa. She had thought then that Gwen had treated him poorly – even dishonourably, to use her own words. But now her friend was clearly unaware of the irony involved in her remarks and was instead positively glowing in his presence. Thinking on it, Paula was pleased Gwen had softened towards this craggy individual and was repairing the cynical way she had exploited him earlier.

"What sort of job will you be doing there, Gareth?" she asked.

She liked this gentle giant.

"I'm not exactly sure as yet. General porter and dogsbody, I guess. Lugging suitcases around for holidaying tourists and visiting businessmen will be part of it, I'm told. I'm just there for the peak season and until the university starts up again in October. It won't be the best-paid job in the world but there's not a lot of alternative employment in these parts. It will be something to help pay off the student loan, however."

"And thou wilst share in the spirit of Camelot!" said Lady Gwendolyn gleefully. "That is a reward in itself."

"Yeah, there's some important meeting about that that we've all got to go to in a couple of days' time," replied Gareth. He stood up to go buy a drink, offering another to the two girls. They both graciously declined. That was nice: this time he was decidedly pleased to be sharing their company.

* * *

The World Traveller Hotel Group had invested a lot in promoting an Arthurian image at their newly acquired, refurbished and renamed Camelot Hotel. In addition to the major restoration of a castle-like edifice, albeit with all modern conveniences, no expense had been spared in putting up banners, flags, decorations and any number of feudal artefacts to create an appropriate atmosphere for their opening launch. Now the final detail was to brief all staff on the notions of chivalry and service to others, on the styles of dress and the ideal of Camelot that they were supposed to mimic and promote, especially on the first day when a variety of media and tourist trade agents were invited.

Everyone on the hotel staff, from the general manager down to the part-time porters and groundsmen, had been summoned to attend and no excuse for absence was accepted. World Traveller Hotel Group's head of human relations, Mrs Elizabeth Morley, opened the meeting in the hotel's main banqueting hall and greeted all staff. She emphasised again the importance of everyone in the hotel committing themselves to the company's chosen theme for this hotel – the spirit of Camelot – and then she introduced Dr Rupert Jeffries, the President of the Knights of the Round Table Society, an economic historian who claimed to be an expert on Arthurian legend and who had been invited to come and give his views to the assembled staff about the idealised world that they were supposed to recreate.

Dr Jeffries got to his feet, took his place at the lectern and gave his thanks to Mrs Morley for the introduction. He welcomed his audience. A rather pompous individual, he was accustomed to addressing small groups of academics and also the closed coterie of fanatics who were members of the Knights of the Round Table Society and who had invited someone as important as he to be their president. He rarely spoke to gatherings of working people such as were assembled in front of him. He coughed once or twice, took a sip of water from a glass in front of him and then he began.

"The legend of Camelot is one of the most enduring and compelling stories in Western literature and civilisation," he began. "It may well be that this place never existed, that King Arthur and the Knights of the Round Table are all pure fiction, but this does not alter the fact that the story and spirit of Camelot has been written about for well over a thousand years and continues to exert a pull on people's imagination today." He paused and looked around the hall. Was everyone paying attention? He thought so. He could not see the reaction of one person in particular in his audience who took offence at the remark that Camelot and the Court of King Arthur was all pure fiction.

"Camelot represented the highest Order of Chivalry in a hierarchical society of a royal and mystical Britain. For knights of the realm to attain honour and advancement in such a society meant to dedicate themselves to the service of others; to fight evil; to always act nobly and righteously; to never lie, cheat or pursue material gain and particularly to honour, serve and do the bidding of ladies of the court."

Dr Jeffries asked where did such a notion of chivalry come from. "The word is derived from old Latin *caballerius*, or horseman, from which is derived *cabellero* in Spanish and *chevalier* in French and it is associated with the conduct of the knight or gentleman at court. This code of ethics some say came about with the spread of Christianity through Europe and persisted despite the decline of the Roman Empire, but this is too easy an explanation. Not dissimilar notions of chivalry also existed in other lands: in ancient Japan and also in Moorish society. If it is part of any religion one must ask – why? We must look a little deeper."

The historian warmed to his theme. "The answer, in my view, is that the chivalrous ethic is a product and essential component of agricultural societies where status, wealth and power all derive from the ownership of land and property. The issue of title to land thus becomes of supreme importance. Legitimate title is obtained principally by birthright, or it might be gained as a reward from the king or landlord who has it in his power to confer title for meritorious service. Hence in an age where birth certificates did not exist we have an elaborate code of ethics surrounding and distinguishing legitimate as against illegitimate birth. Secondly, in an age without antibiotics where sexually transmitted diseases were widespread and could not be cured, promiscuous conduct threatened the health and stability of family inheritance. The noble knight and his intended bride should thus be both of pure blood. Thirdly, the fact was that marriage for the nobility was a matter of arranging an approved distribution of ownership, power and prestige in society. It was not a matter of love or sexual attraction, yet we know that such emotion is a basic human psychological drive. Put all these three elements together and thus chivalry becomes the code for the outlet of human passions: The desire to protect the economic and social order; to sublimate the aggressive male instinct in service to the king; to ensure an ordered and legitimate passage to nobility for lower orders by proving one's valour, and most important of all: to honour and serve ladies of the court that allowed for the notion of courtly love – of worship from afar, of the idolisation of the chaste maiden, but not the consummation of sexual desire outside marriage with its taboo on illegitimacy."

Dr Jeffries paused for breath at this point. He took a sip of water from a glass at the lectern and looked around the hall, though he was not yet ready to invite questions. Victoria, the newly appointed receptionist that had started with Gwen and Freddy could not wait for any invitation, however – she raised her hand and immediately took advantage of this hiatus in the proceedings.

"Dr Jeffries, so far you have described chivalry and the spirit of Camelot only in terms of its implications for menfolk. Women do not seem to be of any importance in your world – except perhaps to stay at home and be worshipped from afar. Hardly an inspiring ethic for us to promote!"

"Thank you for that interruption, young lady," replied Dr Jeffries testily, who gave every indication that thanking Victoria was the last thing he wanted to do. "Let me enlarge upon the role of women in agricultural, pre-modern societies. At root, building, enlarging and protecting one's ownership of land and property was a matter of physical combat. When all else fails to resolve disputes, men take to arms. In this age, physical strength determined outcomes. Women did not compete in this arena – they could hardly lift a double-handed sword, for example, let alone successfully despatch an opponent with it. But in ensuring the passage of title from one generation to another, of course, women played an absolutely crucial role. Their health and fecundity was prized above all else. The maiden was thus idolised and as a result matching maidens with pure and noble knights was an exercise in the distribution of power. Women were well-practised in the art of matchmaking. In addition to bearing children and thus playing a vital role in ensuring stability in the transfer of title, if the exercise of physical strength and skill in combat was a key determinant in resolving disputes so ladies of the court grew adept in manipulating this weapon also, that is – their menfolk. Men developed physical prowess. Women developed their intellectual and diplomatic prowess. History is full of examples of women who were feared for their witchcraft, scheming and intrigue – code for their ability to outwit and exploit physical force for their own ends."

At this stage Elizabeth Morley did not want the occasion to stray any further away from the desired objective – to promote the Hotel Group's vision of the spirit of Camelot that they wished all staff to take aboard. She asked Dr Jeffries to sum up. The emphasis on serving the king, on a hierarchical society where upholding the law was important and of earning knighthood through good deeds – all this dovetailed neatly with the desired internal culture and organisation of the multinational corporation, where the directors were the elite and promotion could be earned by lower orders if they defended and complied with directives from above. The Hotel Group wanted more of this.

Dr Jeffries did as he was bade and concluded his presentation, running methodically through the various points he had covered and, in his academic manner, quoting various sources and justifying the logic of his argument.

Not that this had any interest for a certain young lady present in the audience who had come recently and magically directly from the Court of King Arthur. She had listened respectfully and attentively to the account so far but had grown increasingly agitated at how the ideals by which she had been raised and had come to inform her entire outlook had been reduced to some dry and uninspiring monologue. She had been standing between

Gareth Jones and Dai Mervyn, who was another less-than-satisfied listener, and she had hardly been able to contain her frustration at times. She had been snorting, fidgeting and muttering throughout Dr Jeffries lecture, occasionally digging her companions and whispering: "Merlyn, Sir Gareth – this poltroon knows nothing…"

The meeting was finally given over to questions and comments from the assembly – a session that Elizabeth Morley was anxious to control and, of course as the senior employer present, someone that none wanted to antagonise. She invited participation from the floor. There was an awkward silence as no one wanted to speak. Then Tom Hughes, assistant manager and as well-mannered as any knight from a distant age, raised his voice and proffered the opinion that Dai Mervyn was the one person in the audience who was perhaps the most experienced and knowledgeable on the origins of Camelot and its relevance to the site where the present hotel stood. He wondered if Dai would like to give the assembled staff the benefit of his wisdom?

All heads turned to face Dai Mervyn, a character well known to everyone in the hall.

"I thank thee kindly, Tom, for the invitation to speak. 'Tis well known by many that I've lived and worked here for most of my seventy years and I guess I know more about this place's affiliation with the legend of Camelot than most…that is until I met someone recently who has more knowledge of the spirit of Camelot than any I've ever come across and certainly more than myself. Don't let her young looks fool you; she's a-side o' me now. Gwen, I think it's only fair you should say your piece…"

There was a rustle of interest from amongst the gathered throng and the Lady Gwendolyn blushed in response. She squeezed Dai Mervyn's hand.

"That's a cruel trick, Merlyn," she whispered, her eyes twinkling up at him.

"No, 'tis your right. Go ahead, Gwen." He beckoned her to

speak.

The Lady Gwendolyn glanced up at the front of the assembly at the two people she had heard speak but two she did not know in the slightest: the invited historian, Dr Boring Jeffries and Mrs Sourface Morley, the disapproving head of human relations. These two, Gwen thought, had no real idea of what they were talking about. They had reduced a treasured ideal to something merely useful, mundane and about as inspiring as a dinner plate. When Gwen spoke up she could not prevent an outpouring of emotion.

"The spirit of Camelot that I've heard described just now I do not recognise! The ideal of Camelot is something that shines across the entire country, across the entire world that I know of. It is an ideal that has attracted the noblest, the most honourable, the most valiant knights and ladies in the land. And more – the poorest and lowest-born look to Camelot as the light that brightens their darkness; it gives hope to those most maltreated; it gives resolve to those who face hardship, and it gives purpose to the highborn who wish to prove their honour and spread the ideal abroad. Camelot is an inspiration to all who live in a world of barbarians – those who know no better than to fight over futile possessions – and who dream of something nobler, more worthy, something to lift their spirits and attain something good and lasting where all else is mean and shallow and impermanent. Does our distinguished speaker not know of the Feast of Pentecost where, each year the Knights of the Round Table assemble to swear their allegiance to the spirit of Camelot? Such an uplifting, exhilarating, enthralling ceremony that brings tears of joy to all who witness it and which resonates around the citadel and inspires all who live there? To see the strongest, most gallant, most intrepid of knights kneel before his chosen lady, or before the Queen Guinevere, and pledge to do battle against all evil, to oppose all cruelty, but to give mercy unto him that asketh mercy; to covet no worldly goods; to take up no wrongful quarrel; to conquer all base emotion and to serve and protect his lady with his life...all this cannot but move the most stone-hearted observer...though I hear of no reference to this today. There is such a wealth of love, honour and respect that dwells within the heart of Camelot and enriches the lives of all who live there. The shared comradeship and sense of unity, the bond between all those of the citadel, this is truly a magnificent, a magical force of good to set against all evil. There are many who would willingly sacrifice their lives for this ideal of Camelot and those who know not of all this, who have no knowledge or understanding of such devotion are the poorer for it. What do people live to create in *this* world? Where are the tallest and most inspiring buildings in this land and what ideals do they espouse? I have seen nothing to compare to the brilliance, the incandescence of Camelot..."

The Lady Gwendolyn came to a close, her voice draining away. She looked around, the colour in her face still flushed with emotion. Dai Mervyn looked back with affection and no little pride. Gareth Jones just marvelled at her with eyes wide open and would have applauded, given the chance. Everyone else was just dumb, dazed and too taken aback to do or say anything. An awkward silence reigned.

Elizabeth Morley was the first to seize the initiative. "Well, ah, thank you, to that speaker for giving us her view on the spirit of Camelot. Erm...the inspiration of that legend is certainly something we would want to cherish, though the World Travellers Hotel Group does not normally require its employees to lay down their life in its service...ha! ha!..."

She blundered on but now there was a rising buzz of conversation that grew in the assembly. Dai Mervyn, Gareth Jones and one rather emotional Lady Gwendolyn could not listen to any more and so they eased their way to the back of the banqueting hall where they escaped as soon as the speechifying came to an end.

"Well done, Gwen," said Gareth Jones in admiration as they emerged into the morning sun. "You certainly showed up the two of them, on stage there. I never knew you were so passionate about Camelot."

"Gwen's a real expert," said Dai Mervyn protectively, "more so than that dunderhead up front!"

As the gathering dispersed, many people came spilling out of the hall past the three of them. Hurrying by, many looked at Gwen with no little surprise and interest. Her brief and emotional outburst had certainly had its effect.

Chapter 9

THE QUEST

Quests according to the legend of Camelot involved knights, or those who sought to become knights, sallying forth on some heroic adventure – undertaking a series of tests and ordeals, fighting and defeating monsters and giants and any number of fantastic creatures – all in the pursuit of honour and thus to return and win the favour of the ladies of the court and thereby to confirm or attain the status of noble knights of the realm.

Ladies of the court were not required to prove their nobility by such quests – courtly manners and deportment, charitable concern for the welfare of the others and, especially, good birth was what was required. Having a pretty face always helped, of course – as it has done throughout millennia – but Gwen was finding out that how you used that pretty face to gain advancement in the fifth century required an entirely different strategy to how you used it in the twenty-first. The spirited and sexy 'come-on' that she had deployed to successful effect in the Camelot Hotel, Monmouthshire, would be close to getting her branded as a witch in the Camelot of King Arthur.

Thanks to her selfish and, inevitably, her liberated and ahead-of-its-time attitude, Gwen Price was faced with the unprecedented demand of having to prove herself worthy of being kept on as a lady of the Court of King Arthur. She was to undergo her own period of testing, partly devised by Merlyn and partly by herself, and her performance was to be judged by the Knights of the Round Table. She was never actually *told* this – this was not some form of pre-television reality show where contestants were carefully selected and briefed before they entered a specially designed arena – but Gwen nonetheless knew well enough that she was being watched to see if her behaviour was consistent with the spirit of Camelot.

Talking to Merlyn she thankfully had some room to determine her own destiny and in caring for Kate's sickness she came up with her first task: how to contain the spread of an epidemic.

"Coughs and sneezes spread diseases – that's how the flu spreads, Merlyn. Do we know how far this has got now? Amongst the ladies-in-waiting, the queen and all – are there servant girls like Kate going around sneezing and spluttering all over the place? If so, there's going to be a major outbreak…"

"This plague, this 'flew' of which thou speakest…the evil is spread by *sneezing*?"

"Yes. Think of the evil being carried from one person to another by the tiniest particles which are conveyed by touch and also fly through the air. It is very infectious. So if you are talking to or touching a person who's got the evil virus, it means you ought to wear a face mask and wash your hands afterwards. And clean all the surfaces where these people have been and left their mark. Gettit?"

"Thou shouldst go, then, to the quarters of all those suffering this affliction, and to those of their attendants, and minister thy solution."

With Merlyn's help, Gwen gained a couple of attendants and, all equipped with muslin face masks, various cloths, brooms, buckets and using vinegar as a disinfectant, off they went to visit the quarters of the queen, first of all. Half a day then followed of thorough cleaning and dusting through all the rooms, washing and disinfecting the toilets, and checking which people had or had not been sneezing. The nearby rooms of the ladies-in-waiting affected were also similarly treated. Most of the attendants of the queen and her ladies were all housed nearby – the possible spread of the infection could thus be contained – except for one servant girl who had apparently been visiting her mother beyond the castle gates in the shanty town of the many wooden huts and dwellings that were clustered about on the outside of the perimeter wall.

Oh dear! Gwen explained to Merlyn that in such places of densely concentrated humanity, plagues could spread like fire. In fact, for really serious plagues when illness could result in death, fire in such places was the only solution. That's what she learnt in her history lesson about the Great Fire of London, Gwen said, though she mentioned it wouldn't happen for maybe another thousand years of so...

There was nothing for it but to follow the servant girl, check out where her mother lived and try and promote as much cleaning and hygiene in this settlement as possible. If there were any there with symptoms of the flu then it was all the more urgent that the message was got across.

Sure enough, when the servant girl introduced Gwen, Merlyn and their accomplices to the place where her parents lived, there was her mother looking decidedly off-colour. Most probably with the early, and most infectious, stage of flu.

Gwen suggested to Merlyn, that as the most feared and revered magician of Camelot, he should use his authority to frighten everyone in the vicinity to follow her suggested course of action: that the servant girl's mother should come into the castle and be quartered with others similarly afflicted; that all around the place be disinfected so far as possible, and that this plague could only be contained if people did not mix freely for a while and if everyone followed basic rules of good hygiene.

It was a long day. Even when all had been done, there was no guarantee that the actions that had been taken would be successful and Gwen guessed that the flu might anyway turn into an epidemic. With people living so close together, both inside and outside the castle, the chances were that most everyone would go down with the symptoms at some time. She warned Merlyn of this.

"I'm really sorry about this, Merlyn, but I guess I've brought this virus here to people who've got little or no defence against it. But I've done all I could to try and check the spread of it, honest!"

"I see that, my lady. Thou hast done thy best today."

"If nothing else, cleaning those poor houses outside is some good we've done. It might be too late for the flu, but if people keep up with all the cleaning and disinfecting it *will* stop future problems. It will! And make sure they stop rats running every-where! Rats will bring far worse diseases than the flu, you tell 'em! Living on top of any unclean animals and birds is not good for people. Sanitary conditions are essential. Remember – clean-liness is next to godliness. It's good magic, Merlyn. Really it is!"

"Aye, my lady, so you say. We will spread thy message, no fear o' that. In the meantime, thou shouldst care for Kate still and I'll be back on the morrow and we shall see what other tasks can be set thee."

With that, Merlyn withdrew and left Gwen on her own, very tired after all the work but actually quite pleased with herself for doing something that she knew was good for people. The rooms inside the castle, and especially the wooden huts and shacks outside, all appeared a lot cleaner, healthier and more attractive to look at.

Gwen went in to see how Kate was. Lying quietly and resting still. Gwen stroked her head.

"You'll be better soon, Kate, don't you worry. I'll go fetch you some fruit and maybe something to drink, OK?" She bent over and gave her a little kiss on the cheek.

Kate smiled back up at her.

* * *

The next morning, Gwen awoke thinking of fruits – specifically oranges. They were good for vitamin C, which was good for the flu, she'd heard. Gwen had never seen an orange from the moment she had first woken up in Camelot. She knew you could buy Spanish oranges in Tesco but could you buy them in Camelot market? No; not as yet anyway. But underdeveloped as this society was, they had ships that traded back and forth so it was a fair bet if she went to market in Newport she could find oranges. She wondered what Newport was like in these days, if it existed at all. There must be a port there on the River Usk, surely, with ships that came and went, in fact she was sure there had been in Roman times and maybe Newport was just a later construction on top of a Roman original? A new port? Whatever, she would ask Merlyn as soon as she saw him where the nearest port and market was. It was time to go buy oranges!

Gwen checked on Kate first of all. She did seem to be on the mend. Her eyes were brighter; she was not so cold and sneezy; she was beginning to regain her appetite. The remains of apples and pears that Gwen had brought her the night before lay beside her on the floor.

"Do you think you can get out of bed now?" Gwen asked. "I mean, take it easy, but you can go to the toilet by yourself, right?"

Kate smiled weakly at that. She could see her mistress was keen not to go running up and downstairs with bedpans for any longer than was absolutely necessary. "I am feeling stronger, yes. Thank you, my lady. I think I can manage to eat something more substantial now."

Gwen guessed some sort of meat and potato stew would be just great...except there were no potatoes going to be available for several centuries. But she'd go and ask the kitchens to prepare something suitable.

Outside it was bright and early in the morning, it was a sunny and cloudless day, the birds were singing and Gwen reckoned that if Kate could get out in the fresh air it would do her the world of good; that, and a meaty soup. Maybe getting Kate downstairs, beyond the kitchen garden and out onto the grass, away from the horses and manure in the courtyard, would be just the ticket? "How about that, Kate?" she asked. "We can put blankets down and have a breakfast picnic?"

"I...I have never done that," she replied, "but I think it would be lovely."

It was settled. Gwen helped poor Kate down the spiral stairs, carrying blankets and sheepskins, and they crossed over the courtyard and past the kitchens. A number of willing helpers came immediately to their assistance and walked them over to an area of grass beyond the vegetable garden. There was a fresh breeze but the castle wall protected them from most of the wind and it was then just a matter of settling down in the sunshine and asking one of the kitchen helpers to bring across some food.

Bread of three different varieties, milk, eggs, fruit, a strong broth made from the meat that was being prepared for the king – a variety of things were brought over for Gwen and her maid to sample. It seemed the kitchens were delighted to see the two of them together and out and about. *OK*, thought Gwen, sunning herself and looking at Kate – wrapped in sheepskins and smiling at being waited upon – *life isn't so bad here, after all.* Having people of the castle around to help out all the time was a positive delight.

Merlyn appeared whilst the two were feasting. "Good morning, my lady – and Kate. You are both looking well this morning."

"Hi, Merlyn," Gwen responded. "Kate does seem better, doesn't she? Do sit down and join us. I have a question for you."

Merlyn graciously declined, his elderly frame was not ready to sit cross-legged on the ground with these two teenagers.

"And that is?" he enquired.

"Where's the nearest port and market-place, Merlyn? Somewhere I can get oranges"

"Oranges, milady?"

"Yes, you do know what they are, I hope?"

"Indeed I do, milady. It is some time since I have seen any –

the king was presented with some by an emissary from Hispania a number of years ago. Caerleon is the nearest place to us where ships call but to get oranges thou wouldst have to send for further than that – to Bridgestow, or Bristol, as some now call it."

"Well that is my next quest, Merlyn. To find oranges."

"I see. Thou wishest to go *thyself* then?"

"I think so. What do you say?"

"A day's ride to Caerleon would be possible. To cross by ordinary boat to Bridgestow and back is not possible for a lady, I must insist – thou wouldst require a royal barge; a major expedition. But thou might pay a boatman to undertake the trade in that port for thee. A knight and his retinue will accompany thee, of course, to ensure your safety, and secure a fair trade."

Gwen sniffed. Ladies did not travel without protection in these times, obviously. From what Merlyn had said she guessed a lady of some status was expected to have an entourage to go with her. Bugger! She was hoping to go on a shopping trip herself with no fuss and bother, but so be it. That was the deal. It was not for her now to challenge such custom.

"Well, I'd like to do that. Oranges are good for the flu, see. And if you can arrange for me to go on a trip to Caerleon so that I can bargain for some oranges, that would be excellent. I'd love that."

Merlyn narrowed his eyes and looked at her. Gwen could guess what he was thinking.

"Don't worry, Merlyn. I'll be good. Very ladylike, I promise."

"Milady, thou wilst go with a Knight of the Round Table, his squire and attendants. They will care for thee as their queen. Your carriage will be the centre of attention. Just a glimpse at you from tradespeople and boatmen will be like looking into the heart of Camelot. They will talk about what they see for an age. My lady, people in these lands *dream* of one day, someday, entering Camelot and partaking of everything it represents. Very few realise that dream. But you, milady, you will represent Camelot coming to them. Do not disappoint..."

Bloody hell, thought Gwen. *I see what he's on about. Suddenly I'm part of the royal family...* Gwen nodded sagely. Things began to make sense now. She was starting to see herself from others' point of view and she felt a sudden pang of guilt – of being a little embarrassed at what she saw. "I understand, Merlyn. I'm beginning to get what you want of me. I'm sorry if I've let you down before...but this will be my chance to make it up to you, honest."

"Make it up to Camelot, milady. Be a credit to thy knight and all the Knights of the Round Table. To which knight will thou grant this honour of accompanying thee? Who dost thou favour?"

Bloody hell, again! thought Gwen. *Of course –* this *is how it works! They will lay down their lives for me, or something...I gotta be the lady they idolise. Shit! What a responsibility!* More guilt flared up within her.

She made a rapid decision: "Erm, I choose Sir Gareth. I think I should make amends with him too. Show him I am the lady he sort of remembers...or try to."

"Good choice, milady. A good choice indeed. That noble knight has spoken at the Round Table at how he is most affected by thee and is most troubled by the demon that has invaded thy soul. Show him thou art able to dispel his fears and art indeed the fair maiden he cherishes."

Kate had been listening to all this and now spoke up. "If thou art to go, my lady, then I must go with thee. I am feeling stronger now."

"Dear Kate – you cannot travel yet, you aren't at all well. That's why I'm going – to fetch oranges for you to help make you better."

Kate was moved to tears. "Thank you, thank you, my lady...but I cannot stay here whilst thou art on such a venture. If thou couldst wait one day, I am sure that I will be fit to go with thee. My lady, thou art my life – I *must* accompany thee! If thou shouldst encounter difficulty whilst I am left behind I wouldst surely die of shame."

Merlyn interposed. "Far easier, milady, if the two of you were to stay here in Camelot. Why not let Sir Gareth go and trade for these oranges you so desire. He would be only too pleased to undertake this commission."

"No way, Merlyn! It's my idea, it's something I want to do, and I dearly need to go outside these walls and see what the rest of this world looks like. I've never been one to stay at home!"

"Well, if thou dost insist, it will take some time to organise the excursion that you wish. That will give Kate time to rest. And I do agree with her that if thou art determined to go then Kate must go with thee. If not, she would grieve and waste away every second thou art absent. She knows well enough that there is an element of danger in what you propose."

"Goodness, I only want to buy some oranges. Every second this shopping trip gets to sound like a major expedition into the unknown!"

"My lady, there are indeed unknown elements that we must protect thee against. I go now to speak with Sir Gareth. He will undoubtedly request permission to see thee...so might I suggest you make ready to receive him?"

Gwen tidied up the remains of the picnic as Merlyn made his leave. She then ensured Kate was sitting comfortably before arranging herself and spreading her robes about in a graceful circle. She smiled to herself at the irony: here she was, a liberated and somewhat rebellious young woman of the twenty-first century now taking care to sit demurely, combing her hair, emphasising her femininity in the expectation of a visit from a gallant knight, if not exactly in shining armour, then certainly from the Round Table and the Court of King Arthur.

She did not have long to wait. Sir Gareth approached respectfully, quietly for such a big man, and then as soon as he caught

Gwen's eye, he stopped, bowed and asked if he might come a little closer to speak with her. Gwen found herself thinking that this was hardly the sort of approach she was accustomed to in the King Offa. She smiled up at her visitor and beckoned him forward. Sir Gareth took two steps closer and then came down upon one knee in front of her.

"Milady, dost honour me with her favour," he began. "The wise Merlyn has indicated that thou desirest to take an excursion beyond Camelot; am I informed correctly?"

"Indeed, Sir Gareth." Gwen switched on her best smile. It wasn't difficult. But what she gathered herself up to say next made her feel as if she was a princess in a fairy tale: "And I would be indebted to you, sire, if thou couldst consent to be my guardian and protector in this venture. I seek a trade with merchants from the Mediterranean in order to bring back oranges for a medicine I wish to prepare." She tried to stop herself from grinning like the cat in Alice in Wonderland, although she felt as if she was now in Wonderland herself.

Sir Gareth continued with the magic of this encounter: "Milady, it is I who art indebted to thee. Thou proposeth a noble venture and it is the greatest of honours that thou confers thy trust upon me to help carry it out. With thy permission, I shalt go forthwith to prepare a carriage for thee and arrange all matters appropriate. An excursion of this order will involve providing for some nights away from Camelot. Thy maid will assist thine own preparations; I shall take care of all else. With thy leave..." He bowed his head and backed away.

Gwen grinned at Kate and watched the retreating form of her knight and admirer. Of course Kate didn't understand but Gwen's friend Paula would never believe what had just happened. Gwen had to pinch herself at what she was doing. It did not seem so long ago that she'd said she'd never dress up like some character in a fairy tale, yet now here she was entering into it wholeheartedly...and beginning to love it. And better than acting in the hotel in some plastic Disney costume, this was *real*.

* * *

An excursion to Caerleon: this was to involve Sir Gareth, his squire Brangwyn and two yeomen bearing arms, all on horseback. The Queen Guinevere had insisted that her own carriage be used for Gwen and her maid and this was to be drawn by four horses and directed by two coachmen. The trip to Caerleon would take best part of a day, going slowly but on a known and well-travelled route. The party would have to camp out in royal tents on a hill above the river port whilst a boat was sent across the Channel to Bridgestow and back. Brangwyn and one or two others would go in this boat to undertake the trade, probably returning the next day, depending on the wind. Sir Gareth would not leave the ladies' side.

A great variety of people were involved in seaborne trade: some absolutely reliable, honourable and trustworthy; others were more like pirates with whom you had to watch your purse and your back. Gwen was made aware that there was no disciplined Royal Navy in these times; quite the opposite – those who sailed the seas formed no homogenous community; there were no rules; no supreme naval authority; no guarantees. Once aboard ship you were on your own and took your own chances – so the party would have to choose their boat and crew carefully.

The next morning dawned with a buzz of activity in the courtyard. Four horses were being fed, cleaned, saddled up and prepared for their noble riders and another four were meanwhile being similarly groomed and then harnessed to the royal carriage. Horsemen and attendants were running everywhere. The carriage was being loaded with tents, equipment and provisions and an extra two packhorses were then added to follow behind since not all could be accommodated without them. Merlyn and Sir Gareth were standing nearby and were being kept informed of progress and messages were also being regularly sent up to the king and queen – the latter still poorly but having passed the worse of her sickness.

At last the Lady Gwendolyn and her maid were sent for. All were ready to depart. A final flurry of loading the ladies' belongings, the two fair maidens were helped aboard, whips were cracked and with a nice display of horses' snorting and stamping the party drew out of Camelot and onto the well-marked carriageway that led south and towards the coast and river estuary. They were off!

Gwen had never before ridden in a horse-drawn carriage. It was an exciting but bumpy ride. The muddy path across field and through forest they were following was well-rutted and suspension on the carriage was primitive, but the swaying around was not worse than a theme-park or fairground ride and, what with Sir Gareth and his men flanking either side, the coachmen up top calling out to their horses, and the scenery pitching up and down as it went careering past, the whole experience was entirely entertaining, if not exhilarating.

The party made steady progress. It was mid-afternoon when Brangwyn and one of the yeomen rode on ahead to make preparations for the arrival of the royal carriage. The hilltop above Caerleon was first cleared to receive the encampment and Brangwyn visited a number of inns in the town to announce the imminent arrival of the party from Camelot, should tradespeople there wish to compete for their custom. Inevitably, word was passed from one to another around the settlement such that by the time the carriage arrived there was quite a crowd of onlookers waiting to see who was coming and to cheer this gallant knight and his fair lady who were accompanied by such fine attendants.

The camp was a grand affair. Gwen had once been on a school camping trip many years ago to Snowdonia and hated it: small mountain tents, little gas stoves, uncomfortable sleeping bags and rain, rain, rain. This, on the other hand, was luxury. A large royal tent was erected big enough for Gwen to stand up in; every effort was made to make her bed comfortable; other smaller tents were set up in a ring outside and a big campfire was lit to roast an enormous evening meal. There was a train of visitors simply dying to meet the Lady Gwendolyn and offer her all sorts of trinkets, bracelets, sweetmeats, oils and perfumes. Gwen asked Sir Gareth how anything was to be paid for – he waved the question away. For most of the local people, he said, it was simply an honour to present her with something so that they could later claim to be suppliers to Camelot. For some of the more ostentatious items where some form of payment was due he said that whatever she desired was for him an honour to arrange.

Gwen smiled and thanked every kind gesture of each individual who was granted an audience but she felt she could not take everything that was offered her. It was too much. But what a night it was – being feasted and feted by all and sundry. This went on for some hours until Gwen could take no more. She eventually made her excuses and retired to bed. Sir Gareth bade her goodnight and assured her that he and the others would take it in turns to watch over her while she slept. Gwen curtsied and offered her thanks – when she at last snuggled down upon sheepskins and feathers she could hear the men outside speaking in low voices as the campfire crackled and threw shadows against her tent wall. What an experience! She loved it all. She couldn't help but marvel at being treated as if she were a princess…if only she could tell her mother and Paula all about it.

* * *

By the time Gwen was awake in the morning, Brangwyn and one of the yeomen had already set off for Bridgestow. High tide was at first light, the wind was in the west and they had chosen one out of three boats at the quayside in Caerleon which had offered to take them across the short stretch of tidal water that separated Wales from England. Gwen was sorry not to have seen them depart but she resolved to be at the quayside on their return. Sir Gareth had said that, thanks to their early departure, they should be able to conclude the business in Bridgestow and sail back before nightfall. Fortunately the weather was stable and there was little chance the wind would frustrate their plans.

After busying about the campsite and putting things in order, with time on their hands, Gwen and Kate wanted to have a look further afield. With Sir Gareth taking the lead on his big, beautiful, grey charger they rode across the hilltop, visited some Roman ruins, waved to numerous smallholders working in their fields before entering Caerleon in order to take lunch at the largest of the local taverns down by the river.

It was whilst they were finishing the last of their meal that Gwen heard some sort of commotion outside. A number of people were shouting and running and the noise seemed to be getting closer and closer.

Sir Gareth rose from his seat. "Stay here, milady – I shall see what is the cause of such caterwauling."

With his hand on the hilt of his sword, Sir Gareth left the tavern. Gwen was not one to sit indoors like some docile kitten, however. She made for the door to peer outside and see what was going on. Kate came after and hung onto her skirts, not so much to hide from whatever trouble there might be outside but more to make sure that her mistress did not venture any further.

A little man with a long pigtail was running up away from the quayside and a number of sailors were after him, hollering and throwing stones and clearly intent on doing him some harm. The little man had shrugged off the first assault by dodging and tripping up his first assailant but another, more muscular individual had caught him and, just as Gwen arrived at the door of the tavern, the poor fugitive was thrown to the floor. The man on top of him began raining him with blows as others in the posse arrived and started calling for blood.

The little man writhed on the ground and tried to defend himself. A second and third assailant started kicking him whilst he was down.

"Oh, stop them, Sir Gareth! Stop them!" Gwen called out in alarm. There were three now hammering away at the poor victim as if they wanted to break his bones. One raised a wooden staff to deal a serious blow.

Sir Gareth needed no encouragement. This was no noble quarrel but a one-sided bludgeoning of a defenceless captive. He drew his sword and beat the wooden staff away as if it was a matchstick. The first assailant, who was kneeling over the little man, he seized by the scruff of his neck and hauled him off, tossing him to one side. He then stood over their quarry and faced the pack of bloodthirsty sailors who had chased him.

"Who are ye to chase a man like a pack of dogs and not give him a fair chance?" Sir Gareth demanded with a face of fury.

"And who are ye to defend such a miserable infidel who deserves to have every limb torn off and the rest of him to rot in hell!" yelled the first and most muscular of the posse.

"I'm Sir Gareth of Camelot, sworn to defend the meek and the powerless against the hordes of bullies and barbarians who despoil this land." He raised his sword to direct it at the throat of his adversary and then circled it to point at all the others who now had formed a row in front of him. A big man, almost twice the size of the one at his feet, with a fierce expression and a broken nose that had come from earlier battles, Sir Gareth was clearly not a person to be trifled with, even without the silver blade that threatened to decapitate anyone who aroused his ire. With the posse now stopped in full flight and the shouting died down, Sir Gareth could speak in a quieter, but still deadly serious, voice.

"Suppose you tell me of what this poor man is accused and why you people think he deserves to die at the hands of an uncouth rabble such as yourselves?"

"Look at him!" one shouted. "He's a heathen, an evil outsider!"

"He tried to poison us!" another shouted.

"No! No! They bad men. I simple cook. Good cook. No poison!" the little man protested at Sir Gareth's feet.

Gwen gained a closer look at the poor man who was now scrambling to his feet. He was dressed in a grey trouser suit, the leggings of which came down only so far as his calves. He wore no socks but just small, flat, cloth shoes with rope soles. A long pigtail dangled down his back almost to his waist. She recognised his looks at once, though she guessed the others would not. He was Chinese and, she guessed, there were very few in these times who would have seen his like before. People were always frightened of what they did not understand; she knew that only too well.

"He can cook for me, Sir Gareth," Gwen called out. She quite liked Chinese food. "Tell the others to leave him alone."

Kate gasped at her mistress's bold intervention but if Sir Gareth was startled by this lady putting herself in the firing line between two opposing lines of battle, to his credit he did not show it. He looked back first at Gwen, checked she meant what she said and then he turned to face his adversaries once more. He let out a scornful laugh.

"Look, you miserable shoal of codfish – the fairest maiden of all Camelot has no fear of this infidel who you seem frightened of enough to want to kill. Go back now, the lot of you. Tell whoever are your superiors that Sir Gareth of Camelot has taken your prisoner and will grant him his life. Now: begone – all of you!"

Sir Gareth stood feet apart, his sword still held out, defiant in front of all of them. None dared contest him, though as they turned away one or two muttered insults under their breath. Safely at a distance, one called out: "We know who you are! We'll come for you one day! The Saxons don't fear no Camelot!" He hurled a stone in the air.

The stone bounced harmlessly along the road towards Sir Gareth, the little Chinese and Gwen and Kate, still standing, waiting at the tavern door.

Sir Gareth looked seriously at Gwen. "My Lady Gwendolyn, thou shouldst not come out and address a fearsome rabble in the street like that. It is not safe and nor shouldst thou grant them the honour of seeing someone so fair as thyself."

Gwen curtsied in front of the noble knight, someone whose honour she had come to respect but she could not completely surrender her twenty-first-century spirit in this unliberated age. How could she explain this difference of attitude and role of women without invoking a fear of witches?

"Forgive me, Sir Gareth. Thou art of course correct. But I have seen someone like this in a vision: a good man; one who is very different but one who brings much fortune to those who are not frightened of foreign influence. And I always feel safe whilst thou art with me – a valiant knight who cannot stay silent in the face of injustice. I trust in thee completely."

The effusive praise of his noble performance did the trick. He bowed his head and went down on one knee.

"Thy ladyship dost honour me most graciously. I am thy devoted servant."

The little Chinese man watched all this with great interest. Such a show of chivalry indicated that he was in civilised company. He stood stock still and bowed to his waist – first to Gwen and then, when Sir Gareth had risen to his feet, to his noble and valiant saviour.

"Thank you! Thank you! You save my life. Thank you again!" He bowed twice more. "You are good people. I may go with you, yes?" he questioned.

Gwen smiled at Sir Gareth. "We'll have to take him back to Camelot with us now. He cannot stay here...and I want to see what sort of cook he is anyhow!"

"As my lady wishes," Sir Gareth smiled in response.

"Yes, you can go with us now," said Gwen to the little Chinese. "But tell us your name. Who are you and how did you come to be here?"

"My name Chen Ka Wai. I travel many years on ship. Now I go with you. You save my life. Many bad men here."

"They're not all bad here, Ka Wai. You'll see," said Gwen. "We have to wait for friends coming on a boat from Bristol first of all, and then you'll go back with us."

Chen Ka Wai nodded. He understood. He was some years older than his rescuers, but although small in stature he was wiry, resilient and despite quite a beating, not one to complain about his lot. He clearly had survived many escapades in his long years crossing the world and he was accustomed to taking his chances as they came.

The long summer day gave over to a lengthy twilight – time enough for the boat returning from Bridgestow to find its way up river and back to the quayside at Caerleon. Brangwyn and his accompanying yeoman disembarked, toting a large sack and they met their welcoming party on the quayside.

"Oranges?" Gwen questioned, looking at what they were carrying.

Both men nodded.

Gwen grinned broadly and almost danced a jig right there on the quayside. Sir Gareth was just pleased to note that no other ships or boats remained anchored nearby that evening – which meant that the posse of unruly sailors who had been chasing their Chinese friend had now left.

Chapter 10

THE GRAND OPENING

"How can they understand, Merlyn, if they have never seen what I have," asked the Lady Gwendolyn, plaintively. "How can they know Camelot if they have never felt the comradeship, the love of all of us working together for a common ideal? It seems to me as if I am speaking a foreign language to them...but thou knowest of that which I speak. Dosn't thou? Tell me that thou knowest!"

Dai Mervyn, Lady Gwendolyn and a quiet and thoughtful Gareth Jones were all outside the hotel now, walking slowly in the grounds whilst all other hotel employees were streaming out of the banqueting hall and moving off to their various stations.

"I know what you mean, 'least I think so, Gwen. Not directly like, more's the pity for that. But I was born in the War and my parents, they spoke of what you say. All together, working against a common foe: they never tired of telling me. The camaraderie, the fun, the excitement; even in amongst the bombing their spirits were high. Everyone helped out everyone else, they said. The loss of anyone was a loss to all. Bonded them, it did. I grew up with that. Never been like that since then, though. We live in a society now where everyone moves on. People used to grow up with friends and neighbours living next door to 'em. Time was when I knew everybody in the village. Not any longer. Things are so different, so fast-moving, so volatile now. Nobody knows their neighbour, these days. How can you feel at one with your fellows next door if you don't know 'em, eh?"

"'Tis sad, Merlyn. More than that...I feel all alone, cut off, isolated, hopeless. I see all these people, walking by and they *all* seem alone. No one reaches out for anyone here. They are all like islands, every one, and I am one amongst them. I despair!"

"Gwen, my Gwen, in the little time I've known thee, you've made me feel I have a daughter again. You, most of all, have reached out and touched me more than any other in all of my seventy years. Look – here comes Morgan: up 'til now my only friend and companion and he feels the same as I. He loves you too – he can feel thy warmth like I can. So don't you trouble yourself so – you *are* creating the love and comradeship about thee everywhere you go. Sure, there's an awful lot of people you see that you cannot touch as yet – too many, see. People rushing everywhere, all the time. But you are reaching some of us, Gwen. You've made your mark, right enough."

Gareth Jones, second-row rugby forward, big and fearful of next to no one, stopped and looked at Gwen. He spoke up, movingly.

"I've never known you like this, Gwen. I knew you for years in school and, coming back, I met you again not long ago here in the King Offa. You are an attractive girl for sure and many's a boy I've known tried it on with you…but they've all said you were a real hard case to crack. And I once said the same in the rugby club. But I guess I've been wrong all along…"

"I think not, my noble knight. It was some other person thou knew'st before, not me. I know not how to explain this but since my collapse and the loss of three days in my life, I have awoke a different person, in a different time and place. I seem to remember some people and places but all is confusion…save what I know of love and life in Camelot and what is missing here. There are many fine things I see in this world, too many *things*…and a lot of talk like just now, but…but somehow it is not enough. It is all so shallow."

"Not all, Gwen. Not everything. You may have lost one life but you now have a new one; you are entering a new job, a new world, and Camelot is a long time gone. It takes time to create an ideal like that. But if you cannot walk straight back into the world you want, this ideal that lives inside you, then you have to build it up, stone by stone and one person at a time, where you can. Don't be so sad, Gwen – you are already doing that: with me, your mother, now with Gareth here. And Morgan remembers thee! Go stretch your legs and play with him."

Dai Mervyn stood and watched as Morgan leapt away, a great bounding wolfhound, with Gwen and Gareth running after him. *Let them all run and play and laugh and love together,* he thought, *not enough of that in the world, just as Gwen says. What an extraordinary girl. She even takes me back to my own childhood, here in wartime South Wales. Remarkable what she's doing. Reckon I'll have to go and talk to her mother. She'll be as pleased and delighted as I am.*

* * *

The opening address from Dr Rupert Jeffries of the Knights of the Round Table Society was just the introductory session for the main business of the day, which was to fully prepare for the hotel's grand opening when lots of media representatives would soon be arriving as guests. There was much to arrange after the keynote speech, including a detailed brief to each employee as to his or her duties for the duration; to issuing what was alleged to be Arthurian dress to all staff, and giving the finishing touches to the flags, decorations and other paraphernalia that dressed the hotel up into something that might be thought of as the castle of Camelot. One item the hotel group was particularly proud of was the round table that was placed in the board room and conference centre of the hotel. It was a smaller version of that which was on display in Winchester castle, although that itself was just some thirteenth-century impression of what the original was supposed to have been.

When the Lady Gwendolyn saw the table, she smiled. Not at all like the real thing, she had whispered to Dai Mervyn, which was a plain oaken circle, but it was colourful and showy enough for the hotel to advertise and make a big fuss over. And the costumes? Some very modern fabrics and thoughtful designs were involved that made all the staff look as if they were part of a film set, yet tough enough to be working uniforms. And what a relief for Lady Gwendolyn to get out of denims and back into a long dress that she was used to, albeit in a style that again was somewhat more extravagant than the simple and functional robe she knew.

Handling the computer and phones on the reception desk was a problem for someone who had only recently arrived from the fifth century. This was something difficult to explain to the others. But the fact that she had missed the formal instruction on the use of such items because of her collapse and hospitalisation gave Lady Gwendolyn the excuse to be entirely dependent on Victoria and Freddy's know-how. At the same time, her manner of speaking, her heightened awareness of what Camelot represented and the whole Arthurian image she easily projected gave the Lady Gwendolyn something to offer her two colleagues. Tom Hughes had not hidden the high regard he held for this unique young woman and both Victoria and Freddy were well aware of it. So in the end the three receptionists were happy to work together, each being able to complement the others.

And so came the morning of the hotel's grand opening. It was a warm, humid, overcast day with an end-of-the-summer feeling about it. A steady trickle of cars and taxis made their way up the gravelled drive to the hotel and a number of local and national pressmen and women disembarked to come in, look over the place and take up residence for the night. Journalists can be a cynical breed and David White of the Sunday Recorder was more cynical than most. He had been a war reporter for a number of years, dashing between various conflicts in Africa, the Middle East and Afghanistan until age and family responsibilities took their toll and then his media company decided his international interests could be better employed by making him a travel and tourism correspondent for their national newspaper. This in David White's opinion was an asinine and unworthy use of his abilities, and though admittedly less life-threatening, he felt it was a decided demotion; and being sent to cover some small hotel's big pretensions in the Welsh borders he considered almost beneath contempt. Nonetheless, he followed the guided tour given by the hotel's assistant manager along with the other hacks in his party and, despite his almost permanently bored expression, his professional eye quickly picked out one or two employees he might interview that could give him a more penetrating appraisal of this enterprise than the company propaganda he was being fed.

An old groundsman with twinkly eyes and an amused expression was the first he went to see.

"Dai Mervyn? Pleased to meet you. I'm David White of the Sunday Recorder. So – what do you think of all this about Camelot they are trying to sell here, Mr Mervyn? Isn't it all a load of hype to encourage tourists to part with their money?"

"Aye...it could be that...then again maybe it isn't..." Dai wasn't giving anything away.

"It isn't just fancy dress, then? You think there is more to this hotel's affectations than just a website and some pretty restoration?"

"There is a lot of fancy dress, as you put it, right enough. They've spent millions on promoting the image. Beneath it all, is there more to Camelot here than meets the eye? Aye...right enough there is, too"

"How so?"

Dai Mervyn took a long look at this first journalist of the day – no doubt another who had been everywhere, seen everything and now believed very little of anything anymore.

"People these days know it all now. Nothing much I can tell 'em," he sniffed.

"C'mon, Mr Mervyn. I guess you've seen a lot in your time. So is there, or is there not anything to this Camelot story here?"

"Historian's will tell you that Camelot is a Celtic legend that has grown over the centuries, that its beginnings are lost in time, it could have been hereabouts, or in Cornwall, or in the North, or it might have been nowhere at all. But I've come to think more and more recently that its origins are right here. This land you're standing on has seen more blood spilt than most places – it is a battlefield where castles have been built up and knocked down again over millennia. But Camelot is one whose imprint still remains."

"Mr Mervyn, I've been to many battlefields in the world where blood had been spilt and where nothing remains but scorched earth, rubble and ruined lives. There is nothing to glorify in such places. What makes this place special?"

"Hope! The fact that it has survived; the fact that the castle that once defended this land against invasion is now a hotel that welcomes visitors from overland and overseas. That is something special. Fortifications that tell of thousands of years of conflict dot this landscape...but they are ruins now, or else rebuilt as tourist attractions. And Camelot lives on here as the beacon of light that has shone through the centuries."

"Spare me the poetic imagery!" David White laughed.

"You can laugh – but I can show you people here who are inspired by what Camelot represents. For one very special person in particular, this place is not just a hotel."

"Well, thank you, Mr Mervyn. Do show me that person."

Dai Mervyn caught sight of Gareth Jones, standing in the distance outside the restaurant, helping some cameramen set up their gear to start filming. He waved an arm to attract his attention and called him over.

"Gareth, can you take this gentleman to meet with Gwen? He wants to know more about Camelot." Dai gave his young colleague a wink.

"Of course, Mr Mervyn. Do come this way, sir." Gareth Jones

was as polite as ever. He led the way back into the hotel foyer and up to reception. As he went, David White took the opportunity to question him.

"So who is this Gwen? Someone like Dai Mervyn who has lived in these parts for many years?"

"No, sir," Gareth replied. "She's my age and has only just started work here like the rest of us. But you'll see when you meet her. Camelot has transformed her life, sir. That's the only way I can explain it."

That was a surprise. The man from the Sunday Recorder was intrigued; even more so when he saw the attractive young woman of innocent expression standing, smiling at him from behind reception.

"Gwen, this gentleman wants to know more about Camelot. Can you speak with him?"

David White was introduced. The Lady Gwendolyn came out from behind the reception desk and curtsied low before him.

"Welcome to Camelot, sire. How can I be of assistance?"

Well, that was novel, thought David White. *She's been well trained.*

"Yes, young lady. You can help me if you can explain if Camelot means anything more than just some image that the hotel wishes to project."

The Lady Gwendolyn lowered her eyes then looked back up at her interviewer with a troubled expression. She looked next at Gareth who stood beside the journalist, then turned to face David White once more. This man bore a disinterested, somewhat bored expression as if he was asking something that duty demanded but he was actually not really bothered about.

"It is difficult to explain to those who have no knowledge of what Camelot represents, sire," she said seriously. "But it is so much more than just an image, a story to tell to our guests, sire."

"So what does it represent? What more than a story?"

"Camelot, sire, is an ideal by which to live. It represents the sense of community, the code of chivalry that binds people together and directs our endeavours to promote that which is good and that which can defeat evil. The Knights of the Round Table yearly pledge their allegiance to King Arthur, to serve Camelot, and to support each other in their common commitment to take up arms against all the dark forces that would otherwise overwhelm their world. 'Tis a noble and valiant ideal that inspires all who are poor and fearful and powerless and have only hope to keep them warm at night when darkness is all around."

The much-travelled ex-war correspondent snorted. "Look here, young lady – I've seen at first hand the brotherhood in arms of men who face death on the battlefield and I wonder if you have any idea of what you are talking about. You've given me some trumped-up poetry of idealised knights in shining armour. A fine story; a fine lesson you have learned to parrot to allcomers but there is no truth in it; there are no ideals that remain in a real war. Just men who are disillusioned, angry, frightened and surrounded by pain and blood and dismembered bodies."

The face of Lady Gwendolyn flushed at this accusation. The insult to her own credibility and more – to the only ideal that made any sense to her in this crazy, faithless world – hurt her deeply. She spoke slowly at first but with rising passion as she replied: "Thou judgest me falsely, sire. I speak only of what I know, of what I have seen. Since I lost my mother as a child I have seen men regularly gird themselves up for battle and go out to face all forms of evil. I have seen older knights speak with younger and counsel them to face their fears. I have seen one, sire, who knew he was going out to face certain death. I saw his squire return, broken-nosed, bloodied and weeping at the loss of his mentor. I wept with him, as did others, but I also saw the glory in his eye that grew there as a result of that sacrifice. 'Twas Camelot that put it there. How dost one measure the value of

Camelot? There is no greater love that I have seen than the love of those who are willing to commit their lives to it, sire. It belittles their memory, their sacrifice, to deny such valour. I know not what thou hast seen and spoken of, milord, but if it is men who fight and die and know not why then I can only surmise they have no knowledge of Camelot. I stand here today, sire, in this place, this...this hotel *where Camelot once stood*, sire, as a testament to all that that citadel still represents and I weep that so few like yourself really understand!"

The Lady Gwendolyn finished with fire shining through the tears in her eyes. Then she curtsied once more, span round and left the two of them, David White and Gareth Jones, looking open-mouthed at her retreat. She couldn't go back to reception just yet; she had to find the ladies' room first to cry her heart out at everything that she had lost. Camelot lived inside her but only the merest shadow remained outside. She was feeling utterly desolate.

"My God!" was the first comment that the journalist could make. He stood floundering in the middle of the foyer like a beached porpoise, wondering what on earth he had just witnessed, and refusing to admit to himself that he had seriously underestimated this young woman he had just watched disappear. Where had that extraordinary female come from? What conflicts had she seen? Or was she some deluded schizophrenic who lived in some other world? He turned to his companion for an explanation.

"Who is that girl? And where is she from?"

Gareth Jones was not one to let down a friend. He was similarly wondering what had happened to the Gwen that he once knew and whether or not she was now mentally disturbed, but there was no way he was going to voice such fears to this unsympathetic outsider.

"Gwen Price, sir. I knew her at school here...but that was some time ago and she is...er...very different now. Excuse me."

Gareth Jones bowed and backed away.

"You can say that again," murmured David White to himself as he was left on his own.

* * *

As the day wore on, a number of the visiting press completed their tour of the hotel. They had made up their minds, and made up their stories and had no need to stay any longer. Others, meanwhile, had booked in for the night, had unpacked, had dined in the restaurant and had then repaired to the bar to drink, swap impressions and generally enjoy the five-star hospitality that their employers were paying for. Hotel staff came and went as the early shift was replaced by those on evening duty. In reception, Victoria had volunteered for the four pm to midnight turn and so the Lady Gwendolyn was free to go home that afternoon to see her mother, to rest and reflect on what had happened. Dai Mervyn offered to drive both Gwen and Gareth Jones back into the village since he was responsible for pushing Gwen into the limelight and had heard something of what Gareth had reported back, so he wanted to make sure that she was OK.

The Lady Gwendolyn was not OK. Once she was seated amongst friends and the Land Rover had crunched its way over the gravel and left the hotel behind, then her chin lowered, her emotions rose and her voice began to quaver.

"Oh, Merlyn, I've tried to put on my best face and not show my feelings but in truth I have been treated most rudely. This first man Gareth introduced me to made fit to ridicule me and claim I knew little of what I spoke. I assured him that I did indeed know of Camelot and of the life therein. Then later came there others who insisted I repeat what I had spoken of earlier – pressing their attentions upon me, demanding, clamouring for a response with clearly no notion of the offence they gave."

"And what did you say to this rabble, my dear?" asked Merlyn, negotiating a gloomy corner in the road under darkening skies. "Did you repeat to them what they wanted to hear?"

"Very little, I confess. I was surrounded by barbarians who had no understanding of chivalrous conduct and clearly would scorn any remarks I made." She struggled to hold her voice steady. "To recount the glories of Camelot to such philistines would be to witness what I value most in all the world being torn asunder by a pack of wolves. I could only say that it was important to hold onto the highest ideals if one wanted to recreate Camelot here today and did they not agree that such idealism was worth striving for?"

"Well said, my precious one. Well said indeed. I am only sorry that it was I that started all this. Me being so proud of you and all, I should have known better than to put you in the firing line of such uncouth invaders. Gareth here told me a little of what happened with the journalist I sent you – o' course he was bound to talk to others. I'm so sorry, my dear. It was all my fault."

Dai Merlyn pulled up his old Land Rover outside Gwen's house. The heat in the late afternoon had now built up to be clammy and oppressive and its sullen mood seemed to embrace them all. Dai looked at the pensive young woman sitting next to him and, daughterless as before, he wished he could do more for her, break the sadness that seemed to have captured her soul, lift her spirits and somehow make her shine again. But maybe that was beyond him. Maybe a younger man could do that for her. He opened the passenger door and helped this princess descend. Then he asked if Gareth too would like to get out here as well. The Lady Gwendolyn seized this opportunity as he hoped she would.

"Please come in with me, Merlyn, Gareth. I am going to have to talk about this day again with my mother and I would be glad of your support."

Merlyn shook his head. "Nay, my love; I'll not do that. If

you're OK now I'd best be getting back to Morgan who'll be wanting a feed and I'll take yet another stroll around the estate to watch those ruffians don't trample all over where they don't belong. But you go ahead with Gareth here. He'll take care of you, am I right?"

"Yes, I will. I'll come in with you Gwen, if you wish."

Such concern shown her by these two men at the end of a turbulent day partly made up for the rough treatment the Lady Gwendolyn had felt she'd received earlier. She waved goodbye from the front door porch to the Land Rover as it grumbled its way down the road, then turned and led Gareth into the interior of her mother's house.

Ceri Griffiths had put the kettle on as soon as she saw the Land Rover outside so when Lady Gwendolyn introduced Gareth to her mother the offer of tea and Welsh cakes came immediately.

"Hello, Gareth," said Ceri. "I haven't seen you in a long while – not since you and Gwen were at school together. Do come in and take some tea."

"Aye, Ms Griffiths. Nearly six year ago now. D'ye remember, Gwen?" He was still anxious to understand what had happened to the girl he grew up with.

"Thou knowest I do not, Sir Gareth," his companion's face was tortured, "thou art talking of another Gwen, not I." Lady Gwendolyn looked up at the mother she thought she had lost and once again the impossibility of her situation threatened to overwhelm her. "I have been spoken to today most contemptuously, as if I were some malicious child spreading falsehoods. But I know only how to speak the truth, no matter how foreign my sentiments may sound. This world is so difficult for me!"

"Did those media people not believe you, Gwen?" Ceri was most concerned. "What did you say to them?"

Gareth answered for her. "I introduced one journalist to her, Ms Griffiths, and Gwen spoke of knights going out to battle; of how they are ready to sacrifice themselves for Camelot; of how she wept for one going to his death... Gwen, you said you had seen all this since your mother had died. How's that?...I...I don't understand. "

"No more than I, sire. But 'tis all true. I know not what magic has brought me here but I vow to thee that before my swoon I lived at Camelot just as surely as I live and stand here before thee now. And folk there do not treat strangers so roughly as they do here. Thou hast heard me speak of the love, friendship and comradeship that surrounds one there. 'Tis all true. If only it existed here..."

"It does, Gwen, my only one. I love you dearly, even more now that you suffer so." Her mother came forward to wrap her arms around her and hold her close.

Gwendolyn burst into tears. "Yet this is the most difficult of all!" she sobbed. "I saw thee taken from me when I was but a child. But here you are! What magic can do this? Thou art my mother, I see that as plainly as I see my face in yours. And yet I do not belong here! This is not my world. How can I bear such contradiction?"

Ceri Griffiths looked across over the top of her daughter's head at the young man who was looking on with concern and confusion in his face. "We've been through this a number of times since she came out of hospital, Gareth. What can I say? Only that I've come to believe her. She is my daughter from a past age. The daughter I had before and that you knew at school has disappeared and has transformed into this one. I've found a new, entirely lovable daughter!" She lifted up Gwendolyn's face and kissed her.

The Lady Gwendolyn smiled back. She dried her eyes, thanked her mother and turned to face her friend once more. "I know this must be a puzzle to thee, Sir Gareth. For certainly it is incomprehensible to me. Thou must understand I have struggled with this for days and days now. I wake in the morning and look about and see a world that I do not recognise; I wonder where is the one I have left behind. I have wondered if I am going crazy, as surely as others must have looked at me and thought the same. But hear this – for there is yet more magic that I have not told thee of before. Not all is left behind in Camelot for there are others here that in some way have come with me. I see them here as I saw them before. I recognise Merlyn – who others call Dai Mervyn. And…and I recognise *thee*, Sir Gareth. Thou art the one I have watched from afar at Camelot. Thou didst live there with me as thou dost now, here! Thou wert the squire who survived the battle that claimed your knight that I spoke of earlier. It was thee! I watched thee, bloodied but unbowed, carry back the body of the man thou loved and served with such honour. I watched from above the courtyard when thou knelt before King Arthur and he didst knight thee. Thou art the most courageous, the most valiant, the most gentle yet most fierce in defence of Camelot of all those that I have seen at court. And truly there are many ladies of that court who have watched thee as I have, though none of us have come close and shown their sentiments, nor won thy affection. Until recently, that is…" The Lady Gwendolyn lowered her eyes. "Until the day that I spoke with thee in *this* world…in the tournament of rugby…" Her cheeks coloured.

Gareth Jones looked at this blushing young woman before him and yet again he was lost for words, lost in admiration, completely surprised for the third time in as many days by what she had to say. He was a big man; broken-nosed and not always successful with women, but confident enough in university; sure of himself in most company as he was on the rugby field…but this attractive, sensitive and articulate young lady had an outlook on life that turned everything he knew inside out. She wasn't crazy, it seemed…but she was making him so.

"G…Gwen…" he stuttered. "I know nothing of Camelot…"

"Perhaps not, Sir Gareth. But I knew thee there, nonetheless. Perhaps it is a different thee there as it is a different me here?

These are conundrums that none of us, not even Merlyn, can fathom. How is it I lost my mother in Camelot but found her here? But whatever mysteries are being played out between us all, I see thee the same noble knight now as I did before. Only closer; more magnificent." She curtsied before him. "Thou hast captured my heart like thou hast captured those of many other admirers."

Gareth looked down at Gwen, the girl he once thought he knew, and then up at Ceri Griffiths. He was flabbergasted. Ceri grinned. She recognised what he was going through – the same complex of emotions that both she and Dai Mervyn had experienced.

"Beautiful, isn't she? If this is what Camelot does, I'd like to go there! Worth knocking yourself out for, don't you think?"

Gareth Jones still couldn't speak. He stood back from the table where tea had been served; he hadn't touched a drop, nor could he now. He needed to get out and think. A last he found his voice.

"If you don't mind, Ms Griffiths, Gwen, I think I'd better be going. I think I need to walk a bit and work things out. This has been a most...er...a most awesome day..."

Ceri smiled. "Of course, of course. Gwen, see him out will you?"

The Lady Gwendolyn accompanied Gareth Jones to the front door. She shyly opened it and went with him as far as the outside porch. The weather had not improved: still dark, heavy and overcast. A storm was undoubtedly brewing.

"I thank thee again, Sir Gareth, for thy support today. I shall see thee again in the morrow?" She looked up at him, her eyes shining.

"I'll be there," Gareth replied. He looked down at her and bent over to give her a farewell embrace, but stopped short. He looked again at her open expression, into her clear, cloudless eyes. She was not at all the cool, teasing, unattainable, fundamentally selfish female he had known before. She was altogether deeper, sincere, vulnerable, generous and more courageous than he in expressing her feelings. She was irresistible. He put an arm around her waist, drew her to him and kissed her softly on the lips.

An electric storm blistered between the two of them.

Gareth let go of her, slowly, reluctantly, his heart beating.

The Lady Gwendolyn almost fell. Her legs shook. Everything inside her seemed to be trembling. It was her turn now to be speechless, stupefied, shaken to her core. Such things did not happen in Camelot. Courtly behaviour was more ritualised; affections were announced at a distance and permission was requested to approach a little closer. Not too close, of course. But this kiss awoke emotions deep down inside her that she could not control. Her body reacted in a way that she had never felt before, as if someone other than herself was in control...and that person, that Gwen Price, was telling her to throw her body at him and indulge in the most intimate of liaisons. The temperature on the front porch soared and it wasn't the weather that caused it.

Gareth stood very close and lowered his head once more. "You mother is right," he whispered. "You're beautiful." He kissed her again.

Chapter 11

LANCELOT, GUINEVERE AND THE KING

When Gwen and her entourage returned to Camelot they found Sir Lancelot dismounted in the inner bailey and speaking with Merlyn, a little way in front of his workshop. The two had to draw aside to watch the royal carriage and its mounted guard enter the castle and wheel round in a wide circle before coming to a halt. Gwen was wise to custom now and remained seated inside until one of the coachmen descended and held the door open for her to emerge. Sir Gareth was already waiting for her so she paused to allow Kate to bustle forward, holding various items of luggage before curtsying before her knight and protector and thanking him for his gallant service. Sir Gareth bowed, thanked her in return and requested her leave to attend to the horses and unpacking. It was all very prettily done. Merlyn signalled his approval from the other side of the courtyard. Gwen gave him a big smile and then crossed over to see him.

"Welcome back, milady," Merlyn called out, nodding to acknowledge Gwen's efforts at being ladylike. "I trust thy excursion was successful? And look, another here is safely returned from a quest in the north: Sir Lancelot has been risking life and limb in his search through the misty mountains."

Gwen bobbed down once more. "Greetings, Sir Knight." She grinned at him. She had not got close to Lancelot before and she noted he must be in his late thirties, with dark eyes and complexion and he was even hunkier than she had thought on first acquaintance. "Hast thou fought off any dragons or other fearsome creatures in your long sojourn?" She couldn't resist flashing him the old 'come-on' look in her eyes.

Sir Lancelot did not catch the teasing note in her voice and nor could he have known that Gwen had once been to the misty, rain-drizzled Snowdon massive when she was younger and that she knew well enough that no such monsters lived thereabouts. Only stocky Welsh slate miners and sheep farmers with their various dogs lived nearby. The proud knight he was, however, he bowed before his queen's favourite lady-in-waiting and smiled back into her glittering eyes.

"Nay, milady. I have not drawn my sword in anger in all this past fortnight. But I have returned with Welsh gold gleaned from the rivers I have crossed and have now asked the trusted Merlyn here if he might fashion some jewellery for our beloved queen as a token of my devotion."

"Gold, you say. Goodness!" Gwen was impressed.

"Aye," said Merlyn. "An unexpected but most valued reward. But what of thee, milady? Hast thou brought back what thou sought?"

"I have, Merlyn. And I have also returned with my own unexpected and I hope most valuable find. Here he comes towards us: Chen Ka Wai – the Chinese cook!"

The wizened little man had slid off the back of one of the pack horses that had been carrying him and he now came pattering over to meet his hosts. As before, he stood a little distant at first and bowed to his waist twice to each of the men in front of him.

Gwen waved her hand towards her companions: "Ka Wai, this is Sir Lancelot, the most intrepid knight of Camelot, if not of all Wales and England, and with him – our most honoured magician and physician, the famous Merlyn, whose name will most undoubtedly ring through the ages." It was a grandiloquent introduction. Gwen was beginning to get the hang of all this chivalry business and threw herself into it with a flourish.

"I wonder, Merlyn," Gwen continued, "if you might introduce Mr Chen here to our kitchens? I can't wait to sample the Chinese food he prepares."

Chen Ka Wai was hopping up and down impatiently as Gwen was speaking. He had been looking all around the castle and courtyard from the moment he had arrived and he was now clearly quite agitated about something.

"Not just cook, mistress. Not just cook. There are many things here interesting. Mr Merlyn, sir, this your place behind?" He pointed towards the workshop with its bench cluttered with all sorts of bottles, glasses and liquids of various colours and consistency. "And Mr Merlyn, sir, what you building here? Sword in sky?" High above the courtyard the Chinaman had caught sight of the lightning rod that was being constructed to lead from the tallest tower down into the ground.

So he was not just a cook, Gwen realised. The way he was bursting with curiosity and enthusiasm she guessed he must be a sort of mini-Merlyn; someone who was used to producing his own kind of magic. Maybe it was best that he didn't go straight to the kitchens after all but just stayed here for the time being and had a look at Merlyn's workshop.

Merlyn quickly came to the same conclusion. The elderly magician was quick to see the potential of having this Asian assistant: between the two of them they could perhaps cook up all sorts of potions and remedies, one of which – with the help of plentiful oranges – might assist to bring down a person's temperature and help with the flu that was now spreading one by one through Camelot. Not exactly an out-of-control epidemic, but nonetheless, after passing from the queen and her ladies-in-waiting, it was now beginning to reduce the manpower of the castle. King Arthur himself was complaining of aches and pains and had taken to his bed with fever.

"Milady, Sir Lancelot, with thy leave methinks I should begin first with preparing some medicament for the king. The gold, sire, I will lock away for the time being. Mr Chen – come with me: I should like to hear of what concoctions thou hast heard of in the land from whence thee came..."

Gwen was left for the moment with Sir Lancelot. Kate, Sir Gareth, Brangwyn and the others were all busy unloading the carriage and packhorses. The sack of oranges, Merlyn had already commandeered. Maybe, Gwen thought, maybe it was time for a little flirting?

"So, gold for the queen, Sir Lancelot? Is there no other lady of the court worthy of thy attentions? Have you thought of no other in all the time you've been away?" She shot him a coy sideways look beneath fluttering eyelashes. This was a provocative taunt since Sir Lancelot could hardly concede he was solely enamoured with the king's wife.

"My Lady Gwendolyn, thine own fair image did invade my dreams for many a night whilst I was far from Camelot. Thy beauty didst likewise dominate my thoughts whilst bargaining for gold with both troglodytes and giants who inhabit and mine the mountains in the North. But, milady, how canst I return with gifts only for thee and ignore thy mistress, the queen of this citadel? 'Twould be a most ungallant, unchivalrous gesture. But indeed it pains me much to shower golden gifts on another whilst my eyes cannot tear themselves away from following your faintest shadow."

This of course was all lies and hogwash, as Gwen full knew, but it was delivered with such panache that she felt she ought to reply in kind. "Sir Knight, thy pain is sufficient recompense for me. Thy sentiments so gallantly expressed win my heart completely. Surely thou shalt haunt my dreams now, and many of my waking hours, in the manner that thou accuseth me..." With that, she curtsied low before him, casting her face down, more to stop herself grinning than in a show of modesty.

Gwen's words had had their effect, however. Sir Lancelot's proud head rose. He felt that he had won the devotion from this young admirer that he duly deserved as Camelot's most famous warrior; that his own feelings for the queen had been well-covered, and indeed this favourite of the monarch who bowed beneath him, this highly attractive lady in her prime of femininity now seemed to be a potential conquest. He was well-pleased with himself.

Whilst this little charade was being acted out, Sir Gareth had approached – though as chivalry dictated he waited at a distance. He could not come any closer without invitation from his lady and nor would he interrupt the courtly advances of Sir Lancelot, the senior knight and many years his superior. He struggled to control his emotions, however, seeing the fair maiden who had chosen him for favour evidently wilting now beneath the charms of Camelot's prime lady-killer.

Gwen rose and turned to see Sir Gareth watching her. His face was a picture. Brilliant! Nothing like having two knights compete over one to make a young girl feel like she had the world and all its menfolk at her fingertips.

"Sir Lancelot, here stands my lord and protector who has been with me these last two days and who faced down an ugly crew of ruffians to win me my Chinaman." She held out her hand to Sir Gareth to beckon him forward.

Sir Gareth duly bowed and took a couple of steps forward, his insides seething. The Lady Gwendolyn was all smiles and intimacy towards Sir Lancelot and she was now calling for her guardian knight as if he were her favourite wolfhound to salute his superior. He, of course, had no option other than to do his lady's bidding. He stepped forward two more paces and went down upon one knee before the king's first knight and lieutenant.

Sir Lancelot showed his pleasure. "Well done, Sir Knight! Thou bringest honour and credit to Camelot yet again. Dost thou knowest who were these ruffians of which my lady speaks?"

Sir Gareth gave no hint of the emotions running within him as Sir Lancelot referred to the Lady Gwendolyn as 'my lady'. The hierarchy at court ruled supreme. He answered truthfully – though with a blank expression: "Saxon barbarians, sire. They came by ship to Caerleon, though I believe they have now departed."

"'Tis just as well. Such folk always bring trouble – the king and I have fought them before. They are a greedy and envious people in my opinion – bent only on destruction and capturing the riches of others. Congratulations again, my friend, for standing firm against such an uncivilised rabble."

A muffled *'kerwhump!'* – like a dragon's cough – disturbed any further conversation. Smoke billowed forth from the workshop behind into which Merlyn and the Chinaman had earlier disappeared. The two of them now emerged, staggering out into the courtyard – both with blackened faces but with white smiles.

The two knights, having heard nothing like this ever before and fearing some outlandish attack, had both leapt up brandishing their swords. Gwen guessed, however, that something entirely different had been going on.

"Don't tell me, Merlyn, that you've been preparing the king's medicine, 'cos I would reckon that *that* mixture you've just ignited would blow out his insides!"

"Ahem, milady, a most unfortunate accident! Forgive me, sires, for causing any alarm. In truth, the king's medicine is already prepared – it needed only a little orange juice to make it more palatable. In the meantime, Mr Chen here was showing me an entirely different concoction…"

"Yes. Different concoction. Different ingredients. Different result. Most interesting…" The Chinaman was busy dusting himself down and nodding thoughtfully.

Gwen grinned. She could see this was just the beginning of a whole new chapter in Merlyn's magical reputation. Better to leave them to it, she thought – things might get dangerous in there for the next twenty-four hours or so.

"Dear Merlyn, please allow me to take the medicine you have ready. And perhaps a bit more of the orange juice? I'll go and take it to the queen's quarters straight away and we'll see if the king will like it. If it doesn't blow his head off, of course!"

Merlyn did as he was asked. A few minutes later Gwen had left her two knights behind and was climbing the large central staircase of Camelot, accompanied by Kate who was carrying a tray with two large goblets of orange juice and herbs up to the royal suite. They were welcomed enthusiastically by Queen Guinevere.

"Lady Gwendolyn, how it pleases me to see thee safely returned from thy excursion. Merlyn tells us that thou didst ride to Caerleon on some errand. Was my carriage to thy liking? Didst thee receive a royal welcome? And pray tell, what is it thou hast brought us?"

"Medicine for the flu, your Majesty. I heard that King Arthur is now suffering. Perhaps you...I mean...perhaps thou shouldst drink a little if thou art still afflicted. It...er...it pains me awfully for bringing this evil virus to Camelot. I feel terrible about that. So I thank thee most sincerely for the loan of thy carriage. The trip to Caerleon was entirely successful, as I hope the king will see when he drinks this..."

Gwen silently kicked herself for being still so nervous speaking to royalty. She ushered Kate in first, who dutifully curtsied low before the queen and held up the tray for royal approval. Kate, of course, had been raised at Camelot and knew instinctively what was expected of her when in royal company. For Gwen it was still nerve-wracking. She was aware that she was supposed to be one of the queen's closest confidants but she struggled to fulfil that role, not knowing quite what language and comportment was appropriate and frightened that somehow she would be found out as some interloper in disguise. Fortunately, however, the queen did not appear to notice her difficulties and simply folded her arms into hers and took Gwen into the royal chambers, calling out enthusiastically to her husband.

"See here, my King: the Lady Gwendolyn has returned and brought us this potion of most divine flavour to ease thy ailment!" She took a sip from one of the goblets as she ordered Kate forward.

King Arthur was lying across a large, curtained four-poster bed and looked feverish and bad-tempered. He rose up on one elbow and beckoned the three women to approach. Gwen and Kate stood back while the king reached out for the goblet that the queen proffered. He took a quick drink as if to see it was to his liking and that it was not going to poison him. His face relaxed a little. It met with royal approval. He looked keenly at Gwen.

"You prepared this, milady?"

Gwen curtsied. "Not I, your Majesty. 'Twas Merlyn who prepared this potion from oranges that I went to find in Bristol…"

"Thou didst well!" The king looked up at his wife. "My Queen, I wish to speak with the Lady Gwendolyn now. If thou wouldst favour me by retiring for a moment…?"

Queen Guinevere bobbed down graciously and then backed away out of the bedchamber. Kate followed as far as the door where she sank down to the floor, out of earshot but ready to be called for if needed.

The king coughed and spluttered an apology to his young attendant. "Milady, excuse my ill temper, but I regret that this castle is indeed suffering from an evil affliction which I fear thou hast brought amongst us!"

Gwen nodded, her face fearful of what might be coming. "Yes, sire, I am indeed sorry, I didn't mean…"

King Arthur waved a goblet-filled hand as if to dismiss any excuse. He took a deep draught of the potion, still spluttering as he did so.

"No matter, milady. What is done is done. This plague is all about Camelot now, though there are those like my dear Queen who have now recovered from this affliction. I am told that there is some mischievous demon within thee that causes this grief but at the same time thou art battling to overcome it. What say'st thee to this charge? Art thou battling with success?"

"Your Majesty, I hardly know what to say. I do not intend any harm...but it seems that since my own collapse I...I have sort of upset any number of people and ways of doing things here. It's like I've forgotten all about the customs of Camelot and have fallen into this world from another time and place. I cannot explain it, sire, but I am trying my best to make things better... Really I am – like this orange drink for you, sire..."

"And the sword above the battlements to attract a dragon's fire. Yes, I have seen thine efforts, milady. Fair maiden, I see that thou art truly engaged in a magical transformation, a battle for thine own soul. Merlyn has spoken thus and I see it for myself now."

A noise outside in the antechamber caught King Arthur's attention. A voice he recognised drew a scowl upon his face.

"Milady, wilst thou instruct thy maid to draw the door shut to this bedchamber? I do not wish to be disturbed." He was clearly annoyed and, feverish as he was, his face coloured rapidly.

"Kate, will you shut the door please?" Gwen called out. "And if you will let me attend thee, your Majesty, I think that with your temperature you should not have these curtains drawn so close and if the door is to be shut then you need as much air as possible from these windows!" Gwen quickly busied about, pulling aside the drapes on the bed and those that obscured the light from the long slit windows.

Despite his sour mood, the king could not resist a wry smile at this young woman fussing over him. "Merlyn hath said thou art full of ideas to address all manner of ailments and occurrences in this castle. What art thou doing to me? I am sick and in fever and thou strips back the bed and the window as if thou wishes me to die of cold!"

"Your Majesty – you suffer from high temperature! How is that to come down if thou art wrapped up like a babe in swaddling clothes? I'm trying to sort you out. Have I not been away for a day and a night to fetch you some medicine to lower your fever? And all you can think of is to shut the door and heat up some more in here!" Gwen grinned. She quite liked scolding the king and lord of all Camelot.

King Arthur growled. "The door is shut because 'tis Lancelot without. No doubt he wants to report back to me on his quest but I fear 'tis no more than an excuse to visit the queen and fawn all over her. He was once my most loyal and trusted knight, the first amongst equals of the Round Table...but his infatuation with Guinevere much tests my patience..." A fit of coughing and spluttering suddenly overcame him. "And worse! I fear my beloved wife is responding to his advances. This is unforgiveable. If this continues one or both of them must be banished! It...it is *unbearable!*" The king roared in anger and his face turned blood red.

Gwen hurried to the bedside. She raised the goblet to encourage the king to drink again.

"My King, leave Sir Lancelot to me. I'll do what I can to turn his head in my direction and away from the fair Queen Guinevere. You just see if I can. How does that sound? Will thou trust me to do that? To save thy Queen for thee? I'm anyway sure that she loves thee more than any other and if I can capture Lancelot's attention she'll soon see where her true love lies..."

The king caught hold of Gwen's arm. "Ye thinks that that can be done?" He looked at Gwen with sudden interest.

"If I'm as bad as you all think I am then I'm sure it can be done," Gwen grinned. She rather liked the thought of royal approval to go and chase the hunky Sir Lancelot. Then she paused and looked at the king conspiratorially: "Even more so, your Majesty, if I might suggest that you praise my youthful looks to the queen and arouse her jealousy..."

"By God, milady!" King Arthur cried aloud, this time with laughter. "Thou art indeed full of the most mischievous ideas...but if thou canst accomplish this and win back the heart of my dear Queen to me then I shalt forever be in thy debt. I'll even forsake the cold and accept thy blandishments to freeze halfway to death in here! Go to, my lady! Go to!"

The king raised his goblet in salute, finished the last of the orange drink and bade her leave to go about her business. Gwen sank to the floor in one final curtsey and turned to go, remembering just in time *not* to turn but rather to back away in the king's presence. Getting used to this Camelot was really quite a challenge. She was beginning to revel in it.

Kate opened the door and Gwen emerged from the king's bedchamber to find the queen and Sir Lancelot waiting outside. By the look of them, they had been having something of an argument. This was an opportunity to exploit.

"The king was so grateful, so appreciative of the potion I brought him!" She raised her hand to her brow, feigning much emotion. "Kate, did thou see'st his reaction?" Gwen looked round at her maid and gave her a sly wink.

"Indeed, my lady," Kate dutifully replied. "Thou art truly honoured by his attention."

Gwen smiled at the others, smoothed her dress down and did her best to show off her figure.

"Sir Lancelot! Art thou here to see the king, the queen…or wert thou following my shadow to these chambers?" She flashed a teasing look at the knight.

This time, Sir Lancelot caught the look in her eye. He bowed in return. "No, my lady, on this occasion I fear it is not thy footsteps but those of King Arthur that I am chasing. He is ready to receive me now?" Sir Lancelot looked at Gwen and then Queen Guinevere, as if waiting for permission. The queen did not actually snort, nor toss her head, but with the slightest movement of her bearing gave every indication that this man was out of order, looking to her junior for permission to see the king. She glided wordlessly forward, nose in the air and passed Gwen on the way into the king's bedchamber. She closed the door behind her with a determined and proprietorial clunk.

Gwen shimmered across the floor and bade Kate to follow her.

She stopped before leaving the antechamber and turned her head to look over her shoulder. It was a classic pose, accompanied by a delicious wiggle, designed to arouse the passions of a man who she guessed had been away from female company for a fortnight or more. Of course, for a ladies' man like him that was not certain, but then – as she had constantly been reminded since arriving here – there was nowhere else on the planet in these times with the same style as Camelot, and Gwen was determined to flaunt that.

"Sir Knight, my lord, I confess my disappointment that thine eyes have not seen fit to follow me like thou hast alleged. Must I content myself only with the attention of others?" A flash of sparkling white teeth smiled at him. "When thou hast finished in the king's chambers...do not tarry here..." Gwen blushingly lowered her eyes. It was more than a subtle hint. The clear implication was for him not to stay with the queen but to search for another.

Sir Lancelot did all he could to stop crowing like a cockerel. He began to make a move in this young creature's direction but Gwen resumed her smooth waltz away and out of the royal suite, pausing only momentarily to sway her bottom at the exit, this time confident that someone's eyes were indeed following her all the way until she disappeared from sight.

The two young women descended the grand central staircase. Kate was bursting to speak. Like the good servant she was, she had affected invisibility whilst in the presence of the king, and in the antechamber with the queen and Sir Lancelot, but she had missed nothing and was beginning to understand and appreciate the artful ways of her mistress. Whilst they hurried down the last flights of the staircase and along the corridors to their own quarters, Kate could hold her tongue no longer.

"Truly, my lady, I have not seen thee like this before...not before thy swoon, nor since. Thou hast initiated a most delicate courtship. For a lady to encourage a knight in so bold a manner is…is…very unrestrained! But if thou dost achieve the king's desires it will be magnificent! For Camelot, and for thee."

The two passed alongside the courtyard. There was a distant 'kerwhump!' again from a certain workshop that momentarily caught their attention, but did not distract either of them from the seriousness of their conversation.

"Thank you, Kate. I think I am going to enjoy this. Sir Lancelot will be quite a catch, don't you reckon?"

"Indeed, my lady. He is the senior knight of Camelot whose reputation has travelled far. There are many ladies of this citadel and elsewhere who seek his company and, I've heard it tell, a fair number have received his favour. But take care, my lady. He has broken many a heart."

"Not mine, Kate. He won't break mine." Gwen spoke force-fully. She was determined to stay in control of this liaison and, thinking on it, she was pretty sure she did not really fancy the man, anyway. He was nearly twice her age, after all. They reached the spiral staircase that led to her's and Kate's quarters and began to climb.

Gwen did not notice the look of another knight, some distance away across the flagstones that she and Kate had just crossed. It was a broken-nosed big man, expressionless, standing alone and thoughtful, sadly watching all the movements of the Lady Gwendolyn and Sir Lancelot.

Chapter 12

INVASION

As it happened, and not entirely to the surprise of Gwen, Sir Lancelot turned out to be a real rogue. Chivalrous to a fault at a distance, after a week of subtle and daily manoeuvring, once he had at last gained entrance to Gwen's bedchamber alone he behaved like a wolf unleashed. Gwen had to use all her wiles to prevent him from grabbing hold of her and throwing her onto the bed, there to have his sexual advances rewarded. She was having none of that, thank you, for a variety of reasons. Firstly, there were no contraceptives in this day and age. Secondly, she had no idea where this dirty dog had been and who he had slept with recently. Thirdly, she guessed that once he had got what he wanted with her then the fascination would wane and off he would go back to try and seduce the queen. No, that was not the plan. And anyway, Gwen concluded, handsome though he was she really did not fancy the man anymore and was not going to waste her newfound virginity on this selfish and unappreciative bastard. Not that that stopped her from continuing to flirt with the beast and have him follow her around like a salivating hound.

Gwen felt sorry for Sir Gareth whom she met on a couple of occasions and who looked at her despairingly but never close enough to talk too. He was too much the chivalrous knight to ever approach without invitation and now he no longer hovered near enough to attract one. For him, she was a lost cause. For Gwen, engaged in a noble quest, the dilemma began to hurt her – seeing how the man she had come to appreciate was condemned to suffer in silence but she could do nothing about it.

Meanwhile, Merlyn had been closeted away in his workshop for days and she had seen nothing of him. That was something she decided should cease. She went down there and knocked on the door.

"One moment!" a voice cried from the interior. Then a minute later: "Who is it?"

"Someone who wants to see what the devil you are up to before you blow us all up to kingdom come!"

The door opened a crack and a quizzical eye peered out. "Who sayeth that I am going to blow anything up? Where did thee get that idea from?"

"Oh, come on, Merlyn! This is just about the oldest cliché in chemistry. Mad scientist peers over strange experiment; waves a magic wand, and Boom! The door flies off in a puff of smoke and the scientist staggers out with his clothes in rags."

"Milady, as always I do not know where thou deriveth such strange notions. Never in my long years have I ever heard of such a thing. True, my Chinese friend here has come up with some interesting experiments and much smoke and noise hath on occasions been generated. But nothing remotely like releasing forces to remove the door…'tis made of solid oak…"

"Just the thing! The more solid the better. Let me in and have a look at what you are up to."

"Milady!" Merlyn protested but Gwen would not be dissuaded.

Things were certainly looking interesting inside. Gwen knew what she was looking for – anything remotely like gunpowder – and various small piles of powder were on the nearest bench that might serve that purpose. She did not know enough about the chemistry involved to make anything like it herself, but she had watched as boys in her school had opened up a couple of rockets and spilled the stuff out. She had seen it fizz and burn up rapidly when lit. She wondered if Merlyn and Chen Ka Wai's powders had done the same.

"So what exactly are you experimenting with, Merlyn, Ka Wai? What are you trying to do down here?"

"Make fire, mistress. Help make fire when kitchen is wet. Also now make smoke. Maybe use smoke to hide people? What you think, Merlyn?" The Chinaman turned to address his older companion – clearly he liked making up all sorts of wizardry.

To Gwen, that sounded rather like theatrical magic: all smoke and mirrors. Not much future there, she thought.

"What about making rockets? China's famous for that."

"Eh?" the two men didn't understand.

Here we go again, thought Gwen. *Ideas way ahead of their time! I'll see if I can explain it...*

"Look – if you pack that powder into a tube, pack it in tight, and set fire to the open end, then it fizzes and fires something awful and shoots out like crazy. Well, it might do, if you've got the right powder. The thing is, if the fire shoots out one end, then the tube flies off at the other end. See? Gareth Jones could tell you all about it, I'm sure. Not the Gareth here, of course. He hasn't seen it any more than you have. But that's how you make rockets. Put the tube on a stick, stand it up pointing to the sky, light the bottom end of the tube and off it flies up, up and up until the powder is all gone. Here, let me draw it for you..."

Merlyn looked at the Chen Ka Wai and both nodded. Gwen had caught their interest. Fireworks are not difficult to draw, thankfully, since Gwen had never been a good student – not of art or science, or anything. But a few arrows to show direction of movement and the two men soon got the idea. Gwen issued a warning.

"If you've got the right fuel and you do pack it in tight then it really goes bang! If you do *not* leave one end open then I do mean BANG! Doors fly off, roofs go up in the air, people get hurt, see?"

Merlyn was quick as always. "I see, milady. If the force you explain is enough to push this rocket thing up into the air, as you say, then that force enclosed in tight space must struggle to escape. Like sneezing – you must give it an outlet! I fear to think of what might happen if you did not let it escape."

"Yes, yes! Most interesting! Most interesting!" Chen Ka Wai was already hopping up and down.

Gwen smiled at the two of them. Give small boys gunpowder and who knows what damage they will do. "Merlyn, please! You know this might be very dangerous?"

"Fear not, milady. Experiments like thou suggesteth will take place outside the castle..."

"Yes, but take care. Keep well away when things go bang! I don't want to gain the reputation again of unleashing some awful force that hurts people...least of all you."

Merlyn nodded sagely. The Lady Gwendolyn's plague had now passed its way through most of the menfolk in Camelot and, as well as the king, many a knight was laid low. Her attempts to limit the outbreak were appreciated, as was the medicine that, now exhausted, had helped alleviate some of the symptoms, but it was true that her reputation was not the best in Camelot.

"Fear not, milady. Mr Chen and I will continue as before with our various concoctions but we will say nothing whatsoever of thy advice and influence. Whatever happens – and we will indeed take all precautions – no blame will be directed at thee."

"Well, thank you, Merlyn, but it is not just me I'm worried about. Remember to look after yourselves!"

"Indeed, milady. Now if thou wouldst be good enough to retire we shall see which of these powders burns the fiercest..."

Gwen did as she was bid. She'd done her best to warn of the dangers and now just had to leave them to it. She left the workshop, rather hoping that fun and games would indeed be the result and no one would get hurt in the process.

It did not take long before the two scientists, not entirely mad but not entirely sane either, had taken a table and various implements and packages out of the castle and had set up stall on a small grassy rise some fifty yards from the castle walls. The rest of the afternoon was given over to a pyrotechnic display of varying degrees of success. There were fizzing and spluttering noises and much smoke. There were, on occasions, no noises at all and no action. There were a number of half-hearted bangs. Then, at last, there was a *whoosh!* and one rocket flew crazily into the air, zig-zagging all over the place in a quite alarming fashion. Cheers, as well as shouts of alarm went up from a number of people lining the outer battlements. Finally, as if to mark the end of the display, there was one almighty *bang!* and the table tipped over as bits of cardboard tubing and pieces of pottery flew everywhere. The two men emerged from behind the table, picked up whatever they could and returned to the castle, appearing to be quite satisfied with what they had achieved.

Gwen had witnessed most of what happened. It was not difficult to miss, such was the buzz of activity amongst people lining the walls and gazing out at Merlyn's table. Word had even reached up to the king, who had risen from his bed and gone to the window to see what his friend was up to.

Fireworks, even less successful ones, were an entertainment for people who had never seen them before. The same could not be said for the flu – which had affected some much more seriously than others. The running of the castle had been seriously impeded with the simultaneous loss of a number of important hands. The kitchens, in particular, were badly under-staffed. Gwen, with Merlyn's help, had insisted that anyone who seemed to display even the slightest symptoms should not be involved in preparing food. As a result, Gwen and Kate – now fully recovered – offered to help out themselves. This gesture on Gwen's part was refused at first – a lady-in-waiting toiling in the kitchens like any of the servants was considered not at all appro-priate – but Gwen insisted and got her way. Challenging Camelot's social conventions was, she argued, not so damaging as letting some go without food.

Such behaviour on the part of the Lady Gwendolyn did, of course, raise eyebrows. Not so much with the Knights of the Round Table, many of whom were too flu-bound to notice, but particularly amongst the ladies of court. Some of the younger ones admired her. Others, mostly older, thought her ways were outrageous – threatening the very fabric of their society.

A far greater threat, however, emerged outside the citadel's walls. It was a day when storm clouds were again building in the West. At Camelot, the sky was overcast, the air was warm and humid and rain came in short showers, sweeping across the land, followed by shafts of yellow sunbeams escaping breaks in the cloud cover. Around midday, an alert guard at his post at one corner of the castle raised the alarm. A large gathering of men could be seen on the horizon, advancing from the south. Shouts from the battlements joined the original cry: Camelot was called to arms to repel a possible invasion.

Hearing the alarm, Gwen could not stay in her room. As before, in the night of the electric storm, she had to go up to the top of the central tower to see what was going on. Kate, faithful as always, would not leave her side and so, alarm or not, she followed her mistress's footsteps. They found Merlyn in front of them, having come to the top of the keep for the same reason.

"This is not good, milady." Merlyn was clearly worried. "There are hundreds of men out there, and look – they are preparing for battle! Swords are being brandished and there is some activity I cannot quite see, some big weapon they seem to be preparing!"

"But surely they cannot mount these walls, Merlyn? Our archers and other men at arms can hold them off?"

"I trust so, milady...but there are many here not strong enough for battle just yet. Forgive me, but I must go to muster what weaponry I can. There is no doubt we will be in for a fierce fight." He stopped and turned before descending the spiral staircase. "Milady, on this occasion, for no reason must thou leave this tower. Whatever these barbarians throw at us will never reach this height...but elsewhere below thy life will be in danger. Believe me! Either stay in thy chamber with thy maid, or with the other ladies-in-waiting, or remain here. Nowhere else is safe!"

Kate nodded in agreement and held onto Gwen's skirts. "We will not leave here, sire," she replied, looking hopefully up at her mistress. "And besides there is nothing that we can do to help thwart these barbarians."

Shit! thought Gwen, looking at what was coming at them. *Merlyn is right. This does not look good.* She could see hordes of men spread out across the fields in front of the castle, still some half-mile distant. They were marching deliberately, determinedly towards her. The yellow, gloomy light reflected occasionally off helmets, shields and swords like the hesitant flickering of Christmas lights, but these visitors were bringing no presents. There was absolutely no doubting their malevolent intent.

Gwen heard a clamouring at the gates below, as a number of the residents of the shanty town outside the walls came rushing to the front entrance, demanding shelter. A small opening in the biggest gate was flung aside and there was a squealing and panic as a number of children, animals, women and finally some men squeezed their way in. Clearly they feared what was coming.

A steady, monotonous tapping of a drum was heard within the castle. Gwen realised it was the turning out of the guard: lines of armed men walked steadily, feet in time with the beating drum, to take up various positions along the walls. Archers took up the highest points, their faces resolute, their actions well-rehearsed, each one stringing his bow, loosening his arrows and then holding bow aloft, signalling they were ready. Gwen could not help but notice that there were a number of positions along each wall that were unfilled and there were, in addition, a number of men that looked far from well.

In the courtyard far below, horses were being led out. Knights in armour were assembling, standing in lines, each with an arm resting on his horse, being fitted out with assorted weapons by squires and attendants. Gwen picked out Sir Gareth by his grey charger and she also recognised Sir Lancelot, but there seemed to be not many others. Were they all ill? Gwen felt absolutely awful. Was she really to blame for this sickness that had so weakened Camelot's defences?

A noise behind her signalled the arrival of others to the tower. It was King Arthur, raised from his sick bed, accompanied by Sir Kay and two page boys. Gwen looked at the monarch in surprise.

"I cannot lie abed whilst there is trouble afoot," grumbled the king as he came to stand, holding himself up by the wall beside Gwen. "If I have no strength to ride into battle then at least I can direct operations from up here. Now, what do we have in front us?"

Lines of armed men were still marching slowly towards Camelot. A low chanting issued forth from a hundred throats. An eerie, unsettling sound, as the distance steadily closed. Then, apparently at some command, the marching stopped. The lines came to a halt and from some way behind, another party of men could just be seen assembling something and then advancing through the centre to reach the front of their army.

The king grunted. "Well, they seem disciplined enough. What are they up to?"

"That, my King, looks like they are bringing forward a battering ram," answered Sir Kay. "It seems they have come well-prepared."

The low chanting started up and the lines of men began to move forward once more. This time there were a group of thirty or more in the middle, walking slowly and carrying a huge, long battering ram, undoubtedly made up of several heavy tree trunks.

"Aye! And I've heard that sound they are making before. They're Saxons. A bunch of barbarians that would dearly love to take Camelot before moving on to capture the rest of Wales. We will have to stop them!" the king rasped. "Tell the archers to target that group in the centre. We must stop them at all costs from reaching the castle gates!"

Sir Kay moved forward and bellowed to the men manning the walls below him. "Tell the archers to target the group in the centre! Fire when they are in range. Pass the word along!"

Gwen heard the command being passed around the castle walls, one man to another, on all four sides, to all those that could see the army approaching and even those who still could not. When that order had circulated then there arose a strained silence, which seemed to slowly spread like an invisible shroud across the waiting citadel. Tension was rising.

Sir Kay returned to the king: "Sire, the knights below are anxious to go out and engage the enemy. Should I give them the order to mount?"

"Not yet, Sir Kay. We do not know this enemy's strategy at the moment and we cannot afford to show our hand as yet, especially if we are understrength. Leave them be for now. Is the enemy within range just yet?"

"Not quite, sire."

It was a very anxious and nerve-wracking time, just standing and watching an army more than twice the size of that mustered at Camelot walking slowly, menacingly forward, step by step and yet doing nothing to stop them. The group in the middle, with the battering ram, were the slowest moving of all but the commander of this Saxon horde must have given instructions that no one move in front of them. They all kept their line, kept up their chanting and – one pace at a time – gradually crept forward. It was mesmeric; awesome; petrifying to look at. It was an altogether terrifying experience for Gwen who had never seen anything like this, nor had ever expected to. The world she had come from knew nothing of warfare like this. Yet out there, in front of her and getting ever closer, these people were come to rain death and destruction upon everything she knew at Camelot; to attempt to tear limb from limb of those she had grown to love.

An archer, on the highest turret on the wall below them, raised his bow and an arrow flew into the air, tracing a perfect arc to come zeroing down to land somewhere amongst the centre of the army. They were in range! That lead archer must have been the head bowman since as soon as his arrow landed there was a rush of hissing as every other archer loosed his weapon and the sky seemed to be marked by scores of pencil lines of arrows in flight, all falling amongst the men with the battering ram.

The line stopped advancing. Gwen could see people staggering and collapsing and could only guess at the mayhem that was occurring. Numbers of arrows were all flying into the same area and anyone there could perhaps avoid one or two shafts from hitting, but not more and more and more as they kept coming. After a few seconds' delay, the shrieks and cries of wounded and dying men came through the air to the castle's defenders. For Gwen this was an awful sound but for the men lining the walls of Camelot there was an immediate barrage of cheering and shouting in return. This was a war of nerves, of courage and of will-power as well as a war of blood-seeking weapons.

King Arthur turned to Sir Kay. "Tell the archers to hold back. Let us wait until the line starts marching once more. When those downed have been replaced and the battering ram starts its deadly move forward then I'll give the signal to fire again. Do it!"

Sir Kay nodded and did as ordered. The command was again sent down to the walls and passed along, one by one. Everyone waited. Within Camelot, no one spoke a word. The tension was again palpable; fearful.

The chanting broke out once more. The line started moving. Slowly and closer the army approached, then the king nodded to Sir Kay and he bellowed forth the command: "Fire!"

Another forest of arrows took to the air. Another rain of death descend upon the advancing soldiers but this time shields had been collected and concentrated on the centre where the attack was anticipated. A few arrows got through to their target; the front line stopped again, but this time the damage inflicted was much less. The pause in the enemy's advance was relatively brief.

"Sir Kay, tell the knights below to mount up. We must try another tactic. And tell the archers to change their target now. They must aim for any of their opposite number in the front line before us. We will send our knights to attack the centre and to defend them from enemy archers we must first fell as many of their bowmen as we can. Tell the knights to await my signal to charge."

"Yes, my King!" Sir Kay hurried forward to lean over the top of the tower and bellow once more to the archers lining the walls. The change in the orders was made urgently clear.

The command was then sent down to the knights below in the courtyard to mount up. The noise and intense activity within the walls of two lines of knights preparing for battle released the awful, gut-wrenching silence about Gwen but, as she watched the armoured horsemen bend, turn in their saddles and arrange an assortment of weapons about them, her heart started racing within her and tears filled her eyes. There was Sir Gareth, big, brave, broken-nosed Gareth, right at the front – of course – holding a spear which had just been handed up to him and preparing to go out and fight to the death. Sir Gareth, the noble, gentle, so chivalrous knight who was her lord and protector, resolute and determined as always, now about to ride forth and face countless enemies…did he know how many? Did he have any idea of what he was about to go out and confront? He was so far away from her but she must shout to him:

"Sir Gareth, Sir Gareth! Take care! I love you!"

It was the sudden revelation of her own feelings for him that did it: Gwen dissolved into floods of tears. It was hopeless. He probably couldn't hear. Did he know that she loved him and not Sir Lancelot? Probably not – she hadn't known it herself until then. But he must not get hurt, no matter what. Part of her would die if that happened.

The archers were directed to fire once more. This time the arrows sprayed out in diverging lines to fall amongst others who had no shields but who were themselves preparing to fire their own weapons as the army came closer to the castle walls. As the change of targets brought surprise and some little commotion to the advancing hordes, so King Arthur hauled himself forward to shout down to the gatehouse and order that the gates be opened and that the knights should ride out.

An explosion of men shouting and horses stamping and then a dozen knights on horseback galloped out in two lines which fanned onto the battlefield – lances held forward, plumes and colours streaming, swords and shields bouncing on flanks; it was a stirring, exhilarating and awe-inspiring sight, except for the men on foot some two hundred yards away at whom they were charging. For them it must have been mind-numbingly horrifying.

Gwen could see Sir Gareth standing high in his stirrups, leaning forward, lance pointed straight at the centre of the opposing army, his helmeted head unflinching as arrows flew about him. Sir Lancelot and Sir Bors she also recognised, but no more of the others as they raced away from her, in a tight V formation, each covering the other, thundering along, the earth flying up after them as they at last reached their goal.

Mayhem again! Screams and shrieks filled the air. The battering ram was dropped to the floor as soldiers and horses dissolved into one another, though in the thick of it the knights on horseback could clearly be seen above the poor men on foot who were being hacked to pieces. Gwen hated it. Bodies were falling, blood was everywhere, it was murderous, stomach-turning butchery. She didn't want to look but she was desperate to keep sight of Sir Gareth who was wheeling and rounding his grey horse and charging into lines of Saxon warriors. Again and again he urged his horse forward and struck down one side then another at men below, some who offered resistance, others who were simply desperate to escape.

Cheers and shouts of encouragement rang out from the walls as the people of Camelot rose as one to support the Knights of the Round Table. But at the same time, both ends of the lines of the Saxon army were hurrying round, as fast as possible, coming to the aid of their fellows in the attempt to encircle the knights, crowd them in and eventually outnumber them. Men on foot carrying axes, swords, pikes and even wicked-looking agricultural scythes were running as quickly as they could to cut off the retreat of the horsemen. Gwen screamed out in alarm. She couldn't help herself.

"This Saxon horde know what they are doing!" King Arthur muttered grimly. He looked at Gwen, white of face and panic-stricken at what she could see unfolding before her. "Fear not, my lady, these knights also know what they are about. They are each one experienced in battle. They will not so easily be caught." As he said these words he hoped dearly that they would come true.

Things at the centre of the battlefield were getting intense. The light was deteriorating as the clouds lowered and, at a distance, the noise reaching those watching was frenzied, horrific and blood-chilling. For the knights in the middle of it all, the sight and sounds of the carnage must have been all-enveloping. And every second that passed, their predicament became more and more dangerous as the hordes of Saxons came circling closer. Gwen was weeping in fear.

At last one knight and then another turned his horse round and beat a path back out of the cyclone, fighting their way back towards safety. Others began to follow that lead. As they did so, the onrushing foot soldiers concentrated their efforts on the knights that remained. Where oh where was Sir Gareth? It was now impossible to see who was who and, with a sudden curtain of rain that came sweeping into the fray, it made the confusion complete.

Cries rent the air again as knights rode out and into men running towards them. More bodies falling, arrows and spears flying, horses rearing and plunging. Clouds rolled across and drew a veil over the savagery that was taking place.

Then a thundering of hooves came out of the mist and Gwen began to count back each of the knights as they returned to the protection of the castle. Three, four, five silhouettes appeared first. Dark figures on horseback, drenched in blood and rain, thundered up the rise towards the entrance, the gates open and welcoming. Six, seven, eight, then a pause, then two more…ten in all – none of the knights were now recognisable but still no grey horse. Gwen's heart was thumping, her hands clenched against the stone battlement of the tower, her eyes peered into the blustery, circling mists; where was he? *Please let him be next!*

Then at last two more came galloping back, just as the clouds descended and closed the visibility to thirty yards or less. There they were: one black horse and one grey, feet pounding, steam flying from nostrils, men bent over black in the rain, racing home. As soon as she saw him Gwen was up and running, she thrust aside her maid's attempts to stop her, she ran down the spiral stairs as fast as she could go, down one flight, then another, then another, desperate to reach the courtyard below. It seemed to take an age before she could reach the flagstones at the bottom and then she burst out into the open just as the heavens crashed above her and rain poured down steadily. Chaos confronted her. Men were running everywhere; orders were being shouted, the big heavy castle gates were creaking aloud as they were being closed; horses were stamping and staggering all around her and knights, exhausted, some wounded, were dismounting and stumbling into the arms of their attendants. Sir Gareth? Where was he? Was he hurt?

It was impossible to cross the courtyard and find him. What

appeared as chaos was actually people running back and forth treating the wounded, assembling arms, calming down the horses; everyone with a job to do and desperate to discharge their duty as efficiently as possible. Rain was drenching Gwen, mud was spraying everywhere, there was blood flowing on the ground and now there were even one or two knights vomiting in front of her. And then just to complete this scene of utter damnation, with an awful hissing sound, arrows began to fall.

Gwen felt a hand on her shoulder, dragging her back. It was Merlyn, wordless but with steel in his eyes, dragging her under-cover, back into the kitchens. Beside him stood Chen Ka Wai and with them were a number of catering staff, staggering under the weight of steaming, bubbling cauldrons of some evil-smelling substance that they were trying to drag out across the bailey. It was boiling pitch.

Gwen wrestled herself free. She refused to follow orders; she was not going to fly to safety at the first sign of danger. She had to find Sir Gareth. Merlyn, of course, was not going to struggle with her – he was organising a work party to ferry great vats of pitch up to the walls, there to be used as a weapon of last defence. He had saved this reckless, wilful young woman from being skewered by the first salvo of fire, now he had to return to his own duties and leave her to her own devices. She could surely see the dangers; his own business now must be attended to.

Arrows rained down. The archers outside had approached clearly close enough to fire at the defenders manning the battle-ments atop the walls, knowing that even if they missed, their arrows would continue their trajectory and perhaps hit others below in the interior. The battle had reached its climax.

Out on the far side of the courtyard Gwen saw a big man raise a shield and shelter himself as he remounted his horse.

"Gareth!" Gwen screamed. She ran out and threaded her way across the courtyard, dodging men, horses, arrows everything in her desperate attempt to get close to him. She dreaded the thought of what he was about to do.

He couldn't be going out again, surely? The enemy were now right outside! Gwen saw one other knight remount as well. She could not see who it was. But the two men turned their backs to her as she was still struggling to reach them. They ordered the gates to be open; they urged their horses forward, and then with a lot of splashing and manoeuvring they rode out through the narrowest of gaps, away from the courtyard, through the gatehouse, onto the battlefield and out to face the surrounding army. Gwen screamed after Gareth again as, to her horror, she saw the great oaken gates now swing shut and be locked, barred and reinforced. Those two knights had gone out to face hundreds and with no chance whatever of return. It meant certain death.

Bang! A great crash of thunder erupted above her. Lightning flashed. The rain poured in torrents out of the black clouds above, but Gwen did not care. She sank to her knees in the mud and cried out to the heavens in despair and utter, utter desolation. He had gone. She had not been able to reach him. He had gone. He had ridden out to kill and be killed!

Chapter 13

No.5 RAGLAN ROAD

The Lady Gwendolyn clung to Gareth Jones on the front porch of number 5, Raglan Road, as if paralysed. She dared not move. If she did, she was actually frightened of what it would lead to next; such was the uncontrollable passion that was gripping her. And Gareth had put his arms back around her so he was not moving either.

A rumble of thunder and then a crackle of lightning broke the magic. They fell apart. Lady Gwendolyn's eyes were round with wonder but she was still speechless. Her mind was racing; her blood was surging through her veins; she had stopped breathing. She just stood there goggling at him.

"Wow!" Gareth was the first to react. He felt as if the lightning, still far away, had somehow reached out and struck him. He had been with girls before but nothing like this. He had slept with girls before but the emotional contact had been minimal. This was altogether different. It was an inferno that had just ignited, here and now. His and her eyes were locked together. The flames were white hot, burning from one to the other.

"Gwen...Gwen..." he stuttered. His brain was refusing to function. He had wanted to walk and think and sort out the confusion in his mind but now he had trouble doing any of that. He just wanted to hold her and kiss her and kiss her again. He was totally bewitched by her.

But there was something niggling at the back of his brain and he had to get it out in front. No matter how gorgeous she looked – and she was still looking at him with those big, open, beautiful eyes – he just had to dig up that doubt, that issue that was worrying him about her and wouldn't let him just cave in and wallow in her loveliness.

"Gwen…we have to talk….will you…will you walk with me a bit?"

Lady Gwendolyn nodded silently. She would walk with him anywhere at this moment.

Gareth turned and shook his bewildered head as he led the way to the front gate, opened it for them both and then started walking slowly down the road, holding his hand out for Gwen to hang onto. A big man and his little lady – both still in the Arthurian costumes from the hotel – strolling in the heavy, early-evening air looking as if they were on their way to a fancy-dress party. One hundred yards down, there were fields at the end of the lane, and a stile which gave on to a footpath, stretching off to some distant woods. Gareth stopped by the stile and looked at her intently.

"Gwen, what do you really know about me? Very little, I'll bet. You seem to know all about some character, some knight from Camelot…but that's not me. The man you know…he's in your dreams. You say all sorts of lovely things about that man but you're thinking of him, someone else, he's not me. How can you say anything about me? Do you know who I am?"

As he was saying this he was thinking: *Do I really want to prick this bubble? If she looks at me and sees someone else, I'll make do with that! I'll be that other person for as long as I can…just so long as I can have her and keep the dream going for as long as possible. After all, it's not as if I have gorgeous girls throwing themselves at me every other day of the week. Let me hold onto this one for as long as I can!*

Gareth's concerns, his questioning of who Lady Gwendolyn was, what she was talking about, the same conundrum always, this brought her out of her own stupefaction. Her mind reasserted some control again over her body so that her hypnotic desire just to be close to him relaxed a little.

"Sir Gareth…to me, thou art truly that noble knight I speak of. That is what I see in thee. I know that here, in this…this new world of mine…where people speak so funny, if they speak to one at all, I know that there are no knights of Camelot anymore. But I know thee; I know *you*, the sort of person you are, I see into your soul. I recognise you from before…"

"But how can you, Gwen? Neither the old Gwen I knew in school before, nor this new Gwen that seems to have fallen into my lap from out of heaven, neither of you know much about me – who I am, where I've been, what I've been doing. For all you know I might be some half-crazed axe murderer who's been burying bodies in the woods over there for the last two years. You simply don't know me!"

He smiled down at her at the thought of it all, waving his arm in the general direction of the trees behind him. He was, he realised, trying to put her off him, challenging her conception of him, trying to see if she really did know him like she said she did and was not merely falling for some idealised, cardboard cut-out of a character.

Lady Gwendolyn put her arms up and held him. Her eyes were laughing. "Nice try, Sir Gareth! Isn't that what people say here? Nice try! Thou art…sorry…*you* are no murderer. It is not there in your soul. I cannot see such falseness in thy face. You are too honest and true to be other than you are. And thou art everything that my heart tells me. 'Tis true, I have seen thee in my dreams of Camelot, as you say, but I also see you here in front of me and I know that I am not mistaken. Thou art still the one who hath captured my heart. Thou art my love. I am thine…I am *yours*."

The Lady Gwendolyn still struggled with this modern English idiom that had no intimacy; no way of marking the difference in speaking to someone so close and personal from someone unrelated, distant, impersonal. She could not think of Gareth as someone unrelated and distant. In fact her body was telling her once more it wanted the closest relations possible with him. She clung to him again.

Gareth put his arms around her and kissed the top of her hair as she buried her face in his chest. *Well there it is then,* he thought. *Don't question it any more. She says she knows me and loves me as I am. Christ! Just enjoy it while you can...until the wind changes and she comes out of this dream.*

The trouble for Gareth was that, unlike Gwen who seemed to know him from her dreams before and loved him then and now, *he* knew Gwen before and, much as he fancied her physically then, she was really not a very nice character. Absolutely adorable now, yes...but would that last?

His doubts she immediately picked up upon.

"I do know thee, Sir Gareth. Of that there is no question. I see into thy soul and love what I see there. But I also see thine own fears. Thou art troubled? Fearful that I might change? My love, I ask of thee what thou hast asked of me: Dost thou know *me*?"

Amazing, Gareth thought. *How does she do it? How does she know what I'm thinking?*

"I dunno," he answered truthfully. "There is no doubting who you are *now*. I've already told you – you're beautiful. What I can't get my head round is where this you has come from and whether you will stay. I guess I should talk to your mother, and to Dai Mervyn. But – hell! –whatever anyone says, I'll take the risk! Who knows what the future holds? I'll love you while I can; while you are like this: so absolutely loveable. If I don't take the risk, I'll gain nothing. If it all turns out wrong in the future...well, that might happen with anyone, anytime, mightn't it? Do I know you? No, I don't think I really do....but it's going to be one hell of a time finding out!"

He grinned. He lifted up her head and kissed her lightly on her open mouth. Wham! The effect this had on the Lady Gwendolyn was the same as before: her whole body rose towards him and she could not think nor talk any more – there was just this overwhelming desire to be at one with him. Somehow within the turbulence that erupted inside her, she was beginning to realise that this body she was inhabiting was not the one she had grown up in, and it was telling her of life and passion it had experienced in this world that her head and heart born in fifth-century Camelot had never known.

Of course, the fire that arose in Lady Gwendolyn immediately aroused the same in Gareth. A big, physical man he needed little encouragement. There was only one direction this was now going to lead, and that was over the stile, across the fields and into the woods beyond. But fate was not yet ready to allow them to consummate their desires. There was a monstrous roll of thunder, a brighter, closer flash of lightning and then rain began to fall in torrents.

"Shit, shit, shit!" swore Gareth. There was no alternative – caught out in the open, the few trees about them offered little shelter. They had to run back up the lane, back to number 5 Raglan Road. Their passion would have to wait.

The two of them held tight to each other and they set off, laughing as they clumsily splashed through puddles – it was not easy for two, ill-matched in size, to hold hands and run together in a synchronised manner through the drenching rain.

One hundred yards to go, the rain came down beating ever harder, the thunder crashing now right on top of them and lightning dazzling, crackling all about them. Fifty yards remaining and the Lady Gwendolyn had to let go, to gather about her the soaking long dress the hotel had given her, and skip over the river that was now coursing down the gutters beside the road. She skipped, but her foot slipped and *crash!* – down she went in the rain, sliding and tumbling onto the pavement, Gareth desperately trying to catch her, but to no avail. She banged her head on the kerbstone, thunder and lightning now seemed to flash around inside her skull and then she saw only blackness.

Chapter 14

GIRLS OUT OF THEIR TIME

With the huge, oaken, barred and bolted gates between her and the man she had lost, as she knelt there in the mud, blood and rain, despair slowly turned to anger within Gwen's breast.

She raged at herself for not getting here more quickly; she raged at him – the big brute of a man, stupidly going out to some pointless sacrifice, and most of all she hated those bastards outside who were now thumping on the gates, having at last brought their great battering ram up to the castle.

Thunder seemed to be rolling around now inside the walls of Camelot and a tremendous flash of electric blue lightning lit up everything in a split second. Gwen looked up and saw rain falling from the heavens, sparkling in the light. Arrows were coming too but they were falling behind her into the centre of the bailey. She dragged herself nearer to the gates, her insides still seething. Atop the central tower of the keep another bolt of electricity split the skies to strike the newly-erected lightning rod and again illuminate everything in an instant. The brilliance caught archers on the battlements, attendants running in the courtyard, shields being held aloft – all as if frozen by the strike. Just as instantly the flash disappeared, leaving only silhouettes about her in the murderous, late afternoon darkness as Gwen at last hauled herself upright.

To one side of her, a wooden staircase led up to the gatehouse battlements where she could see Merlyn, Chen Ka Wai and others carefully manhandling great steaming cauldrons – absolutely focused on their task at hand whilst all else around them was chaos. That was the place to go. Gwen had just started climbing when a fearsome, timber-splitting crash shook the gates beside her. The ram was in action and threatening to break through. She hurried upwards, gathering her soaking wet dress higher about her to more easily move. As she did so she saw four men above her, swathed in cloths to protect them from the heat, tipping the first of the cauldrons' contents down the aptly named murder holes above the approach to the gates.

Shrieks and howls issued from below. The battering at the gates stopped. Boiling oil cascading down upon the men beneath her was causing pandemonium. *Good,* thought Gwen viciously. *Let them suffer!*

The battering ram was the Saxons' main hope to enter Camelot and there to make their superior numbers count so, despite the wounded below, men burnt by the oil were quickly replaced and the thundering on the gates resumed with little delay. Shields were deployed above heads as more cauldrons were summoned forth above and their contents tipped over them. This offered some defence, so fewer howls and cries followed and the determination to keep going, battering their way forward, was not slowed for long.

Merlyn was cursing aloud. "The rain is cooling the oil too quickly – we must set it alight somehow!" But carrying boiling oil and pitch from the kitchens by hand was tough enough. Doing the same with cauldrons that were already alight was impossible. What to do?

Gwen had climbed to the top of the staircase but she was separated from Merlyn by a number of men, discarded cauldrons and black pitch spilt and solidifying on the stone floor. She shouted across the battlement to him: "Merlyn – use rockets, grenades, explosives – whatever you've got!"

He looked across and their eyes met. He understood. Thunder crashed around them, the rain was still pouring, arrows still flying, but he understood. Gwen saw him bend down to speak to Chen Ka Wai and the latter turn away.

Meanwhile, out on the battlefield, the mists were swirling and the evening twilight was approaching steadily. Gwen searched amongst the numbers milling about below her to see if she could see horses. There – away to her right, Sir Gareth was still fighting, charging and bludgeoning his way through archers, pikemen and the soldiers who were trying to protect the men at the back of the battering ram. The other horseman following close alongside Gwen could now see – it was Brangwyn. Of course! Only his loyal squire would be certain to support him in this crazy, last-ditch attempt to foil the enemy, no matter if it was certain suicide.

Another fearsome crash below as the ram thumped into the gates. Then more thunder and lightning rent the air above – it seemed as if the gods were conspiring to bring down Camelot along with the Saxons. Gwen looked through the rain towards the central keep where the double-handed sword made into a lightning rod pointed skyward. How was it bearing up under this assault?

Well that was doing well. *How ironic!* thought Gwen. *I at last can show people that I am not some evil witch but someone also who can help protect Camelot...only to achieve this at the very time the barbarians invade.* Anger surged within her again.

A horse screamed out on the battlefield. Gwen's attention was immediately seized by the awful sound. Her blood turned to water as she dreaded to look. There, only a short distance away, Brangwyn's horse had been impaled on a pike and the rider himself was toppling as she watched. Three Saxons rounded to attack him but another horseman was quicker to rally: Sir Gareth swept to his aid. His sword arm went up and down rapidly, viciously, with all his strength: once, twice, and then he paused and reached down towards the fallen rider. A big strong man, he had felled two Saxons but the third pikeman now came at him.

Gwen's heart was in her throat, her breathing had stopped, her eyes were locked on this individual combat whilst all around archers on both sides were firing at one another, the battering ram was crashing below her and lightning lit up scenes inside and outside Camelot as if flickering and frozen in an old silent film. Except there was uproar about her, not silence. She was suddenly aware that Chen Ka Wai was next to her, lining up rockets and various earthenware pots and a metal canister on the stone floor.

"Ka Wai – fire a rocket over there, quickly! Where Sir Gareth is!" she was absolutely frantic.

Clever man – he needed no explanation. Sheltering his weaponry from the rain, pointing one rocket in the desired direction, he conjured up a flame somehow and – whoosh! – off it roared through the half-light.

The effect on those below who saw it streaking down from the gatehouse and into the melee some twenty yards distant was immediate. They were petrified. This was like a dragon's breath! Sir Gareth's great grey horse reared and plunged, frightened out of its wits. Not its rider, nor Brangwyn spread-eagled below, nor the Saxon who was about to thrust a pike into Sir Gareth, none of them could do anything but duck for cover.

Whoosh! Another rocket set off, zig-zagging furiously over people's heads. Merlyn had attached short, sharp, wicked-looking spikes on top of the four or five rockets they had prepared – each about six-foot long and packed with gunpowder – and this second one found a target – some poor warrior some distance away who screamed terrifyingly as it speared him into the ground, still belching out fire and flames and black smoke.

Merlyn meanwhile was not idle. He picked up one of the pots, lit its fuse, waited while it spluttered into life then rolled it down one of the murder holes.

BANG! An explosion below. The battering ram stopped at once. Looking down, Merlyn was cursing again. Splinters of pottery had caused mayhem amongst a number of men at the head of the ram, the black pitch that was spread about all over was smoking, but it was not alight. Other men below were rushing to minimise the damage, their advance had not been stopped yet.

There came then a great crash of thunder, and lightning suddenly dazzled the scene all around. The central keep of Camelot was lit up in a strange eerie blue light – the sword/lightning rod a thin black line pointing heavenwards right at the top in the centre of it. Electricity buzzed and crackled in the air like the night Gwen first saw the electric storm and, just like then, her hair seemed to stand on end. People standing in rivers of rainwater round and about at the foot Camelot were lit up by electricity – some badly frazzled, others not. It affected Saxons and Celts randomly.

The intervention of awesome forces of nature stopped all fighting for a moment...all except for Ka Wai and Merlyn who ignited and then threw what they had left, two more pots and then the metal canister, down onto the throng of barbarians beneath. There was one noisy bang...and then one almighty BOOM! that blasted Gwen off her feet. Fire immediately ripped along the battering ram, tore through shields, flared up the outer wall – everywhere the black pitch had solidified. The immense blast even blew great holes in the castle gates. Stunned as she was, Gwen struggled back onto her knees but she did not need to look down to see what had happened. She didn't want to. There was blood and body parts flying through the air.

An eerie silence followed, broken only by the steady pattering of rain. An awful moaning issued forth below and outside the gatehouse. Then King Arthur's voice was clearly heard, bellowing down from the top of the keep:

"Open the gates! Knights of the Round Table – mount up and ride out! Out! Out you go!"

Camelot went onto the attack. Tired men and horses were fitted out with swords, shields, spears and lances and once again, with plumes flying, they cantered across the courtyard, through the smoking crater that welcomed them immediately outside, past blackened corpses that looked as if they had been flung around by a ferocious dragon, and thence onto the battlefield of

Hades.

Fires were still burning in places, there were wounded and dying soldiers crying out, the battering ram had been tossed aside, smoking and splintered, and all able-bodied men seemed to have fled. Dark mists shrouded much of the distance so the knights spurred up their mounts to fan out and search. They did not expect to find much resistance.

Gwen came hastening down the wooden staircase to reach the gates below. Once more she was desperate to find him. Her heart thumping, her blood racing, her heart in her mouth, would the agony ever stop? She had to reach him – *Please, God, let him be alright!*

She ran out of the castle in the direction she had seen him last. She stumbled over the scorched and pitted earth and refused to look at whatever ghastly, gory scenes were around her – her eyes were searching only for one horse and for one rider. Gwen staggered now through mud that tripped her and seemed determined to slow her progress. But there! There was his grey horse – but standing alone, head lowered, nostrils steaming in the cold, clammy wetness that clung to everything. It was not the cold that chilled her marrow, though. It was the sight of his big body, crumpled on the ground below his horse, beside that of Brangwyn who was down on his knees, trying to speak to him.

Gwen flew those last few yards and flung herself down.

"Gareth! Gareth! I'm here! I love you! It's your Gwen! It's me…oh, Christ…please…please be OK …"

His eyes were flickering. She frantically searched his body – his helmet was dented, where was he hurt? How bad was he? He looked up at Brangwyn and saw sadness in his eyes. *Oh no! Please, God, don't let him die!*

There was an arrow imbedded in his side. The flight of it was broken off – perhaps when he had fallen – but the arrow head was buried in him somewhere. Had it pierced the ribcage? She pushed her fingers into his clothing, fought with chainmail and leather and buttons in a frenzied rush to get to his flesh. She was frantic with worry and had to steel herself to be disciplined in her search and not just to go crazy with frustration, rip her fingernails on his armour and fail to gain access to his body.

All the time she was looking at him. His eyes opened. He gave a twisted smile. A twisted smile and a broken nose – God, how she loved this ugly brute! "Gareth…I love you…do you know that…? Do you?"

"You're…you're Lancelot's lady…" He had strength enough to argue. That was good.

She kissed him, her hands still feeling inside the leather jerkin he wore. "No! I never let him near me. I wouldn't let him lay a finger on me. I only tried to lure him away from the queen. Understand? You are my only knight and lord! Aaagh!"

She found the wound. There was blood pulsing out of his side and his clothing was pinned into him by the arrow. Feeling as gently as she could around and beneath the wound, his ribs seemed strong. It had not broken through. Had it gone up into him from *beneath* his rib cage? She fervently hoped not – that would be serious. The angle of the arrow seemed, however, as if it had struck him from above. What a relief!

Sir Gareth was beginning to come round. "Milady…I'm fine…only concussed…please let me be."

Gwen could not believe it. How could he say he was fine – he had an arrow sticking in him! But the relief to hear him talk, to understand what had felled him – a blow on the head – and to know that the arrow was not life-threatening…the relief was enormous. Her spirits began to rise.

"What do you mean you're fine? You're half dead! I am NOT going to leave you be." Gwen slipped her hands, now stained with his blood, out from his clothing and reached forward to examine his head.

Sir Gareth's grey charger began to react when it heard its master's voice. A lively stallion, it stamped its front feet just at the moment that Gwen moved her position. She felt a blow on the back of her skull and promptly collapsed down on the ground beside him.

* * *

Seconds passed. Lady Gwendolyn dizzily came back to her senses to find a horse looking down at her, and Brangwyn. Brangwyn? Where had he appeared from? Where…where was she? Her head was spinning but the blow had been slight and she soon collected her thoughts. The big, grey horse she realised she recognised – it belonged to Sir Gareth! Looking up at it now, the said horse backed away in the rain and the mud. Mud? Scrambling to her knees, Lady Gwendolyn looked wildly about her. It was still raining, darkness was falling fast but this was no twenty-first-century roadside and here was Sir Gareth lying wounded beside her. Wounded! His blood was soiling his armour and the ground beside him. Indeed, there was blood everywhere, some on her hands, and here she was crouched over Sir Gareth on a field of battle. No doubt about it. Where was she? Outside the many-turreted walls of Camelot! Beloved Camelot!

Sir Gareth – how badly was he wounded? Fear struck her heart greater than any other emotion at being returned to the citadel she loved. Her head ached somewhat from her fall; she was once again bemused at where she was and how she had got there, but above all else, the man she loved was bleeding beside her.

"My lord, thou art hurt! Thy blood stains the earth beside thee! I cannot bear it!"

"My fair Lady Gwendolyn, thy pain is greater than mine own, I swear to thee. I am concussed but 'twill pass. My wound is…is not serious. But thou hast been struck by my steed and laid low before me. And more: 'tis dangerous here, milady. This is no place for thee. Brangwyn, my loyal and most trusted fellow –

help us both to rise."

The three stood up on the blasted field – Sir Gareth in the middle, bent over a little with the arrow still piercing his flesh and Brangwyn on one side, Lady Gwendolyn on the other. The scene of carnage that lay around them was ghastly to behold for someone who had just woken up from hallucinations of the future but Camelot and safety was only a short distance away and her arms were around a man who, until this day, whether in the fifth or the twenty-first century, she had only been able to worship from afar. She slipped her arms up under his leather jerkin to feel for his wound, but more than anything it was his warm flesh, the heat of his body, that impressed her most of all. For him, he knew the force of the arrow had been spent on breaking through his chainmail, the little that was now stuck into him had less of an impact than this woman's hands that were testing his flesh. This was a new, intensely pleasurable and much-to-be-encouraged experience.

Sir Gareth quickly assessed that, with no enemy in sight and with other knights abroad and searching for any remaining threat, the three of them were now in no danger. He addressed his squire: "Brangwyn – attend to my horse. I fear that thine own will serve thee no more. I shall walk back these last few yards with my lady." He stopped and smiled down at her. "Fair Gwendolyn, as always thou astonisheth me. What other damsel from Camelot runs onto the field of battle to attend to her knight? Dost thou have no fears for thine own safety?"

The Lady Gwendolyn grinned back up at him. How could she explain that she had just been thrilling to his kisses in another time and place and now didn't want it ever to stop? "My lord, I will follow thee anywhere. I have spent an age wanting to get close to thee and I fear that my passion could wait no longer. Beaten, bloodied and faint from thy wounds I will have thee thus whilst there is still something of my lord left for me!"

Sir Gareth tried to laugh but it hurt doing so. "What time and place is this, my lady, for thee to confess thy passion? Look – there are the bodies of Saxons strewn all about. There is mine own blood mixed with theirs at our feet. Is this a fit place to declare our love?"

"Chide me not, my lord. My love for thee knows no rules, no time; it knows only that thou art hurt and that I must be with thee. Let us hurry to Camelot where I might tend to thee more tenderly and let no other come between us!"

Sir Gareth smiled to himself. He was exhausted, injured, hurting and barely able to walk but this woman's confession of love and desire was like a drug that overcame it all. He would have carried her up in his arms and off to her bedchamber straightaway if he could...but drug or not, though his thoughts wanted nothing else, his big, muscular frame was strong no more. He limped across the blackened crater, past the splintered gates and eventually into the inner bailey. He slumped against the wall beside the spiral staircase that led to his lady's chamber. He could walk no more.

Kate appeared suddenly out of the gloom. "My lady! Where hast thou been? How canst thee run out amongst the fire and arrows raining down in the heat of battle?" Her frightened, tear-streaked face was white with worry.

"Kate! My Kate! How much I have missed thee!" Lady Gwendolyn caught her maid up in her arms and whirled her around, delighted to see her again. Her face was creased with smiles – even more so seeing the confusion on her maid's face who clearly did not understand her mistress's reactions. "But, dear Kate, my lord here is in need of assistance – canst thou summon two men to aid his climb up these stairs? He shall not return to the knights' quarters. I will tend to him above. Go! Find help quickly!" She kissed her confused servant on the cheek and pushed her away.

It took a few minutes before Kate returned with two of Sir Gareth's attendants. Gently, gingerly they helped him up the confines of the spiral staircase, along the passageway above until he could at last reach his lady's rooms and lie upon a bed. Then Lady Gwendolyn bid them all away, entreating Kate to bring hot water from the kitchens and thereafter to find Merlyn and bring back bandages and poultices to apply to her lord's wounds. Next, she lit several candles, brought them close to examine his big body and proceeded to strip him to the waist, cutting away that which she could not remove without disturbing the arrow still embedded in him.

Sir Gareth lay on his side, bone-tired, in pain but delighted that this fair maiden had declared that she was now his and was determined to ease his suffering. He had a lump on the side of his head that had been responsible for his concussion and he still had trouble keeping his wits about him, but lying down and having this lovely lady take his clothes off was something that needed no explanation. Hot water was brought into the bed chamber. Kate was embarrassed to see a half-naked man lying there and so quick to disappear again as soon as possible to find Merlyn.

Alone with her heart's desire, Lady Gwendolyn proceeded to wash him down, running her hands all over his chest, side and back, on occasion pressing her lips to his flesh as she did so. He had lost a fair bit of blood, straining to climb the stairs, and blood and dirt caked his body so there was much to clean off him. Holding his left arm aside, she examined his wound. Most of the shaft of the arrow had been broken off; the head had pierced through his flesh and was lying next to his ribcage. To pull it out she had to delicately cut through some of the blue and swollen flesh, then wash the wound as thoroughly as she could, allowing more blood to flow out, hopefully cleansing the interior as it did so. She knew that it was not the arrow now that was the problem but whatever dirt and debris that it had left behind inside him. She examined the open wound, lowered her head and licked away whatever foreign material she could amongst the blood that was emerging.

Sir Gareth lay as still as he could, flinching as little as possible as his lady probed the damage done to him. He could hardly believe that she had buried her face in his side and was cleaning him with her tongue. Not that he could feel too much – the area was numb with pain – but looking down upon the back of her head he could see what she was doing.

Satisfied she had done as much as she could, Lady Gwendolyn turned to wash the blood off her face and then again to wipe his wound as clean as possible. She would have to stitch up the hole that now remained in his side. Pinching his torn flesh together with her hands she reached up to look at him, the knight she loved in whatever world she found herself in.

"Thou art so courageous, my lord. Not a sound from thy lips whilst I have cut and punished and bled thee. And now I must push needles into thy flesh and pain thee more."

"My beloved lady, thou couldst never pain me. I fear that I am weak from loss of blood and my head still spins with concussion, but if thy lips should touch mine own like thou hast touched my wound below that will suffice as the most efficacious medicine ever known in Camelot. I will float; I will dream; my wound will never hurt again…"

She kissed him and almost let go of the wound she was holding together as the desire in her quickly rose again. Her cheeks flushed, her temperature climbed, she would have let go of his flesh, but refused to. She must mend this man first before she threw herself onto him and all caution to the winds.

Kate reappeared with bandages and medicines. Still holding onto Sir Gareth's side, Lady Gwendolyn asked her maid to find needle and thread from her belongings in the chest at the foot of the bed. She noticed now that her bedchamber had been turned around and all her belongings rearranged. Someone other than herself with entirely different tastes had been inhabiting this world but any questions about that would have to wait. First things first: she had to close and bind this puncture in her knight and lord.

"Kate, I will need thy help now. Thread this needle first, pass it over to me, then prepare to clean the blood away from my lord's side as I tie his wound together. See!"

Half an hour later and the Lady Gwendolyn was pleased with her handiwork. She had watched a similar operation before, as a maid like Kate, but this was the first time she had done it herself. She had instructed Kate as she had been instructed herself and hoped that Merlyn, the master physician, would be as pleased as her when he saw what she had done. Was she being selfish, wanting to do all this herself instead of calling someone more experienced than her to attend to this wounded warrior? But *she* wanted him, all of him, and didn't want the rest of Camelot to have him – a very twenty-first-century ethic, she little realised.

Sir Gareth lay there still, unmoving, trusting his two fair surgeons, not so much as uttering a whimper as his flesh was stitched up like they were sewing some cloth shirt. And now poultices were applied and bandages wound around him, four gentle hands turning him and binding him until his two guardians were satisfied. He risked turning and lying on his back now, his left arm tucked down and holding the poultice tight against his wound. He smiled.

"Ladies: my most sincere and humble thanks for thy kind and sensitive ministrations. No knight has ever been so sympathetically cared for as thou hast cared for me. Milady – thou art an angel from heaven sent to recover me from the Devil's own battlefield, but I cannot overstay my welcome in thy chambers any more, I must rise and leave thee in peace now…" Sir Gareth made an attempt to climb to his feet.

The Lady Gwendolyn was outraged.

"I do *not* give thee leave, Sir Gareth, to move from this bed! You give me thanks as if I am a mere maid to Merlyn and not one that has declared her undying love for thee. I will *not* be dismissed as some squire or attendant. And thou wilst stay where thou art until I release thee!"

"My lady, I mean thee no wrong! I only wish to serve thee as any true knight and must not presume to stay in thy rooms for longer than is appropriate..."

"My lord, it is I who shall be the judge of that!" She turned to her maid. "Kate, thou must leave me now. Thou hast served me as faultlessly as always. I am delighted to have you back with me once more but I shall call you next when I need you. Thou art my loyal and faithful servant." She kissed her on the cheek and dismissed her.

When the door closed, Lady Gwendolyn turned back to her knight who had moved no more, admonished as he was.

"And now, my lord," she said as she lowered herself to kneel beside him, "thou ungrateful warrior who wishes to bid me goodnight, I have not finished with attending to thee yet!"

She immersed a cloth in the water that was still warm in the basin by the bedside and began to wash him again. Loosening the remainder of his clothing she stripped him of his leather breeches and stockings and began to bathe his legs. When she reached up to his loincloth she gently removed that too, and continued bathing him as he, for the first time, now began to move restlessly and moan aloud...though not in pain. She dropped the cloth on the floor, removed her dress and got onto the bed, kissing his body as she did so. Careful not to hurt him too much, she then climbed on top of him and blew the candles out.

Chapter 15

WELCOME TO CAMELOT

Gwen's head hurt. For a few seconds the world seemed to be turning round and round and she fought hard to regain consciousness. She felt the rain on her face and suddenly came to. Gareth! She found herself in his arms, his worried face looking down upon her. What was he doing? It was he that was injured, not her! But her head was still hurting and looking around she did not recognise at first where she was.

"Gwen! Look at me! Are you OK? You've really banged your head!"

His arms were holding her, gently encouraging her to sit up. It was dark, the rain was still pouring and she was getting soaked by a river of rainwater flowing down the road. Road? Everything suddenly came into focus. She was half-sitting, half-lying in the road just down from her house in the middle of a thunderstorm. She was back!

"I'm back! I don't believe it! Gareth...are you OK?" She ran her wet, cold arms up under his shirt and felt for the arrow that she had seen sticking in him.

Gareth jumped, laughing. "Gwen, for Christ's sake! Can't you leave off for a second – your fingers are like ice! Let's get inside, quickly."

Gwen held on to him. She couldn't believe he was uninjured. On the battlefield she had felt blood pumping out of him. She felt for his wound and there – there she felt something: a lump on his side where the arrow had gone in.

She looked up him, worry creasing her face again. "What's that? There! You're hurt!"

"Get off me, Gwen! That's just an old rugby wound where I got trampled on...get up now, come on. You've had a nasty fall!"

He lifted her up onto her feet. "There, let's get you inside and look at your head…"

Gwen wouldn't move. "You got *trampled on* in rugby? What bastard did that? What sort of game do you play where people do that to you?"

"Gwen, don't just stand there in the pouring rain! Has the knock on the head made you crazy…?" He could not believe this gentle, loving woman was now standing, trying to argue with him only yards from her front door instead of running for shelter.

Gwen threw her arms around him and kissed him with all her strength. Her head was still spinning but there were all sorts of other feelings crowding through her brain and, anyway, she had got used to the rain and lack of creature comforts in Camelot. First things first: the man she was panic-stricken about; the man she thought had gone out to his death; that big, ugly mountain of a man was standing in front of her, now uninjured, and she wanted him.

"Yep!" she came up for breath. "I'm crazy alright. Crazy for you!"

Gareth laughed and picked her up. He walked the last few paces in the rain to the wooden gate at number 5, Raglan Road, carrying Gwen in his arms. He kicked the gate open and awkwardly staggered through it and up to the front porch. There, he tried to put Gwen down but she hung on to him, her arms tight around his neck.

"Ooh, Sir Gareth, thou art so strong and brave!" She tried kissing him but he wasn't having any.

"What's got into you? Behave yourself!" He knocked on the door and finally managed to set this crazy woman on her feet.

Ceri Griffiths opened the door, her eyes wide in surprise. "You're both soaked. Come in quickly," she said. "What on earth were you doing, going out in this downpour?"

"Mother! It's you! I'm back!" Drenched in the rain as she was,

Gwen rushed to cling onto her mother.

Her mother smiled and let her daughter press her soaking wet clothes against her. "Come on, dear – you've only been gone a few minutes and now look at you! What have you been doing, the two of you, as if I didn't know!"

Gareth grinned. "Well you said it, Ms Griffiths. You have a beautiful daughter!"

"Gwen, dear, we'll have to get these soaking wet things off you and wrap you in a towel. In fact..." she looked at Gareth, dripping in front of her, "you'd both better come inside and do the same before you catch your death of colds."

Gwen looked up at her mother, her eyes shining with happiness. "Mother, if we both take our clothes off in the same house together then you'll have to wrap me in concrete, not towels, to keep me off him!"

Ceri Griffiths laughed. Thinking on it, perhaps that was rather a risky thing to say, she considered.

Gareth was as fascinated as before with the twists and turns this girl was performing with his emotions. "Gwen has had a nasty blow on the head, Ms Griffiths. She slipped over just outside and went down with a bang."

"No, Gareth, Mother, I really am OK. Don't worry. It is just that I'm back home again. I...I have been away for so long it seems. In another world. You wouldn't believe it..."

The three all looked at each other without speaking. Water was still streaking off two of them, making little rivulets on the carpet in the hallway. An awkward pause.

"Gwen, go upstairs immediately, dry yourself off and change. Come downstairs only when you are ready and we can talk about this later. Gareth, don't move! Stay here and I'll find you something to change into. Gwen – off you go this instant!" Her mother took charge, spinning her daughter around and pushing her in front towards the stairs.

There was an airing cupboard on the landing upstairs where

Ceri Griffiths kept the towels. She pulled out two of the biggest and returned to the hallway.

"Take your top off, Gareth, and dry yourself with these." She handed the towels to him. "I'm afraid I have no men's clothes in the house to let you have – I got rid of all those years ago and anyway those that were here would never have fitted you..."

"Don't worry, Ms Griffiths. It's good of you to let me have these." He stripped off the Arthurian shirt he was wearing and the tee shirt underneath. Both were saturated. He towelled his upper body dry right there, standing in the hallway. His trousers were equally wet from the knees down but he could suffer that. Polite as ever, he was effusive in his thanks to Gwen's mother.

"Thank you so much, Ms Griffiths...but I suppose I had better be going. I'm making a mess of your carpet..."

"No, Gareth, you can't go until Gwen comes down. You had better come inside and wait." She ushered him into the front room and he stood there, rather awkwardly, by the front window. They both looked at one another and knew what each was thinking. Which Gwen was it that would come downstairs?

They did not have long to wait, Gwen was desperate to see them both. She came skipping downstairs, barefoot and in a jumper and jeans, her face still alight. She came into the front room and span around, taking it all in.

"I'm back! I'm back!" She was bursting with emotion. "And a proper toilet upstairs!" She grinned at the two others, staring at her. *They must think I'm crazy,* she thought. She wanted to rush and kiss them both again but their faces were too serious. She stopped.

"Is everything OK?" she asked tentatively.

"Erm, Gwen...you said you've been away, in another world, that we wouldn't believe it. I think we would, if you'd like to explain..." Gwen's mother held her hand and directed her to sit down in front of them. Her mother sat facing her; Gareth, still rather wet, preferred not to. Both were looking intently into

Gwen's face, trying to read her expression.

Gwen suddenly felt very nervous. "I don't know how to say this..."she began.

"Try us," said Gareth.

"There was a thunderstorm, a castle, I was rushing outside ..." She looked at her mother, trying to explain. "Sir Gareth was hurt..." Gwen looked up at Gareth, pleading with her eyes. "I was trying to get to you, to see where you were injured, you were *bleeding*...then I got hit on the head – by your horse, I think."

"Gwen, how long ago was this...and *where* were you?" Her mother was searching her eyes.

"Just...just minutes ago. There was this terrifying battle..." Gwen put her head down and covered her eyes with her hands. Images of men dying and blood spilling everywhere came back to her. Merlyn's face grim and steely as he set fire to the grenades; Sir Gareth riding away from her; her desperate rush onto the battlefield, seeing his body lying on the ground. She exploded into tears. It was all too much.

Her mother put her arm around her and Gwen raised her head, tear-stained and confused.

"Don't ask me how it all happened. But I was there. I was!" She looked round at Gareth, standing above her. "I thought you were dying...I did!"

"*Where* was this Gwen?" her mother still asked, although she had guessed the answer.

"In Camelot," she answered simply. "There! I've said it. I know you won't believe it, but I was there, with King Arthur, Merlyn and...and ...Sir Gareth. And I'm not crazy. Really I'm not. It wasn't a dream! I *was* there!" She looked at her hands, to see if there were any traces of Sir Gareth's blood under her finger-nails...but she couldn't find any. "And now I'm here again..."

"We knew it," said Gareth. "We both knew it! So...the old Gwen is back." He was upset and his voice showed it. He didn't know where to look or what to do. The girl he had kissed and who had declared her love for him less than thirty minutes ago had already vanished. "Shit!" he swore.

Ceri Griffiths wasn't finished. "Gwen...you say we won't believe it...but we *do*! We do believe you. And do you know why? Because all the time you say you were away we had another Gwen with us here. She said she was from Camelot. It was you here all the time...but it wasn't *you*. It was a new you..."

Gwen looked up at her mother in utter surprise. Her eyes opened in wonder. "No! Don't tell me...don't...but *do* tell me...how did she speak? What was she like? Did she speak of Camelot? What did she say?"

Gareth broke in. "She was beautiful. Your mother said that. You were beautiful, open, honest, *so* expressive! We all loved you. Dai Mervyn as well. You were like his daughter come back to him. He told me that even his dog, Morgan, loved you. And yes – you, or rather she, she spoke as if she had just walked out of the past...'Dost thou know me?' was the last thing she asked me. Then she fell over and I picked *you* up." His voice was flat, expressionless. He was hurting inside, his emotions turning his stomach in knots.

"You, or she, told us that Camelot was this warm, supportive community where everyone really cared for one another, whereas here, people are so distant and she felt all alone. Except she...it obviously wasn't you...she said that she had lost her mother as a child and could not understand how she could find *me* here...I really loved her...I mean, you!" Ceri began to feel her own tears beginning to rise.

Gwen was stunned. Speechless. These two were as overcome with emotion as she was. What sort of person had replaced her in the affections of those here? Somebody clearly who had had a big impact on them. Gwen tried to think of what Kate had told her when they had first met – of how her mistress had loved Camelot and how she, Gwen, saw nothing. How her mistress had lost her mother, killed by Saxon invaders many years ago;

how Sir Gareth absolutely doted on her. Yes – she had been slow in realising how much he felt for her and she guessed she had treated him badly for days until just recently when she had woken up to her own feelings about him. And here were these two now, implying much the same – how the Gwen who had replaced her was far quicker to appreciate and love them than she had ever been. She leaned forward and put her arms about her mother.

"I love you, Mother. I'm sorry. I'm lucky to have you, I realise now." She looked at her and nodded. "What the Gwen who took my place here said is true. Camelot is like that, right enough. When I was there, at first I saw only the things it didn't have. *Things* mostly. I didn't see what it did have until much later. And I guess I used Sir Gareth at first and didn't see how lovely he was until I nearly lost him." She got up and went to hold his hands. "But I love him now!"

Gareth was still stone-faced. Same story as before, he thought. "What Gareth did you know there? He wasn't me! I haven't moved from this place. Do you know *me*?"

"You *are* the same. You big lovely, ugly, brute. Just as distant and standoffish at first here as you were there. Very polite and proper. I remember you used to look at me at school like you looked at me in Camelot. From afar. And I treated you badly in both places! I must have been a bitch to you but you were still good to me. And then I saw how good and proper and courteous you were with *everyone* in Camelot and realised you were like that here as well, before. And when you were prepared to sacrifice yourself to protect us all, like you had protected me, that's when I realised how lovely you are. Here as well as there. So don't tell me I don't know you! Gareth Jones...I do know you and if you don't bloody well kiss me now I'll burst into tears again!"

Gwen promptly burst into tears. Gareth gently kissed her. "I do know you...I *do*!" She looked at him, tears coursing down her cheeks. "This has all been too much!"

"Telling me," he grimaced. He looked down at Ceri, holding Gwen's head into his chest, comforting her while she cried. "I don't know whether I've kissed the same girl twice in half an hour, or kissed two *different* girls…Talk about going crazy!"

* * *

The morning came with Sir Gareth still sleeping, weary from battle and in need of complete rest. Lady Gwendolyn rose and looked down at his craggy features, now softer in repose. She had worshipped him for years but it had taken a trip to the future for her to get up close and confess it. Evidently this knight had fought harder and longer than any other – though she had not seen it – had been hit on the head and struck in the side, so it was no wonder that he was in need of more sleep than her. She had not witnessed the Saxon invasion first-hand but was in no doubt that Sir Gareth would have been first onto the battlefield in the attempt to repel all and any of them.

But now she was back in Camelot! Again, she had no idea how it had happened but she had travelled through time to find the same man here as she had found there and this time, injured as he was, she had been able to stay with him, dress his wounds, save him from losing any more blood and have him to herself all night long. He lay there sleeping in her bedchamber after making love and she was in heaven.

She silently left the room to look outside and find Kate. There she was, in her own small servant's quarters next door, waiting patiently to be summoned. Lady Gwendolyn swept into the room and knelt down, putting her arms around her.

"Kate! We must whisper so as not to wake my lord, but 'tis so good to see thee again. I have truly missed thy smiling face and support whilst I have been spirited away in some truly bewildering world. Hast thou not missed me too?"

"Milady, milady – how hast thou been elsewhere? And here all the while another that is thee, but not thee? I fear some awful magic has possessed thee and thou hast acted most strange…such that I have worried so about thy safety and sanity. Merlyn himself hath said a mischievous demon is inside of thee."

"No demon, my Kate. Powerful magic, perhaps. But thou sayest that I have been acting strange? How so?"

"My lady – thou hast gone out to face dragons whilst they thunder above us. Thou hast travelled to the coast and would have faced Saxons in the streets of Caerleon had I not held on to thy skirts. Thou didst go with me to the kitchens to prepare food like any servant…and thou didst run out onto the field of battle just yesterday to be with thy knight…so many ways that I do not recognise in thee…"

Lady Gwendolyn sat back in wonder. All that? But this must have been whilst she was struggling to cope in this future world that frightened and made no sense to her. All that time, then, someone must have taken her place here who made as much sense to Kate as that world made to her.

"Kate, whatever happened before is past. I am now how thou knowest me. The same and no different. Save that I have endured an experience so bewildering that I cannot describe it. Kate – I have seen my mother! My mother whom I lost as a child before even I knew thee! This I vow is not madness. Nor was this heaven wherein I found her. Least, if that is heaven it is more like hell than I ever imagined. But it was my mother as sure as this face is mine own. I saw there Merlyn and Sir Gareth too. All in this other world; they were there – in many ways different; in many ways the same. The most fearful magic has been at work. But hist! A movement next door! My lord is awake! We will talk more later. My Kate, I must fly!"

The Lady Gwendolyn returned to her own chambers as quickly as she could, just in time to see Sir Gareth stumbling naked out of bed.

"My lord!" She rushed to his side, the right side, to help him stand, meanwhile lifting her hand to hold his head down so that she could kiss him.

He allowed her to do that, smiling beneath her lips that pressed all over his face.

"My lady, still thou continueth to surprise me! I wake in thy chambers after such a night. You come to me without hesitation, and I unclothed before thee, with such love and a fearlessness in showing it that doth shake me to my core. These last hours thou hath aroused such passion in me that no pain could subdue and we are more than betrothed, but now like man and wife. The very walls of Camelot have shaken and will continue to tremble if others learn of what has passed this night. My lady, allow me to kneel before thee and pledge myself to thee that I have not been able so to do until this moment."

Sir Gareth sank painfully on one knee to the floor, took her right hand and raised his head to look at her. "Lady Gwendolyn, my lady, I vow to serve thee and protect thee so long as there is life in my body. Mine heart is henceforth pledged to thine own; my spirit is tied to thine; my body yours to command. Forgive me for failing in strength to pledge my honour to thee before this night. This night whenst thou hast honoured me with the greatest gift that any maiden can bestow. I am your knight, your lord and your protector for ever. I am yours."

With that he kissed her hand.

Lady Gwendolyn placed both hands about his head and lowered her own to kiss him once more. "Most noble and gallant knight, I am yours as thou art mine. My love for thee knows no limit but thou art still injured and so I command thee to return to this, our bed that we have shared, and I shall examine your wound once more. No sire! Do not protest. Thou must do thy lady's bidding!" She smiled at him. There was a twenty-first-century spirit rising in her and she was going to have her way. Once she had pulled up blankets to cover her knight's naked lower half, she called Kate in to see her.

"Kate, wilst thou run and fetch more hot water and tell Merlyn to come? I wish that he visit our bedside to look at the surgery we have performed on this wounded warrior. Quickly, Kate, whilst I remove these bandages."

Kate ran off, her cheeks colouring as she heard her mistress refer to "our bedside" – a confession of intimacy that had not been sanctioned by marriage. But she would fetch Merlyn and say nothing about this, the loyal servant that she was.

When Merlyn arrived, Lady Gwendolyn had removed all the bandages and the poultice to reveal the stitching in her knight's side. She reached for the hot water that Kate had brought and commenced to clean the wound yet again for Merlyn to have a closer look. He commended the surgery.

"Well, milady, thou hast served thy knight well. The wound is clear, the swelling is slight, there is no trace of infection. Thou has practised my trade with success. You did not wish to call me last night?"

"Wise Merlyn, I thought that thou had enough business to see to and with one less wound to concern thee thou wert free to attend to others. And my lord is *my* lord. What good would I be to him if I could not comfort him myself?"

"What sayest thou, Sir Gareth? Wert thou not concerned that thy wound needed a more experienced hand?"

"I do not doubt thy experience and thy many skills, wise Merlyn. But I do doubt that your lips would have provided the same service as my lady's! My wound thou wouldst have attended to well, that is certain, but thee could not have lifted my spirits so well as my beloved Lady Gwendolyn."

Merlyn smiled. "Of that, sire, I must concur. Milady, again thy actions surprise us all, this morn, as before. Last night thou didst ignore again all my injunctions and ran headstrong below into danger, yet again straying where no lady should go. Is it the thunder and lightning that affects thee – like I know how some react to the full moon?"

"Well said, Merlyn," laughed Sir Gareth from the bed as his wound was again being bandaged by Lady Gwendolyn and Kate. "Perhaps my lady is the daughter of some hot-tempered dragon?"

At that, Lady Gwendolyn threw down the bandage she was holding and her newfound spirit flared.

"If I did not care for the two of you so much I should box your ears! But one is injured and the other so elderly that I fear to damage his fragile senses! There is no dragon nor demon's seed within me. My spirit is all mine own and I have learnt much recently on how I must use it to fend off the heartless taunts of others! My love, my lord, thou treatest me so unjustly. I shall not touch thee again 'til thou hast retracted thy cruel words and begged my forgiveness!"

"My lady, my love and betrothed, mine own and future wife, I do herewith withdraw every word that injures thee and humbly beseech thee to forgive my erroneous jest! Thou knowest I mean thee no harm but do indeed wonder at such devotion that leads thee into fields of conflict where thy very life is threatened."

"Milady," Merlyn interrupted, "thou knowest I have said that there is some mischievous spirit within thee that leads to all manner of surprises. Thy good intent is no longer in doubt. From King Arthur down to the lowest servant both within and without these walls of Camelot we have all seen and wondered at the truly remarkable changes thou hast wrought. From drawing the sting of dragons, to administering medicines, to working alongside servants and finally to rescuing an infidel and helping he and I to produce the most fearsome of weapons – this citadel will never be the same. Thou hast even driven the queen back into the arms of her king and left Sir Lancelot without solace and less stomach to fight. Sir Gareth here didst shame the senior knight with his superior strength and courage on the field of battle. Ye hast done all that!"

"Wise Merlyn, the Saxon invasion was beaten from the moment the first fiery flame shot out from the walls of Camelot. My strength was not needed. The lightning that lit up the keep, the great explosion that followed, the flames that fired forth and more that encircled the walls – all convinced the barbarians that we had summoned dragons to attack them. I heard them cry, I saw them run: Brangwyn and I had none left to fight from that moment on. Mine own efforts were puny compared to that which thou wert able to employ. My life is saved because of thy magic. As my lady is my witness, fallen and concussed as I was, there were none of the enemy left to dispatch me, only my squire remained, equally unhorsed on the field of battle."

The Lady Gwendolyn listened and marvelled at these stories. She knew that someone in her guise but other than she had done all that they had recounted. Yet somehow she was not surprised. That Gwendolyn they spoke of was a visitor from a future time who had taken her place, just as she meanwhile had replaced her in turn. And now, back in Camelot, after all her strange experiences, Lady Gwendolyn felt at one with that other self: more in command of her life and situation than ever before. And had she not demonstrated that already to her chosen knight, to all of Camelot, as well as to herself? She had taken her fallen warrior from the field of battle, repaired his injuries and spent the whole night making love with him – all this within hours of first being alone with him: truly a bold and convention-shaking practice that no lady of court would ever admit to. But she felt no shame. Quite the opposite – she felt fulfilled. There was only one sorrow: she knew she would not see her mother again; but the fact that she *had* seen her and known her was a gift from the future that she would never, ever forget. There was much in that foreign world that had frightened and distressed her – the size, pace, impersonality, the absence of community most of all – but there remained something in the future that gave her hope: that one could still find love and inspiration on an individual level, if not

in a community as a whole. With her mother, Merlyn, Gareth –
love there was no stranger to that world.

She looked around at the others sharing her bedchamber with
her now. She was happy to be back. Lady Gwendolyn felt that
she had it all: both the loving and supportive company of
Camelot *and* one special individual whom she would marry and
she knew she would love her entire life.

* * *

Ceri Griffiths, Gareth Jones and Gwen Price all looked at one
another and no one could speak for the emotion that swirled
around between them. Ceri, the more mature amongst them, was
first to put voice to her feelings.

"Gwen, my love, you are my only daughter and always will
be. Whatever you do, wherever you go, I will always love you.
Understand? No one will ever, can ever replace you. I don't
know how it happened but you've been through so many
changes just recently. Haven't you? Tell me how you are now.
How has all this left you? How are you feeling?"

A white, crumpled face looked back at her mother: "Numb!
Confused! I don't know what I feel inside now. I was so happy at
first being back, with Gareth, with you. Now I don't know. I feel
as if you love someone else other than me…and that there is no
place for me here. Not in Camelot either. I'm…I'm lost."

"My love, my love, what have I just told you? You're not lost,
you're home! My lovely, sensitive daughter…you're home. I love
no one else other than you!"

Gwen couldn't stop weeping. "But I saw the look in your eyes.
And in Gareth's eyes. You were hoping I *hadn't* come back. That
the other me was still here"

"It is *you* that is still here, Gwen. That other you is still *you*.
My love: you have been through such a lot, such an amazing
adventure that it has left you exhausted, emotionally drained.

But you're still my daughter and when you've rested and recovered, you see – we will *all* see how we come out of this. It's affected us all. Look at me. Gwen. Look at my eyes – see what I feel for you there…"

Gwen looked at her mother. She nodded tearfully but at last she was reassured. She was, however, almost too frightened to look at Gareth. She at last turned her tear-reddened eyes towards him.

Gareth at the same time wondered who he was looking at now. It was not at all like the hard, cold Gwen he had known before but neither was it the person who he was last in this room with and who had told him he had won her first in Camelot. Maybe that was as well? He wanted to win a girl here in Monmouthshire, not in some dreamland. But – Christ! – her kisses had somehow unhinged him. He wondered if that would ever happen again, after this. Maybe that was the best thing to do – give it a rest and see what happens tomorrow. After all, they both had to go back to work tomorrow!

"I think, Ms Griffiths, we all need to rest and recover. I said earlier that this has been an awesome day. I didn't know the half of it! I dunno about you, but I will never be the same again after tonight. I'm going to walk home now and try and make sense of it all. No, Ms Griffiths, I don't need a lift home. I want to walk, raining or not. I'll have my clothes back, though. Good night, Gwen. I'll see you tomorrow…I hope."

Which Gwen he would see he didn't know, but he wouldn't mention that. He took his wet clothes back and, shivering, put them on. At least they were not muddy: he'd worn worse in a game of rugby. Now it was a twenty-minute run home; he made his excuses and left. No kiss for Gwen this time. Maybe tomorrow…

* * *

It was a long, sleep-deprived, turbulent night for all of them: three people struggling to come to terms with everything. Then next morning, very early, the phone rang in Raglan Road. It was Dai Mervyn, calling to ask how Gwen was after her traumatic day of work.

"Hello, Dai," Ceri answered. "It's not easy to explain how Gwen is...except to say that she has changed. Dai, my Gwen doesn't know about what happened in the hotel yesterday...she says she's just come back from some battle in Camelot. Yes. I know. Difficult to understand. Except talk to Gareth – he was here last night with her and we were all crying. Dai, it's my daughter as she was...but it's not how she was...you'll have to see her to understand. What? OK. Of course, come as soon as you can."

Ceri went up to see her daughter and got out her Camelot Hotel uniform for her to wear. The Arthurian dress she had worn yesterday was still wet, hanging up in the utility room. Gwen, meanwhile, was in the shower, silent and subdued.

Ceri put breakfast together, very simple but with Gwen's favourite cereals, and waited for her daughter to come down. The strain on Gwen's face when she at last came to the breakfast table was as plain to see as storm clouds across the sky.

"Is this what I have to wear now?" she asked, looking at her mother and then at her uniform. How could she go to work in the hotel as if nothing had happened? Going back there would be a struggle that she didn't know how she would cope with.

Ceri went across and hugged her. "Yes, my love. Don't worry. It'll be fine. Dai Mervyn's on his way to pick you up. He wants to see how you are."

"Does he?" Gwen looked up quickly, her voice shaking. "Does he want to see *me*...or the girl that was here?"

"You, my love. It's still you and only you. Look, there he is now." The Land Rover was pulling up outside.

Ceri went and opened the front door and diplomatically

retired to leave her daughter waiting in the hallway. Gwen wasn't sure what to do, although she did want to see what Merlyn looked like in this world. She couldn't remember.

There he was, the same face smiling at her as she saw in Camelot. He paused at the rear of the Land Rover and let Morgan the wolfhound out, then he opened the gate and they both came up the garden path. Gwen stood there and couldn't move. She just looked at Merlyn with tears welling up again in her eyes. When would this end?

"Hello, Gwen, my precious. How's thee then?" Merlyn looked kindly at her. Morgan came up and licked her hand.

"Merlyn... Do you know me?"

"Aye, my precious. That I do."

"But...but...we've hardly seen each other!"

"Did you know me in Camelot?"

"Oh yes. You...you were always telling what to do. And I never did what you said. You were so patient with me..."

"Well then, you knew me there, and I knew you here, see. So we both know each other, don't we?"

"If you say so."

"Aye, I do. Morning, Ceri!" Dai called out. "We're just off then. I'll bring her back this afternoon, no worries!"

He put an arm round Gwen. "C'mon, precious, let's go. Welcome back. All will be well; but thou must work at it! Welcome to Camelot...back here..."

END

Also by Tony Cleaver

Understanding the World Economy 9780415681315
Economics: The Basics 9780415571098
Frogs, Cats and Pyramids 9781782794103
El Mono 9781909716179

At Roundfire we publish great stories. We lean towards the spiritual and thought-provoking. But whether it's literary or popular, a gentle tale or a pulsating thriller, the connecting theme in all Roundfire fiction titles is that once you pick them up you won't want to put them down.